You're the Only One I Can Trust

A Novel
by Michael E. Petrie

abbott press®
A DIVISION OF WRITER'S DIGEST

You're the Only One I Can Trust.

Copyright © 2012 by Michael E. Petrie.

All rights reserved. No part of this book may be used or reproduced by any means, graphic, electronic, or mechanical, including photocopying, recording, taping or by any information storage retrieval system without the written permission of the publisher except in the case of brief quotations embodied in critical articles and reviews.

ISBN: 978-1-4582-0355-7 (sc)
ISBN: 978-1-4582-0356-4 (e)
ISBN: 978-1-4582-0357-1 (hc)

Library of Congress Control Number: 2012907641

Abbott Press books may be ordered through booksellers or by contacting:

Abbott Press
1663 Liberty Drive
Bloomington, IN 47403
www.abbottpress.com
Phone: 1-866-697-5310

Because of the dynamic nature of the Internet, any web addresses or links contained in this book may have changed since publication and may no longer be valid. The views expressed in this work are solely those of the author and do not necessarily reflect the views of the publisher, and the publisher hereby disclaims any responsibility for them.

You're The Only One I Can Trust is a work of fiction. Names, characters, businesses, organizations, places, and incidents are either the product of the author's imagination or are used fictitiously. Any resemblance to actual persons, living or dead, actual locations, or actual events are entirely coincidental.

Any people depicted in stock imagery provided by Thinkstock are models, and such images are being used for illustrative purposes only.

Certain stock imagery © Thinkstock.

Printed in the United States of America

Abbott Press rev. date: 06/28/12

For my loving and understanding wife, who encouraged, nourished, and helped facilitate the writing of this novel.

Special thanks to my friend of many years, the late Paul Fick, Senior Deputy District Attorney for Riverside County, California

There is always some madness in love; and also some reason in madness
—Friedrich Nietzsche, German philosopher (1844 - 1900)

Nothing takes the taste out of peanut butter quite like unrequited love
—Charles M. Schulz, US cartoonist (1922 - 2000)

You can't always get what you want, but sometimes you get what you need
—Rolling Stones

Prologue
Griffin Gambil

June 2000

Griffin Gambil was having the absolute time of his life. A wealthy sixty-year-old man, clearly still in his prime some might say—though it is unlikely anyone younger than fifty would make such a statement—Griffin was still a relatively handsome fellow. He suffered from neither the middle-age spreading of his mid-section nor the hair loss so common to men his age. Even though he seldom exercised, Griffin remained fairly trim, a condition he attributed to the stress of the business world which, he claimed, burned calories faster than jogging.

His dark hair, peppered with just the correct amount of gray, gave rise to a sophisticated "older gentleman" appearance. Pricey designer clothing completed the persona of the well-to-do. Griffin always liked to say the only difference between a dirty old man and a sophisticated elderly gentleman was the amount in his bank account. He would say this with just the hint of a smile, never an out-and-out laugh, so that the listener was never quite certain if he was making a serious observation or speaking in jest.

Griffin had a wife. An attractive brunette-cum-blonde with a remarkable figure that belied her forty-five years. He would have been quite satisfied with such a wife, except that she was sexually frigid as a block of ice. So, he had a girlfriend . . . a mistress, really. For every problem there was a solution, Griffin believed.

Unbeknownst to Griffin, his wife was not as repelled by sexual activity as he would have believed. It's just that she had been fornicating in her mind with another man for so long that she no longer thought of her husband as a sexual being. Otherwise, Griffin's wife had, for much of their fifteen years together, been completely content sharing a passionless life with her husband—he was intelligent, a good friend and excellent provider. She had been content, that is, until quite recently.

Few things in life surprised Griffin anymore. But he was somewhat taken aback when his wife, out-of-the-blue, announced that she was leaving him. She moved out and began cohabiting with a man from her distant past who suddenly reemerged, re-claiming her like chattel that had merely been on temporary loan to Griffin. Stunning though this turn of events was, Griffin tried to take it in stride, convincing himself that it hardly mattered. Without the distractions of a wife hanging around, he could now concentrate more fully on his business. Griffin was in the *business* of making money. Primarily through real estate. He bought, sold, brokered, developed—and sometimes even blatantly cheated people out of—real estate.

Additionally, his wife leaving him for another man was the best thing to happen to Griffin's sex life in years. He could now more easily spend time with his mistress. Physically, Griffin's mistress was everything his wife was NOT—his *wife* was tall, curvaceous and beautiful.

Griffin's wife and his mistress were polar opposites in personality and character as well. His wife had always treated him respectfully and truthfully. This would include the completely forthright manner in which she disclosed to Griffin her affair with another man, and her subsequent abandonment of the marital domicile rather than continuing to live under the guise of husband and wife. Griffin's mistress, on the other hand, abused and mistreated him and, he felt certain, she was a habitual liar. His wife left without taking a dime; his mistress demanded every dollar she could squeeze out of him. Yet, it was the mistress who brought Griffin such contentment as he had never before felt in his entire life.

GRIFFIN GAMBIL SAT IN HIS car, a late model black Cadillac, parked on the street in front of his mistress' house. He flicked on the radio—the "oldies" station. He enjoyed listening to old-time rock & roll performers like the Platters, Little Anthony & the Imperials, Gene Chandler, the Silhouettes—what he called "Doo-Wop music." Music from his youth. The DJ announced "up next—four in a row" from a singer Griffin considered more contemporary than oldie: Phil Collins. More and more, non-Doo-Wop music was encroaching onto the oldies airwaves, something Griffin tolerated rather than enjoyed.

He took pen and paper from the glove compartment and studied the pad on his knee. He and his mistress had been engaged in another of their little erotic games. Games that got Griffin so emotionally charged that he felt he could go out and conquer the whole damn world! He had never experienced anything so intense before with any woman, certainly not with his wife. Games that made Griffin so grateful for the feeling that he often expressed his gratitude by bestowing lavish gifts. This one would be a real doozy!

He listened to the words being sung from the radio, *I can feel it coming in the air tonight—Oh Lord*. Smiling to himself, he responded audibly, "Oh Lord, indeed. I most surely *can* feel it coming in the air tonight!"

At the top of the blank page in his lap Griffin printed in large bold letters, LAST WILL AND TESTAMENT OF GRIFFIN GAMBIL. The rest of the page, in his usual hand, he listed the breadth and scope of his domain . . . leaving everything he owned to just one person, the only woman he ever knew to make him feel so fully alive: his mistress.

"That ought to get her attention," he chuckled to himself. "Hell, it'll get *everyone's* attention if I get run over by a bus before I can destroy this damn thing."

The will wasn't real, of course. He never intended for it to be. He had a *real* will—one drawn up by lawyers, with witnesses and everything—in a safe deposit box down at the bank. This was just new fodder for their game playing. She would be so pleased to see the will—so touched by this grand gesture of his generosity toward her—no telling to what heights they might soar tonight!

A tap on the car window caused Griffin to look up from his bogus will drafting project. Surprised and annoyed at this intrusion, he stuffed the pad of paper back into the glove compartment, away from prying eyes, and got out of the car.

"Look," he said, trying not to vent his impatience too harshly. "I don't know why the hell you're bothering me, but make this quick. I don't have all day."

Those were the last words Griffin Gambil ever spoke. The glint of a gun barrel caught his eye—it was the second to last thing Griffin Gambil would ever see. There was a loud, percussive pop, a spume of red. In the time it takes to pull a trigger, a bullet smashed into Griffin's skull, taking his nose, an eye and much of his face with it. Before the darkness of eternity descended over him, Griffin—looking downward with the single good eye still attached to its socket—watched his own blood spilling onto his Gucci loafers.

From within the car, another song with the pulsating drum beat and voice of Phil Collins kept hammering over and over the final refrain: *No more, no more, no more, no more* . . . .

Part One
The Story According to Ben Harding

Chapter One
Benjamin Harding

Benjamin Harding had never been the sort of man who shared his thoughts or feelings easily. Not necessarily reticent, he'd just never had the time, nor the inclination. And he certainly never fancied himself to be much of a writer. But, while it was all still fresh in his mind, he decided to memorialize the tumultuous events he'd recently experienced. Call it a journal, a diary, a memoir, what-have-you. Ben began to write:

CHANGE. CHANGE IS UNAVOIDABLE, CONTINUOUS and gradual over time. But, sometimes change must be intentional and abrupt. That's how the biggest change in my life occurred—with intent and abruptness.

I was an attorney—with reluctance I admit to still being one. Being an attorney has been the focus of my life for more than twenty years. But all that has changed. Clawing my way up the ladder of legal hierarchy within a large law firm is no longer my mainstay. Sure, I was made a partner after *years* of sweat and toil—untold hours churning out the billable hours, hustling new business, combating constant stress associated with high stake litigation. The job made me unfit company for any decent caring woman. So, my marriage of six years finally bit the dust. I hold no grudges, it was probably all my own doing. Wrapped up in my work and in myself, I was an emotionally absent husband. Thank God we never had children, the guilt of being an emotionally absent *father* might be too much to bear.

I kept the marital residence. My "ex" wanted no part of a house that held only lonely memories; she packed her things and was gone. I had no memories associated with the house. For me, it was merely the place where I went each night to sleep after working all day. I bought her out and continued living in quarters better suited to some upwardly mobile family unit and far too large for the needs of a single occupant. Moving would have interrupted my robotical routine; the house was an easy drive to the office.

So, there I was—well into my forties and living alone—living for my job, my career. Big deal, partner! A non-equity partner at that. To the non-initiated, an impressive title with an old established Newport Beach firm. For those who know better, I had merely raised myself to the rank of an elite drone. A non-equity partner is still only a worker bee after all.

My six-figure salary was another thing that might sound impressive to the uninitiated—until you calculate all the hours I gave the firm. Figured from that perspective, my hourly wage quickly loses any prestige one might attach to it. Okay, so it did allow me to live in a big mock-Tudor house in one of those snooty, private, gated, exclusive South Orange County communities; a place chosen by my former "better half" as fitting and proper for an attorney and his wife—but a place no less impressive sans wife. And I did commute to the office along the pristine manicured streets of this highly affluent and nearly crime-free little Southern California city in my Porsche Boxster—ocean blue with gray leather seats, my favorite indulgence.

Maybe I shouldn't complain—and for twenty-something years I did not complain. I went about my life in a tedious, quotidian, almost antiseptic manner. Dark suit, white shirt, colorless neck tie; corporate law, real estate law, mergers, acquisitions, litigation; tasteless lunches consumed with clients or fellow attorneys while discussing cases; three weeks vacation per year, but not to be taken all at once—oh no, important lawyers like me cannot be spared from the office for such lengthy periods.

But now, that has all changed.

THE FIRST DETOUR FROM THIS path of mundane familiarity came with the death of my uncle, Jonathan Wilfred Harding III. Much to the chagrin of my grandfather—Jonathan Wilfred Harding II—since boyhood my uncle always preferred the moniker of Jack, and that is what most everyone called him. To me, he was always *good old Uncle Jack*, my favorite relative.

Completely unlike his brother—my father—Uncle Jack was, I suppose, the miscreant black sheep of the family. Standing out amongst all my uptight, conservative, hard-working, ambitious, God-fearing relatives, Uncle Jack shone brightly like some blighted beacon of bohemian unconventionality. Already well over thirty when the whole "hippie thing" was going on back in the late 1960s, Uncle Jack moved from our deeply rooted hometown in Illinois to California, where he embraced that youth subculture anyway—in spite of the "don't trust anyone over thirty" Zeitgeist dogma—shunning the mainstream, growing long hair and beard and "going with the flow" of the counterrevolutionaries. Long after the days of dope-smoking gurus and independent free spirits with long flowing locks had been replaced by money-grubbing yuppies, Uncle Jack retained the facial hair and the 60s attitude . . . and continued to live along a little strip of Venice Beach, California called Ocean Front Walk.

The family dismissed him as a crackpot, but I always admired him. Most assuredly, Uncle Jack is the reason why I chose to attend college and law school in California and have remained in the Golden State all these years—albeit laying down my own roots in the more staid Orange County, a place more in keeping with my Midwestern conventionality.

After graduating from high school, much to my amazement my parents consented to letting me spend the summer with Uncle Jack, for what I'm sure they presumed would be the last few idle months of my life before starting college and advancing into the work world.

That summer of 1971 was a summer right out of any teenage boy's fantasy. Two months of living on the beach in sunny Southern California! Uncle Jack taught me to surf the small but consistent wave breaks right in front of his house at Venice Beach. By then Uncle Jack would have been in his late forties, but you would never know it; he could surf with the best of them, bike ride along the beach bike path for several hours, and still manage to party long after we watched the sun sizzle into the Pacific right out our front window. He was more like an older brother than an uncle—certainly not at all like someone from my *parents'* generation.

We would sit on the front deck of the little beach cottage, day after sunshiny day, listening to rock music and flirting with bikini-clad beach bunnies as they cruised past our door on roller skates along the paved path that parallels the ocean for some twenty miles.

So many of the local colorful characters for which Venice Beach is known were among Uncle Jack's coterie of beach buddies and often stopped by to visit, each with their own unique tales to share. Blond blues singer, Ricki Lee Jones, was a struggling artist in those days, frequently venting her frustrations with the music business on my patient uncle. Beach Boys drummer Dennis Wilson sat at breakfast with us one morning after surfing with Uncle Jack and told me about the frenetic "early days" with his famous band. Everything and everybody at the beach just seemed so damned exciting!

Sadly, The Doors singer Jim Morrison died that very summer. Uncle Jack sat up all night embracing a whiskey bottle—something that was actually rather out of character for my uncle—mourning the passing of the *Lizard King,* a man he called friend.

"Jim lived just a bit down the beach, but often he'd crash right here," I vividly recall my uncle saying, pointing a finger in my direction for emphasis and speaking with slurred words from grief and whiskey. "He'd just wander in, grab a beer from the fridge and crap out on that very sofa you're sitting on, Ben. Jim often said 'no one gets out of this world alive,' guess he's proven himself correct. I hope he won't be remembered as just another fallen rock star," my uncle lamented. "He was one of the warmest, most human persons you could ever know."

A decade or so later, Uncle Jack would write to me of Beach Boy Dennis Wilson's drowning accident in the marina less than a mile from the old beach house. Uncle Jack deeply regretted not being there for his friend, as if his presence might have somehow prevented the tragedy.

I enrolled at Berkeley that fall and spent the next four summers with Uncle Jack at the beach house on Ocean Front Walk. College life was hard work, but fun. Summers were outrageous! Uncle Jack was always there waiting for me to drive down from school. Suntanned and trim, he never seemed to age. I jokingly told him that one day I would be a stooped old man and he would still be surfing the ocean out front of his beach house. He told me that *old* is more a state of mind than a physical reality and I think he truly believed that. Often he would say things like, "Time, my dear nephew, is merely an illusion perpetrated by the inane manufacturers of space." Then he would laugh a hearty chortle. He was frequently spouting off one-liners like that, and I seldom understood their profundity, but always listened and laughed merrily along with Uncle Jack.

I loved my Uncle Jack and I loved the summers spent with him in that little beach shack more than anything. But, in the summer of 1976 Uncle Jack took off to sail around the world on a sailboat with some friends—a voyage that would take several years—so he rented-out the house on Ocean Front Walk to strangers. For me, the fun times were over. Stanford Law School, studying for the bar exam and grueling hours spent working at the practice of law consumed my life. Several offers arrived in the mail over the years from Uncle Jack, asking me to join him on his sailing voyages—but I was far too busy. I had become too grown-up to play with Uncle Jack anymore.

IN THE BLINK OF AN eye, nearly twenty-five years had come and gone. Uncle Jack completed his circumnavigational excursion, finally settling in with a woman he met somewhere in the Mediterranean. They eventually married, but never had children, and neither I nor any member of my family attended the wedding ceremony, if there was one. Except for the annual Christmas greeting which arrived like clockwork from various exotic ports, I'd had virtually no communication with Uncle Jack in all that time.

Still, when news reached me of his passing, I was deeply saddened. My knees caved, suddenly lacking ability to support my frame. Collapsing into the leather chair, seated behind my big oak desk, wearing my expensive suit, this tough lawyer had tears rolling down his cheeks. There was no funeral to attend, no grave site to visit. Uncle Jack's ashes were scattered into the sea near his Mediterranean home. I only learned of it after the fact.

And then I was contacted by a fellow attorney, someone with whom I was not at all familiar. Uncle Jack had left a will.

I never imagined Uncle Jack would leave anything to me. Indeed, I never considered my freewheeling uncle to have accrued much of an estate. But there was the old beach house on Ocean Front Walk in Venice. What fun times we had shared there. And now this funky old house from my youth was mine. Thank you Uncle Jack, wherever you may now be. What a kind and generous gesture.

Scarcely more than a shack, even back when I used to spend my summers there, the house is very old—built in 1929 by a silent film producer who used it as a summer retreat, much the same way I did as a younger fellow I suppose—and after years of occupation by renters, in considerable disrepair. Still, located right on the sand at one of the most famous beaches in all of California, certainly it must have *some* value.

Indeed it did. The realtor estimated its value at considerably more than one million dollars! Thank you, thank you—a million thank yous—Uncle Jack!

THAT FIRST DETOUR FROM MY normal life was delivered to me by a lawyer with the reading of my uncle's will. The second detour from my life path was also delivered by a lawyer: I was served with a malpractice lawsuit! Of course, along with the lawsuit was the inevitable complaint to the State Bar. So, I suddenly had to defend myself on two fronts. I'd never before been investigated by the Bar, but heard horror stories from attorneys who had, claiming the Bar tends to favor the complainant and often comes down hard on its own members.

But I was more concerned about the malpractice claim. As if the practice of law were not stressful enough, now some disgruntled client who did not appreciate the outcome of his case was suing me, alleging that I somehow mishandled the matter. This particular client happened to be an overweight, overbearing, follically challenged head of a closely held corporation in the refuse business—more commonly known as trash collection. His company held a three-county monopoly on such service. Ara Ratono was a self-made multi-millionaire, in spite of having little formal education and far more dollars than sense, who continuously found himself in one legal confrontation after another—all the while openly inveighing his contempt for attorneys even as our firm bailed him out of myriad self-inflicted messes.

A widely proliferated rumor that Ara Ratono—or Ari, as he prefers to be called—has mob ties was something none of us at the firm took too seriously—though his arrogant, gruff, ruffian persona did nothing to diminish the connection. Basically, we all recognized him for the huge blowhard he was, but disguised any ill feelings and fawned over him, lest he take those huge retainer dollars elsewhere. He seemed to relish seeing how far he could push the Brooks Brothers set, how much of his crap we'd put up with. He earned his living through his company's collection of trash, and we earned ours by putting up with constant trashing from him.

Ari's most recent courtroom battle was assigned to me. And now, like a schoolyard bully, he didn't like the outcome so he was taking his ball and leaving, taking his game to another firm, the malpractice suit a final piece of his trash lobbed into our court on his way out. Personally, I was tired of his abusive nature, and was happy to be rid of him. The senior partners seeing dollars walking out with Ara Ratono, however, did not share my joy.

I know Ari's not the only person who likes to put down my profession—it's in vogue to hate lawyers. But if people only knew what we go through as lawyers they very well may be more appreciative. And nothing grinds my valves more than the relentless telling of inappropriate LAWYER JOKES! Every time some clod asks what I do for a living, as soon as I say I'm a lawyer, I just sit back and wait. I know it's coming and almost invariably it does come . . . the inescapable lawyer joke or derogatory comment about lawyers! I think that before anyone is *allowed* to tell a lawyer joke, he or she should be *required* to put their life on hold while they complete four years of college, generally a couple more years earning a Masters, three years of tautological servitude in law school for the coveted Juris Doctor degree, followed by six months of intensive bar review study, culminating with the three days of nonstop brain-banging called the bar exam! After surviving all that, if you still think lawyer jokes are amusing, I will gladly laugh along with you. Anyone not willing to pay such dues has no standing to make jokes or comments. Lawyering is a stress-filled profession that requires years of study and hard work before you ever make your first dime—a job that is continuously hampered by the time constraints and conformity to the various Rules of Civil Procedure, Rules of Evidence, Ethical Rules, rules,

rules, rules! My entire adult life I have complied with volumes of so many seemingly inane rules!

I NEEDED TO GET AWAY from it all; escape from the rules, the malpractice lawsuit and pressures facing me at the office. So, I took the afternoon off and drove up the coast toward L.A.—to the Venice Beach house that had recently come into my possession. I'd not been up there in years. Only fifty or so miles up Pacific Coast Highway from Newport Beach, but a universe away in tenor and spirit. Venice Beach is a place removed from many of the realities of the world, a place where the bizarre often becomes the norm. *Reality is merely the temporary result of the struggle between rival gangs of programmers,* my Uncle Jack used to say, way back in an age before computers and programmers were commonplace. Uncle Jack was a man ahead of his time.

Venice Beach is also a place where one can ponder and reexamine one's life. My initial instinct upon learning of the beach house's value was to sell it and pocket that cool million. But once I saw the shack again, I knew I could never sell it. The last of the *old* places still standing along the strip of sand known as Ocean Front Walk, it is now surrounded by modern dwellings and high-rise condo complexes. This fine old building rising up out of the sand with its weathered front facing the Pacific Ocean seemed to me a monument in tribute to my beloved Uncle Jack—although, a monument in dire need of some TLC.

Entering the now vacant dwelling, thick but delicate cobwebs began flittering in the breeze from the open door, threatening to disrupt the intricate bridgework they created which extended from one room to the next. Walking its interior, time breathed in and out as a flood of memories came rushing at me—filling my senses with melancholic feelings I'd not held in decades. The rooms swam with faces, voices and sounds from halcyon days.

I walked out onto the front deck, looking toward the beach, drawing into my lungs the viscous, damp air that hugs the coast. Two girls packed nicely into bikinis glided past on roller blades. One waved and smiled as she continued on her way. Skates have been replaced by *blades,* but the scenery had not really changed much over the years.

I walked back inside. The place needed some work, but its soul was still intact. It was warm and stuffy in the house from being boarded up, so I opened a few windows and removed my shirt for comfort. Passing a mirror in the bathroom, I caught a glimpse of myself shirtless. Yikes! I had no idea I looked that old. My reflection was that of a pasty-skinned, middle-aged man with a protruding paunch acquired from too many years sitting behind a desk. I'm about the same age now that Uncle Jack was when we hung out together, but Uncle Jack never looked so old.

Clearly, I was not aging well. It suddenly occurred to me that time can be your enemy or your friend. Working as a lawyer with myriad time constraints, statutes of limitation, filing deadlines . . . I was always battling with time. For too long, time had been my enemy. Now I wanted to change all that, to make peace with Father Time; to make time my friend. I decided right there and then that a change—an abrupt and intentional change—was in order.

I had never before thought of myself as a millionaire, but I sat down on the sand facing inland toward the Santa Monica Mountains, ocean behind me, surveying my newly acquired beachfront real estate, and did some quick calculations in my head. The Venice Beach house had no encumbrances, title was free and clear. Further, if I sold my home in Orange County, I could pocket a real chunk of change from the equity that had built up over the years. The new tax laws would allow me to keep the profits from the sale of my residence tax-free up to $250,000. That, combined with the savings I had squirreled away and my 401K plan at work, and . . . *Voila!* Suddenly I was worth around two million bucks! From Orange County bourgeois to Venice Beach parvenu in a single afternoon. Could this be true? If so, then what the hell was I doing toiling away as a drone at the law firm?

It struck me that, like some slave from olden days buying freedom from his master, I had enough money to buy *my* freedom. But just because I found myself suddenly worth a few bucks did not mean I should live like some rich, arrogant asshole. Not me. No conspicuous consumption here. Not anymore. I planned to pick up the baton from my dearly departed uncle and to run with it. Uncle Jack had the right idea all along and I intended to follow in his footsteps.

I slept that night on the hardwood floors with the ocean breeze wafting over me and sonorous crashing surf just outside my door. Morning sea gulls woke me with their laughter. Barefoot, with suit pants rolled above my ankles, I sauntered sleepily over to the Cow's End around the corner and stood in line for some morning java. Directly across the street was Starbucks—the caffeine corporate giant. In true anti-establishment Venice Beach fashion, Starbucks was virtually deserted while the mom-and-pop Cow's End had people waiting. By my second cup, sleep cobwebs had been evicted from their nightlong residence inside my tired brain and I jumped into the Porsche to cruise back down the coast to Newport.

Looking disheveled from sleeping on the floor in my suit and with beard stubble erupting over my face, I walked into the office, dictated a resignation letter to my secretary, handed my caseload to the senior partner... and quit! Malpractice insurance would take care of my defense to the lawsuit against me and I just didn't give a rat's ass what the State Bar might do with the complaint lodged against my license. In fact, they could take my California Bar card and stuff it where the sun don't shine! I felt like a man just released from indenture.

Next stop was a local realtor's office to peddle my mock-Tudor gated home and to begin packing. I, Benjamin Harding—at age forty-eight—was reinventing myself. As good old Uncle Jack might have said, today was, indeed, the first day of the rest of my life.

Chapter Two

My first task was to lose the flabby lawyer body I was carrying around. I've never been a fan of exercise purely for exercise sake, but living at the beach offers plenty of incentive for getting fit and makes working out about as enjoyable as it gets. Up each morning at 6:30 a.m.—out of habit, even though I no longer need to maintain such hours for work—the ocean air is almost always crisp and invigorating. At that hour, mine are often among the first footprints in the cool sand as I make my way down to the water's edge.

But upon reaching the water, there's usually a universe of activity already in motion: sea birds pecking in the sand in search of breakfast; surfers paddling out to catch the first waves of the day; couples doing a graceful Tai Chi dance and assuming yoga positions with limber joints I can only envy; and joggers bobbing their way along the damp, compacted area of shoreline where the ocean water greets the shore.

From day one in Venice I took up running, crunching my way atop thousands of tiny sea shells that line the beach. At first, just a nice, easy pace. Horribly out of shape, every muscle in my body seemed to be protesting. Each day going a little farther than the last, until I was able to run *pier to pier* easily enough. From Venice Pier to Santa Monica Pier and back again is about 5 miles. My slow jog took about fifty minutes to cover the distance, but in the process I soon shed ten pounds. My salubrious regimen appeared to be paying off.

I didn't, and still don't, miss my old lawyer life in the least. No deadlines to meet, my life finally my own. What a joy! I even threw away that pesky cell phone that always seemed to ring at the most inopportune moments. The Porsche—an indulgence I simply cannot bring myself to give up, besides there still remains two years on the lease—often sits in solitary confinement in the garage, undriven for days at a time. My preferred mode of transportation is a beach-cruiser bicycle with fat tires that I bought at the bike shop three blocks away.

And, I'm finally able to read books for the sheer pleasure of it. Books that I have put off reading for years due to time constraints. It's terrific. I'm not required to do anything for myself or anyone else for that matter. I don't even need to *think* if I don't want to. I'm able to just *veg out* on the beach—to immerse myself in deep thoughts or contemplate my navel. I can fill my head with visions of scantily clad bathing beauties or just sit and people watch. Venice Beach, I am absolutely certain, must be the best place in the entire world for people watching!

Besides the beautiful sun-bronzed bodies that proliferate at the beach, there's a whole host of colorful locals who provide endless entertainment. Some of these locals I remember from my summers here way back in the 1970s. They have since become Venice Beach fixtures, icons, actual tourist attractions—like the turban wearing, guitar playing, Jimmy Hendrix look-alike who glides along the boardwalk on roller blades; and the "snake lady" who walks the beach each morning with a live boa wrapped around her torso.

The *newbies* are no less entertaining, each in his or her own way: the too-tan hard-body male weight-lifter with a body so finely chiseled he almost resembles some cyborg from a science fiction movie—half human, half machine—as he struts his stuff along the sand, skin oiled and muscles glistening; the equally tanned, pony-tailed, living Barbie doll prattling endlessly into a hands-free cellular phone as she weaves carelessly in and out of boardwalk pedestrian traffic on pink roller-blades, seemingly oblivious to those darting and dodging out of her way; the balding, pony-tailed bicyclist with a parrot perched on the handlebars, feathers ruffling in the breeze and chattering loudly in its own happy cacophonous parrot language—the bird always seems to be enjoying the ride, just like everybody else here at Venice Beach. For the first time since those long ago summers, I'm finding life to be damned exciting!

Anyway, one morning after returning from a run, I sat down to check e-mail on the computer. Amongst the junk, one message caught my eye. I'd been contacted about a thirty-year high school reunion being planned. Good Lord! Thirty years! How many of those years had I wasted in pursuit of the almighty dollar whilst life was passing me by?

The reunion was to be held at our old school back in Illinois. *Would I like to attend?* the message asked. It would probably be fun. It would most likely prove interesting. With no job and no caseload filling my days, I certainly had the *time* to attend. But I sat staring at the screen, unresponsive.

The irony, I supposed, was that most former classmates would likely view my years practicing law to be commendable, while shaking their heads in dismay at my current lifestyle as a beach bum. My hair was already nearly long enough to pull into a pony tail and I was sporting a salt and pepper goatee on my chin—backlash against all those years of compelled grooming.

What might my presence contribute to a crowd assembled to reminisce about our lost youth, enmeshed in small talk about spouses, established careers and families? I had no spouse or children, no career, and cared little for reliving the past. Just a forty-eight-year-old bachelor living at the beach—a law firm burn out victim—I was only just *beginning* to live. While former classmates would likely be sending nearly grown children off to college and planning for their own *golden* years, I felt as if I'd only recently been reborn. Did I really have anything in common with this crowd? What on earth would we have to say to one another?

The e-mail reunion announcement included a few pointed questions for an update on everyone's life. *City and state of residence?* VENICE BEACH, CALIFORNIA. *Occupation?* For lack of a better answer, I typed in LAWYER. *Marital status?* DIVORCED. *Children?* NONE. I clicked the send button and headed out the door for a bike ride.

EARLY AFTERNOON, WITH NOTHING ELSE to do, I checked e-mail again. Three messages—all from former classmates. I had not communicated with anyone from high school *since* high school. Now suddenly, after thirty years, here were three messages from a past life. As it turns out, all from female former classmates. Opening the first, it read:

> Hi Ben,
> *I saw your name on the classmate list and just had to say hello. I nearly flipped when I saw your name. I hope you remember me. Wendy Fredenthall. Remember? We dated a few times junior year. You were one of the cutest boys in our class! I always thought so, really. And now you are living out there in sunny California. Lucky you! And, my goodness, you are a successful attorney! I never knew you aspired*

toward the law. And now, here you are, at the height of your career. You must be so incredibly proud! How long have you been divorced? I've been married three times and have been single the last five years. I have three children, the youngest is 18 and my oldest daughter is 28. I really, really hope you will be coming to the reunion. It would be so amazingly wonderful to see you again. Maybe we can sit together at the banquet table and get reacquainted. Like the old Beach Boys song, we'll have Fun, Fun, Fun!
Looking forward to seeing you again after all these years,
Wendy Fredenthall

At the height of my career? What a hoot! If she only knew. After racking my brain, I finally recalled Wendy Frendenthall. She was a bubbly cheerleader with great lungs. Sounded like she's lost none of her effervescence. I opened the second e-mail message:

Ben,
How wonderful to read your response to our class update survey. I can't tell you how often I've thought of you over the years and wondered whatever became of you. I still remember sophomore year when you took me to my first formal dance. I was so excited and you looked so handsome standing at my door wearing that powder blue tux. Unfortunately, I wore very grown-up high heels and wound up several inches taller than you. I assume you have grown taller since then—just kidding!
And now you are a big-time attorney in Los Angeles. That is so nice.
I'm a schoolteacher, still living in our old hometown.
I really hope you will be coming to the reunion. It will be such fun to see you again.
Best to you,
Doris Lund-Blumberg

I remembered Doris Lund. She was a smart, cute girl with long brown hair and a turned up nose. And I remembered the dance we went to together like it was yesterday. At school she always seemed about my height, but when I picked her up for the dance it felt as if she was wearing stilts! She towered over me in her high heels. I remembered dreading slow dances all evening because it seemed like my cheek was directly at bosom height dancing with her. It was very awkward. I also remembered that her beautiful long hair was trussed up and piled on top of her head in a way that made her look downright matronly, even at age fifteen. I never could figure out why girls who had such beautiful tresses felt compelled to pile it up on their heads in a manner far too sophisticated for their girlish faces every time they attended a "dress up" affair. I found myself wondering how matronly Doris might be looking today at age forty-eight.

The third message on my screen caused an involuntary ripple up my spine, like what the French call *frisson*. The subject header read: *from Samantha*. Could it be the same Samantha who had caused me severe emotional heartburn for both junior and senior years in high school? Samantha Zimmer was, in my opinion, the most beautiful girl in our entire school. She was a couple of years younger, a mere freshman when I was a junior, but she captured my heart so completely that I traveled in her wake like a faithful puppy the rest of high school. Always paying just enough attention to me to keep my hopes up, but never quite following through with the sort of attention I craved from her, I prayed night after night that if I could just have one thing in this life—please God let me have Samantha Zimmer!

By twelfth grade it was obvious to everyone but me that she was "in love" with another guy. His name escaped me as I tried to recall it, but he was in my graduating class, a real jock type . . . and I hated him! When he took Samantha to Senior Prom—the most important social event for all of high school—it shattered my fragile teenage heart.

Amazingly, all these many years later, just reading Samantha's name on my screen still caused my heart to race. I was eager to read what she might have to say to me after so much time.

Dear Benjamin,
I saw your name on the internet—the reunion thing. My God, I can't believe how lucky it was to find you. So much has happened. I really need to see you. As soon as possible. Please. It's important. I'll be in L.A. next Wednesday. Can we please meet?
Samantha

I read the message five times, as if my brain was suffering some sort of neuron disconnect. There was nervous sweat dripping from my forehead. I'm a grown man, how could I be reduced to pangs of adolescent nervousness over this girl from my long ago past? Good grief man, get a grip!

I read it a sixth time and leaned back in my chair, cogitating on the words she sent, letting it all sink into my brain. I wondered if perhaps some sort of cosmic settlement was taking place here. I was finally living the kind of carefree beach life I had always secretly dreamed of, and maybe now the girl of my dreams would be entering this new utopian world as well. But the voice of reason inside my head reminded to be cool and not go reading too much into this thing.

I replied:

Dear Samantha,
Great to hear from you. Next Wednesday should be fine. I'll move a few appointments and make it work. Here's my number, call when you get into town: 867-5309.
Looking forward to it,
Ben

Okay, so I embellished the part about moving a few appointments—I no longer had any appointments. I just didn't want to appear too anxious. But, apparently, Samantha did not mind seeming anxious. Moments later, another e-mail appeared on my screen. It was from Samantha.

Benjamin,
Thank you so much for fitting me in. This means a lot to me. I feel you're the only one I can trust. I will phone you upon my arrival.
Sammie

I'm the only one she can trust? What was that supposed to mean? No matter, in a few days I hoped to find out.

Chapter Three

I had less than a week to finish whipping myself into shape for my meeting with Samantha. When a fellow is afforded a second chance with his former high school heartthrob after thirty years, he damn well better try to look his best. I ran faster and longer each morning on the beach. My lungs feeling like they were going to burst, I urged myself onward with mental images of Sammie reuniting with a tan handsome version of myself and chastising herself for ever letting me get away! I baked in the sun until my skin turned the proper shade of brown, shaved off the goatee, and got a haircut. I was going all out—just as I always had for this girl back in high school. Hopefully, my current efforts would yield a greater reward than in the past.

Wednesday I never strayed outside the house for fear of not hearing the phone ring. But it never rang. As daylight came to a close, I sat on the sofa with a glass of wine watching the giant golden globe descend low in the sky and set into the waters of the Pacific. With the sun all but gone beyond the horizon, the sky took on a bright orange hue. I never tire of watching this nightly spectacle.

And then the phone rang.

It was Samantha. She was at LAX, could I pick her up?

No time for a shower or change of clothes, madras shorts and polo shirt would have to do. Is the *preppy look* still in fashion? I had not driven my car in a week and found myself praying it would have no trouble starting. Somewhere in the back of my mind I recalled something about the car having an anti-theft mechanism that required special starting requirements if it sat for more than a week.

I turned the key and the engine hummed to life. Thank God. Out the back alley, past the marina and driving along Lincoln Boulevard toward the airport, I kept willing myself to calm down and cast my nervousness aside. No use, butterflies had taken up residence in my stomach.

I PULLED UP AT THE curb under the Southwest Airlines sign and it suddenly dawned on me that, after thirty years, I might not recognize the girl of my dreams. In my mind Sammie remained a flawless young beauty with honey hair, peaches-and-cream complexion, and the sweetest blue eyes containing the slightest hint of amber as if sunlight itself found a home there. Hopefully, *I* would be an easier target to spot—the tanned goofball in the dark blue convertible scanning arriving passengers for a sixteen-year-old girl who was now a forty-six year-old woman.

I sat in the car, top down, parked by the curb with the motor running for several minutes, until airport security came and ordered me to move on. One more circle around the airport and I arrived back at the same spot under the Southwest sign. As I was busy scanning the crowd of ever arriving travelers, a woman with a deeply bronzed face—one that made my sun-darkened hue look almost pale—leaned into the car and spoke my name.

"Benjamin?" she said.

Dumbstruck, I studied her. Not at all unattractive, the woman had frosted blond hair that was striking alongside her brown face. Her perfume was heavy and redolent, distinguishable even within the amalgam of car exhausts and bus fumes permeating the night air. Large hoops dangled from her lobes in multiples of three. Freckles darker than the rest of her were scattered along her exposed and puckered cleavage. Perhaps even somewhat trashy-looking by Newport Beach standards, but this wasn't Newport Beach.

"Sammie?" I managed.

She was smiling broadly. "Benjamin! Wow, you look exactly the same. I would recognize you anywhere!"

Now there was a line if I ever heard one. I looked exactly the same as in high school? Thank you very much, but I think not.

"Sammie?" I repeated dumbly. I could scarcely believe it was her. She looked *nothing* like the girl I had known. Not that she didn't look terrific, she just did not look like Sammie. But the hint of amber in her eyes confirmed it, even before she did so verbally.

"Yup, it's me. Been a long time, Ben."

I nodded. "Where's your luggage?" I asked, at a loss for what to say.

"Only have this cosmetics case," she said, lifting a small satchel for me to see.

That seemed strange. It was good news though, because the Porsche really had scant room for luggage. She climbed into the passenger seat and I hurled us away from the curb as can only be accomplished in a true sports car. I busied myself shifting gears and weaving in and out of traffic, waiting for her to speak.

"Ben, is your office nearby? Can we go there and talk, even though it's after hours?"

My office? How did I tell her that I no longer had an office? And why did she want to see my office anyway?

"My house is nearby. Would you feel comfortable going there?" I asked.

"Sure," she said. But the smile disappeared, replaced by a look of concern. She looked to be deep in thought, pensive. I began to wonder if she was already having second thoughts about seeing me again. I mean, it had been thirty years. Maybe the forty-eight-year-old Ben Harding was a disappointment. This female had always been able to create a miasma of doubt in myself, but I decided to let it lie. We drove to the beach house in silence, top down, wind whipping her hair.

I SHOWED HER IN AND motioned for her to take a seat on the sofa. Unfortunately it was pitch black outside, so the million dollar ocean view was all but lost to her. Fetching us both glasses of wine, I sat down near her on the couch. We spent the better part of an hour making small talk, getting reacquainted and reminiscing about the old days back at school in a faraway place called the Midwest.

As she spoke and moved about, the Sammie I had known in school reemerged. I remembered her gestures, the way she tossed her head. She looked older—didn't we all—but it was Sammie . . . *my Sammie*.

With timeless particularity, she managed to solicit the tepid details of my last thirty years. There was not that much to share: work, divorce, followed by more work, until recently moving to Venice Beach and starting my life anew. But, what she told me about *herself* I found to be nothing short of fascinating.

After high school, Samantha had attended junior college for two years and earned an AA degree in Fashion Merchandising. She smiled after telling me that and added, "It probably seems silly to someone like you, Ben. A big time Los Angeles attorney with a Doctorate Degree in Law from Stanford. But we all play the cards that are dealt to us. I had a good body and a flare for fashion. Absolutely. Those were my cards. And it turned out okay, because it got me out of the *boring* Midwest . . . to this day I'm still repelled by the sight of an ear of corn!"

We both chuckled.

"I ended up moving to the Big Apple, working in an industry that I found pretty darned exotic. I became the buyer for a major clothing store chain. I traveled around the country on business, flew to Europe twice a year for the big buyer shows . . . it was really exciting. Okay, maybe not as exciting as law . . . ."

My choking momentarily interrupted her. I set my wine glass down on the coffee table and dabbed Merlot spittle from my chin with a napkin, regaining some composure.

"Mostly I worked between New York and Los Angeles," she continued. "In fact, Los Angeles is where I met my husband."

Husband? I sat rigidly upright, clinging to my composure rebound as best I could, but the impact of her remark must have registered on my face because she quickly qualified it.

"Oh, he's dead now," she stated matter-of-factly. "I guess that makes me a grieving widow. Funny, I don't feel like a widow. Griffin and I were married right here in California and lived as husband and wife for nearly fifteen years. We lived in the West Valley, out in Woodland Hills. In fact, I still keep some clothes and things at our house there. That's why I didn't fly with any luggage."

Gee, I never knew Samantha lived in California. All these years she had been living within a couple hours drive from me. Isn't life strange?

"Griffin was in the real estate business. A real shaker and mover back in the late 1980s when we met. Our first few years of married life were pretty sweet. Then the bottom fell out of the real estate market around 1990 and he lost nearly everything. For the first half of the 90s we lived mostly off *my* income. That was very difficult for Griffin. He was fifteen years older than me and very old-fashioned in his thinking. It shamed him that we actually needed my income.

"But real estate eventually came back around and by the late 90s Griffin was back in the high life again. Absolutely. Financially he made a real comeback. Unfortunately, by that time our marriage had become little more than a formality. I hope you won't mind me speaking so frankly, but sex had never played a big part of our relationship. Griffin and I were more like brother and sister. It was a marriage almost completely devoid of passion, and always had been—right from the start. We cared for each other, but . . . let's just say our marriage was different from most. Again, I hope you don't mind my speaking so frankly with you, Benjamin."

"Not at all. I'm here to listen." A conditioned response that made me cringe as soon as I heard myself say it. It's what I might have said during any client interview.

She continued. "Griffin and I had all the elements of marriage, except for sex. That was mostly my fault, I know. I loved Griffin, but just not as a lover. Putting it bluntly, my passions have always remained attached to one special boy I knew in high school. I have never felt such yearning for anyone before or since. For years I kicked myself for letting this boy get away. He was the one real love of my life! Thank God for the internet, because it allowed me to reconnect with my dear long lost love."

Whoa! Was she referring to me? She had, in fact, located me on the internet. Was I the love of her life that she had lamented all these years? I never had a clue she harbored such feelings toward me. My God, was this her reason for wanting to see me?

"This is the reason I needed to see you, Benjamin."

Chapter Four

My heart was pounding so hard I felt certain she could hear it across the sofa. Perspiration dripped from my forehead. Thirty years since high school and this girl—woman—still caused me to sweat nervously. At last she was confessing to me the words that I had so longed to hear as a boy, all those years ago. Better late than never! I waited speechlessly for her to continue.

"This is the reason I needed to see you," she repeated. "You knew him."

The cognitive dissonance of what I just heard caused any sense of understanding to shut down in my brain. Suddenly flummoxed—I stammered, "Wha . . . what? Who did I know? What do you mean?"

"I mean you knew the boy who was the love of my life. He was in your class. Surely you remember Pete. Pete Spivey?"

Pete Spivey. That was the name I couldn't recall earlier. He's the guy Samantha went to the prom with—the guy everyone but me knew Sammie was in love with. He was the reason I never got to first base with Sammie in spite of my relentless efforts. I suddenly hated him all over again. I nodded dumbly, in answer to her question. Yes, I remembered Pete Spivey.

"After he graduated, Pete joined the military and I lost all contact with him. I was heartbroken, devastated. Absolutely. But I moved on with my life. I mean, I was just a teenager. I dated lots of boys all through junior college, but none turned me on—if you'll excuse my crassness—like Pete.

"By the time I met Griffin I was nearly thirty years old. Griffin was intelligent, ambitious, handsome . . . and adored me. I decided to *settle*. I married him, but the memory of my first love—Pete—never left me.

A couple years ago, I was surfing around the internet and tried to locate Pete. Miraculously, I found him."

Sammie then began relating how they'd e-mailed back and forth, how she discovered Pete was single and back living in the Midwest. His wife had died a few years before. Sammie was sad for him, she said, but secretly delighted to discover he was once again available. They rapidly found themselves in one of those internet romances, words of passion flying like cupid's arrows through cyber-space. Then Pete flew out to California to see her. It was like throwing gasoline on a flickering flame; the old fire flared back up and roared to life! She confided that it was as if all the years had been erased—she felt young again and he made her feel incredibly sexy. They began dating immediately, with Pete becoming a frequent flyer between the West Coast and Midwest.

"This all happened while Griffin was still alive and you were married?" I asked, interrupting her narration.

"Yes, uh huh. But I didn't keep my affair with Pete a secret from Griffin. I confronted him with it right away."

"And . . .?" I wondered how a man with old fashioned thinking might handle such a situation.

"And . . . he was hurt for sure. Absolutely. But he handled it very calmly. Griffin was a realist, he knew there was no way to keep Pete and me apart. And I knew there was no way I could continue living with Griffin. Pete wanted us to have a brand new life together, away from his roots back east, away from mine in California. So, he bought a small tract house in Phoenix, using some money he'd gotten from an insurance policy when his wife died, and I moved in with him there. I know it bothered Griffin a lot, but it seemed the humane thing to do." She said this with all the logic of someone considering euthanizing an ailing pet.

"A few months later, Griffin filed for divorce. He never served me with papers or followed through on the divorce in any way, but he showed me the petition his lawyer had filed."

"He showed it to you?" I asked.

"He brought it with him when he came out to visit."

I must have looked skeptical at the notion of the abandoned husband *visiting* his wife and her lover, because she paused a moment before continuing.

"I know it sounds weird, but it's true. Absolutely. He came out to Phoenix several times to visit Pete and me. He usually stayed at a hotel, but once he even spent the night in our guest room. We remained friends the whole time."

"So, how long have you cohabited with Pete then?" I inquired in a voice more lawyerly than intended.

"I moved in with Pete a few months ago."

"You said Griffin passed away. When? How?"

"He committed suicide, Benjamin. Griffin put a gun to his head and blew his brains out. It was totally out of character for him. Absolutely. Griffin was a vibrant, ambitious man. It's impossible to imagine him doing it."

"Well, in light of what you just told me about you and Pete and all, don't you think . . . ."

"That he killed himself on account of me?" she interrupted rather snappishly. "No, I don't! I told you, Griffin was fine with the whole thing. He actually *liked* Pete."

She paused, looking apologetic for snapping at me, then continued. "I know that may sound odd, Pete and Griffin were as different as night and day—but Griffin seemed to embrace Pete almost as a friend. No way he was distraught over me."

"Samantha, why are you telling me all this? And why now, after all these years, was it so important to see me?"

She hesitated.

"I'm glad you asked," she said, straightening her posture on the sofa. "The real reason I looked you up is because I need a good lawyer."

Again, I choked upon hearing her words. I still had not told her that I had given up practicing law.

"Why do you need a lawyer?" I asked.

"Well, to handle the probate for one thing," she said.

I blew a sigh of relief. A simple probate matter was no big deal. I could easily refer her to a good probate attorney.

"But, it may be considerably more than that. There are a lot of extenuating circumstances that I haven't told you yet."

"Like what?" I wanted to know.

"Like the police are investigating whether it really was a suicide.

Although, the general consensus is that it was. But *I* believe Griffin was pushed into by his girlfriend."

"Girlfriend?" Here was new information.

"Not a girlfriend really. Griffin had been seeing a hooker."

"Define *seeing*," I said.

"Griffin had an ongoing... *relationship* with a prostitute. It had been going on for several months, maybe as long as a year. Lord knows why he needed to pay for the services of a whore, Griffin was a very handsome and well-heeled man. If he wanted another woman, I'm sure there was no shortage of females who would love to meet someone like him."

"Why do you think this hooker might be responsible for his suicide?"

"For one thing, he shot himself on the front lawn of her house—a house that he bought for her."

"He bought her a *house?*"

"He bought her a house, he bought her a car... God knows what else he might have given that woman! Griffin had a good deal of money, but the idea of him *pissing* it all away—pardon my French—on a prostitute just wasn't in his nature. He had far too much respect for money. He loved money!"

"But yet, from what you're telling me, he spent lavishly on this woman. You say that suicide was not in keeping with your husband's character, but neither was spending money on hookers. Maybe you didn't know your husband as well as you thought," I suggested.

She stared blankly back at me, unresponsive.

"Okay," I tried again, "your husband—your estranged husband—died on the front lawn of a hooker's house. But what makes you think she *caused* him to commit suicide?"

"Because she wanted him dead."

"Why?"

"Because he left a will. In the will Griffin left everything to her."

"Everything?"

"Everything," she confirmed.

"Okay, your husband left everything to a hooker. How much are we talking about here? Do you have any idea what the value of his estate is?"

Looking me squarely in the face, Sammie answered—completely devoid of the emotion one might think would be attached to such an answer. "Somewhere in the neighborhood of twenty million dollars, give or take a few million."

Chapter Five

Samantha had not sought me out as an old boyfriend. Not as the love of her life who had gotten away. I'm not sure if I was disappointed or not. She was turning out to be a tad more complex than anyone I would care to be involved with. What Samantha saw in me was someone who could help her with the legalities vexing her current situation. She wanted a lawyer. She wanted a lawyer who would take a personal interest in her and her situation. She was hoping I was that same hopelessly smitten teenaged boy she had known, only with a law degree.

Referring her to a good probate lawyer was out of the question; she was set on yours truly handling the matter. "You're the only one I can trust," she said to me that evening after her fourth glass of wine—a reiteration of her earlier e-mail—shortly before she keeled over and collapsed for the night on my sofa.

I lay in bed thinking for a long while after Samantha had conked out. She wanted me to don my lawyer's hat and handle the probate of her husband's estate, to fight the will leaving everything to her husband's hooker/girlfriend, and in the process to somehow discover what had brought Griffin to commit suicide in the first place. On this last issue, I think she was looking for some sort of validation to her belief that *she* was not the cause.

Unfortunately for her, Samantha was looking for the man I no longer was, and had no interest in being: the diligent and dutiful lawyer, exactly the kind of man I had given up being when I quit the firm and moved to Venice Beach. Unfortunately for me, there was still a fair amount of that smitten teenage boy left. She had the kind of eyes that made me want to help her. That was as true now as it was thirty years ago. I might try my best to wriggle out of it, I hated practicing law and thought I had put all that behind me, but I knew that by morning light I would probably agree to take her case.

SAMANTHA WAS STILL ASLEEP ON the couch the next morning when I sneaked past her to walk outside onto the deck overlooking the ocean, the sun not yet visible from behind the inland mountain peaks as the sky gradually brightened into daylight. Pulling on my running shoes, I trotted across the loose sand toward the water's edge and started my morning ritual of running to Santa Monica Pier. This was my last chance before telling her I'd take the case to think of a way out of it. In cadence with my feet slapping upon the wet compacted sand—left, right, left, right—I mentally sorted through the pros and cons involved.

"Why shouldn't I help out an old friend?" the little voice inside my head asked. Besides, I rationalized, until my house down in South Orange County actually sold, I was still responsible for those hefty mortgage payments and, since quitting my job, could use a few extra bucks. The legal fees for probate matters were set by statute. A lawyer gets a certain percentage of the probated estate arrived at through a specific formula created by the state legislature. No lawyer could demand more than the statutory amount, even if he were F. Lee Bailey. The only exception might be if there were fees generated for duties performed over and above the standard probate matter, in which case the lawyer would petition the court for an *Allowance of Extraordinary Attorney Fees* and the court would decide if such extra fees were justified.

I could handle a simple probate matter easily enough and help a friend in the process. It didn't hurt that the statutory fee for an estate worth twenty million dollars would keep me in surfboards a good long time. After all, I was no longer associated with a firm, and who knew when the next opportunity to earn a fee might come along? And, if the case became a criminal matter—Sammie seemed to suspect there was more to her husband's death than a straightforward suicide—I could then recommend a good criminal lawyer to Samantha.

I turned back toward the beach house to give Sammie the good news, that I'd handle her case. But when I arrived she was gone.

Chapter Six

I had just rinsed off the salt sweat from my run and was stepping out of the shower when a female voice startled me.

"Good morning," Sammie greeted cheerfully. "So this is what I passed up back in school, huh?"

Grabbing a towel to cover my nakedness, we both laughed—I self-consciously, Sammie giggling like a schoolgirl. Standing there in the bathroom doorway, hair pulled back in a ponytail, barefooted, and wearing oversized sweats she must have snatched from my closet, she *looked* downright schoolgirlish as well.

"Where've you been?" I asked.

"Benjamin, I knew you lived *near* the beach, but I didn't realize we were right *on the beach* till I woke up this morning to this fabulous view," she said, waving her hands expansively. "You weren't around, so I went for a nice walk along the sand. How long have you lived here? It's just fabulous!"

"Not long," I answered, trying to dry myself with the towel while maintaining some semblance of modesty. That she offered no sign of retreat and just continued to watch made the task more awkward. Even more awkward still, her presence began lending itself to a growing level of involuntary arousal that I'm sure did not go unnoticed.

"You hungry?" I asked, trying to divert her attention and gain some degree of control.

"Getting there," she replied, eyes darting from the toweled protrusion to my reddening face as I continued my terrycloth dance. The double entendre of both my question and her answer, in light of the immediate situation, somehow totally escaped me. Otherwise, the next words I spoke might have been entirely different.

"Look," I said, "I'm afraid I don't have very much to offer you . . . to eat . . . in the house, I mean. What say we stroll on over to the *Cheese and Olive* and I'll buy you some breakfast? We can talk while we eat."

An audible sigh escaped her lips which, upon reflection, probably indicated disappointment at my inability to recognize an opportune moment. She vacated the doorway with a playfully dismissive wave. "Absolutely. Sounds great," she said over her shoulder, leaving me abruptly alone in the bathroom to complete my ablutions.

The Cheese and Olive is one of those Venice Beach landmarks that has been around forever—or in this case, since 1969—and is a short three-block stroll from my house. Seated at a sidewalk table, oblivious to the throngs of beach goers passing by only a few feet away, I told Sammie that I would take her case. She looked downright thrilled. I then explained to her the basics of testamentary law.

As a married man, Griffin's estate consisted of two distinct types of property: community property and separate property. Under California law and rules of intestacy, absent a valid will, Sammie would automatically inherit all of her husband's community property. This was true even though Sammie had moved out to shack up with her new boyfriend, Pete Spivey, since Sammie was still legally married to Griffin. Griffin did not have the legal right to leave Samantha's interest in community property to anyone, much less a hooker. That much was clear. So, no matter what the outcome, Sammie was in line to receive a sizable estate from the community property portion alone.

She was also entitled to one-half of all Griffin's *separate* property—that property which is not deemed to be community property in California—unless Griffin left it to someone else by will. Via a valid will, he could leave his separate property to anyone of his choosing—even a prostitute.

So, the first issue to tackle would be whether the alleged will wherein Griffin left everything to his prostitute girlfriend was valid. Griffin had a formal attested will, Sammie told me, that was drafted several years prior with the help of an attorney and which tended to mirror the rules of intestacy. That formal will would presumably be found valid. However, any subsequent wills—such as the one that left everything to the hooker—would supercede that prior will unless the subsequent will could be shown to be invalid.

"You understanding all this?" I interrupted my spiel to ask Samantha.

"Pretty much. All the community property is mine and half of Griffin's separate property is mine. So, who gets the other half?"

"Any living parents, brothers, sisters . . . ."

"Griffin's only relative is his brother," she said. "So, I'd get everything, except for half of the separate property that goes to his brother?"

"Unless the will where he left everything to the hooker is found to be valid. Then the hooker would get everything except for your community property, and the brother gets zip."

Samantha nodded that she understood, so I continued the lesson.

The will that the police found in Griffin's car at the scene of his death was what we lawyers refer to as a holographic will. This means it was a testamentary document drafted completely in the handwriting of the decedent. A holographic will must still comply with certain requirements in order to be considered valid, but is not required to be witnessed like a formal attested will. Basically, the only requirements are that the testator—the person creating the will—must have *capacity* and *intent*. In a nutshell, capacity means he was mentally stable at the time the will was drafted, and intent means he intended the instrument to be his last will and testament.

There were several fronts on which to contest the validity of Griffin's holographic will. The most obvious and effective would be if the girlfriend had caused his death. She would then be barred from inheriting anything—thereby rendering the holographic will meaningless. Sammie seemed to believe this was the case— that Griffin's prostitute had, at least, played *some* role in his death. If the police found evidence that Griffin had died at the hands of his mistress, our job would be much simpler.

AFTER BREAKFAST, WE WALKED BACK to the beach house. Sammie took a seat outside on the deck while I went inside to telephone the police and inquire as to the status of their investigation. I informed them that I was the probate attorney and needed to know if there was an ongoing investigation that could affect probate. Absent any real proof to the contrary, I was told, the police were ready to label the matter a suicide, thereby closing any criminal investigation. I could pick up a copy of the official report or they could mail one to me.

Hanging up the phone, I could see Samantha seated outside, looking so peaceful with eyes closed and head tipped back fully exposing her face to the warming rays of the sun, the sea breeze gently blowing her hair. I hated to disrupt such tranquility with unfavorable news, but walked outside and sat down in a chair next to hers.

Shielding her eyes from the sun with her hand, she lazily looked in my direction. "Well, what did L.A.'s finest have to say?"

I told her, and my words were like flipping a switch from tranquility to hostility. Samantha became instantly livid over the news. Bolting out of her chair, she began pacing the length of the deck, spouting off obscenities about the police, and shouting that there was no way Griffin would kill himself and leave his property to a "goddamned whore!"

Then, calming somewhat, she plopped angrily back into her chair. "Pardon my French, but I get furious when I think about that woman and the awful way Griffin died. It was *not* a suicide!"

She sat in silence a few moments, staring blankly out to sea, tugging absently at several tufts of hair that had escaped her ponytail. Then her eyes narrowed in a rather unsettling way, and she looked at me. "If the police are too lazy to do their job, we can do it for them!" She spat out the words with total disgust.

"What do you mean?" I asked.

"Benjamin, you need to give the police evidence so they will declare this a murder."

"How do you suggest I accomplish that?"

"You need to do your own investigation, Benjamin. You're so much smarter than those incompetent donut-munchers. You'll be able to discover the proof that is right there under their noses, but that they've refused to take the initiative to find."

"Sammie, that's not what lawyers do. We only argue legal facts. Lawyers don't go sleuthing around. That's only on TV. Sleuthing is a job for the police. They are trained to sleuth. Besides, we don't necessarily need to prove she killed him. Even if Griffin did commit suicide, there are other ways we can attack the will."

But that did not placate Samantha. She would not rest until the circumstances of her husband's death were cleared up to her satisfaction.

Sammie ranted on about her dearly departed husband. "Griffin was an extremely strong-willed, intelligent man," she told me. "He was a tough cookie and knew how to manipulate people. He always maintained control over situations. Absolutely. There's no way he would have killed himself. It just wasn't in his nature. Somehow this prostitute killed him, had him killed, or pushed him into it. Maybe she drugged him!"

"That may be, Sammie, but what can I do about it? The police have concluded Griffin's death to be a suicide. I'm just the probate attorney, for God's sake."

"At least look into it, Benjamin. At least go talk to this slut and do a little snooping around."

"Lawyers don't snoop around, that's the job for police," I told her again.

"Please, Benjamin, please! For once, think outside the box; do something outside your job description. Do it for me. You're the only one I can trust. Please."

There it was again. That "only one she can trust" bit again. *Why* was I the only one she could trust? Christ! We hadn't seen each other in thirty years! Why would I be the only one she could trust? We continued going round and round until she finally wore me down and I begrudgingly agreed to *look into it* for her. With that, her demeanor shifted instantly— from rancor to gratitude. Throwing her arms around my neck, she hugged me—squeezing so tight I thought I might suffocate—and sobbingly uttered, "Thank you. Thank you so much, Benjamin. You're the only one I can trust."

Chapter Seven

We drove together out to the San Fernando Valley. I dropped Sammie at her house in Woodland Hills—strange name for a place since there are no "woods" adorning those hills, only brown scrub-brush that briefly turns green each year during the rejuvenating winter rains. Samantha would be staying at her former marital residence, the one she had occupied for so many years with Griffin before taking off to the Arizona desert with her old high school flame, Pete Spivey. She still had clothing and various personal items at the house, so an extended stay would be easy for her. It struck me as slightly odd that she had no misgivings about sleeping in the same bed where her estranged husband had spent his last night—perhaps he had even spent it with his prostitute girlfriend—but maybe that was just me.

The Gambil home was a large modern stucco affair with four car garage and circular driveway. A nice house, but modest quarters for someone worth twenty million dollars. On the way, we stopped at the West Valley Police Station and picked up a copy of the death report on Griffin. The address listed in the report as the site where his death occurred was, no doubt, that of his hooker girlfriend. Griffin had died not more than eight miles from his own home, it was an Encino address.

After dropping Sammie off at her house and assuring her that I would continue to investigate the circumstances relating to Griffin's death—that I would not "drop the ball" as she felt the police had—I drove my little blue Porsche in the direction of Encino.

The girlfriend's house was not at all difficult to find. It was located on a well-manicured side street with older but expensive homes just south of Ventura Boulevard and only four blocks from a McDonald's restaurant.

Where else but Los Angeles would stately million-dollar residences be located within onion sniffing distance of a McDonald's?

It was a single story early 1960s vintage house—relatively plain looking for the neighborhood—set back from the street by a rather long driveway. The only ornate feature readily apparent was a wrought iron fence about the curtilage, encircling the grounds with an elaborate ten-foot gate barring automobile access whenever the gates were closed over the drive. But the gates were open as I cruised slowly by. A late model Mercedes Benz was parked in front of the garage. Intending to merely drive by, I was struck by the urge to stop and knock on the door. The open gates seemed an inviting sign and I was curious to see this courtesan whose beauty and sex appeal had inspired a handsome and wealthy man to bestow her with gifts like houses and cars.

Parking in the driveway directly behind the big cream-colored Mercedes, two German automobiles in tandem—my tiny sports car dwarfed by the full-sized sedan—I walked up and knocked upon the front door.

After several moments, a timid sounding female voice, barely audible from behind the door, asked, "Who is it please?"

I answered that my name is Benjamin Harding. I am the probate attorney representing the estate of the late Griffin Gambil and would like to ask a few questions regarding his death. Could I please speak with . . . quickly scanning the police report for the girlfriend's name . . . Connie Cantu?

The door opened to reveal a woman in her mid-thirties with medium length dark hair and almond eyes, Asian. There was something almost purplish about the color of her hair—the sort of deep purple that hides beneath the darker, more dominant color and only appears in certain kinds of light. Other than that, there was nothing particularly striking about this woman. She was not altogether unattractive, but hardly evocative of great beauty either. She wore a snug fitting, short black leather skirt with very high platform heels. The thought quickly flashed through my mind that she must be quite short in stature, the heels only raising her as high as my nose—and I'm not all that tall.

"Ms. Cantu?" I inquired.

"Ye-es," she answered haltingly. "I am Connie Cantu."

"Is this a good time to talk? Do you have a few moments?" I had no real authority to speak with her, but she may have thought that, since I was the probate attorney, she was obligated by law to answer my questions.

"Please to come in," she said, holding the door open.

I entered her home. It took a moment for my eyes to adjust from bright sunlight to the relative darkness of the interior. Furnishings were sparse, but what decorating motif existed was decidedly Oriental.

"You may sit there," she said politely, but with just a hint of a somewhat dismissive tone, motioning me to a large wicker chair in the shape of a clam.

She moved with feline grace, seating herself directly across from me in a chair matching my own. Crossing her legs, her already short skirt rising higher toward her hips, a mordant smile briefly flirted with her dark red lips as she recognized me noticing her shapely thighs. She lifted an already lit cigarette from the ashtray on the black lacquered table next to her chair and raised it to her mouth. I recognized it as a brown Sherman MCD, a pretty hefty smoke.

Wearing a silky, cream-colored blouse draped wispily over her small breasts, the nipples themselves appeared to be the largest protrusions from under the dainty material. Certainly not the tall, busty sex-goddess one might expect from central casting; aside from great legs, she was diminutive—with the breasts of a twelve-year-old girl. It was difficult to imagine a man like Griffin Gambil becoming so obsessed with anyone such as this that he would lavish her with cars, money and real estate. Still, I had to admit, there was something hauntingly alluring about her. Her mien was exotic.

I asked a few questions to confirm the facts already contained in the police report. Then, unsure just where my line of questioning might take us, I cut to the chase.

"Ms. Cantu, there are those who believe you played some part in the death of Griffin Gambil. Rather than my asking you specific questions, why don't you just tell me your side of the story in your own words and let's see where that takes us. Would that be all right with you?"

She puffed carefully on her cigarette, her lips pursed in a puckering manner, dragging the smoke deeply into her tiny lungs. Devoid of facial expression, she sat silently staring back at me—seemingly considering my suggestion to speak candidly.

"Where would you like me to begin Mr. Harding?" Blowing smoke from her small bow-like mouth, she enunciated each word carefully—including the R in Harding, which an Asian from central casting would never do. Any timidity I may have initially sensed in her had vanished, replaced by outright hauteur.

"Tell me about yourself and your relationship with Griffin Gambil. Tell me why he killed himself on your front lawn."

Connie Cantu looked at me skeptically. "Are you certain you would like to hear the *real* truth?"

I nodded.

"Then that is what I shall give you . . . the real truth."

I sat waiting for her to begin her story. Several minutes went by as she made quite a production out of thoroughly extinguishing the brown cigarette, pushing and twisting it into the ashtray until it was shredded, nearly obliterated, and no longer smoldering. Then she turned her gaze on me, staring silently, seemingly collecting her thoughts, choosing precisely what information to share with me.

"Men are usually so easy to control," she began matter-of-factly. "This one just got away from me. You see, ever since I was a young girl, I've been aware of a woman's power over men."

Without being aware of it, I must have raised a skeptical eyebrow because she paused a moment, studying my face.

"Yes, that's right—not a man's power over women, but rather a woman's power over men. All women possess this power. We are smarter, live longer, and hold between our legs the one thing men desire most in all the world," she said, nodding her head in agreement with her own words. "But, for some inexplicable reason, many women are not aware of their power or simply choose not to employ it. This is especially true of Asian women. I am Chinese, with a dab of Filipino. We are programmed from birth to be subservient to men. It is our culture. This was certainly true of my upbringing in Honolulu where I was raised in a very traditional Chinese home. It can be a difficult conditioning to overcome. But, for me, the notion that it was *I* who was the superior when it came to men somehow surfaced naturally. Simply put, I can get a man to do anything—and I do mean anything—just by using my natural goddess-given feminine abilities."

Fascinated, I couldn't prevent a fleeting smile from crossing my lips at her uncommon usage of the term "goddess." It was a smile which she likely interpreted as a condescending smirk, as she abruptly stopped speaking again for a moment. Once I assumed a proper look of respect, she resumed with a uniquely petulant narration.

"There was a strobe light flashing, pulsating with the beat of the music as I walked out on stage wearing a black vinyl body suit and stiletto boots. All my silly male slaves watched in captivated amazement as I danced seductively. I began pouring red liquid candy—cherry flavored—all over my body. My slaves sat enthralled . . . until I spoke the magic words to them, 'LICK ME!'"

I looked curiously at Connie Cantu, trying to imagine the bizarre scene she was describing and how it had anything to do with Griffin Gambil. She paused, smiling wickedly at me.

"That's when I woke up," she explained with a mirthless cackle. "I was thirteen years old when I had this dream. I knew instantly that it was far more than a mere dream—it was a revelation of my true self, of what I was *meant* to be. The next day I used my meager childhood savings to buy a black vinyl corset, fishnet thigh-highs and stiletto heels. I would model this outfit in front of a mirror in my room with the door locked. I loved how it made me look and feel, so beautiful . . . sexy . . . strong and powerful. Of course, I was only playing dress up. No way was I yet ready to live out my dream of dominating men and having them worship me. I was still a child, my mother would have killed me!"

She laughed defiantly at this and I smiled weakly back.

"It would be a few years before I truly came to understand the power a woman holds over a man. I would say to any woman who doubts she has this power, try wearing a very short skirt or low cut top and walk *confidently* into a room filled with men. The key is *attitude*, the clothing are just accessories. A haughty woman clad seductively can cause men to make absolute fools of themselves. Men just can't help it, it's in their genes.

"And to any man who doubts this ability that we women posses, try speaking about any *non-sexual* subject you care to choose with a strong, confident woman who is wearing a cleavage-revealing blouse." With almost imperceptible movement, she parted her legs the slightest bit and my eyes involuntarily focused there. Then, giving me a look intended to prove her point, added, "Or try speaking with a woman who is seated in such a way that it offers a view up her short skirt toward her shapely thighs. Having trouble keeping your mind on the subject at hand, Mr. Harding? This is exactly what I mean."

My eyes darted away from her, self-conscious. Her lips once again curled into that knowing smile; she had made her point.

"Griffin originally contacted me on the internet. I used to have a web site where I acted as cyber-mistress—what's commonly known as an S&M site. I was an internet dominatrix, inviting men to contact me through e-mail. Typically, we would send little S&M-flavored erotic messages back and forth—generally where I refer to the guy as my slave and order him to do certain things. Once I got the guy hooked—I'd tell him how much I would appreciate a *gift* from him, some tribute of monetary significance. That's the way the business works.

"I maintained a mail drop where my male slaves could send money if they wanted to continue our internet dialogue. On rare occasions, once I've developed a rapport with a man over an extended period and feel comfortable that he is not some sort of psycho, I will agree to an *in-person* meeting. I am definitely *not* a hooker and I make it clear, right from the start, that there will be absolutely no sexual contact between us. Even with such a restrictive caveat, men are willing to pay money just to meet with me and have me order them around. It's amazing, it really is, what men will do.

"That's what happened with Griffin. On the internet, he submitted an application for an in-person session with me. He said he would be traveling to Hawaii on business and asked if we could meet then. So, I agreed to meet him at a hotel near Kuhio Street in Waikiki where I often arrange for such sessions. The manager there is a brutish man who I am able to charm into being my defender; he stands ready to handle any of my slave clients who might turn nasty.

"The first time I saw Griffin, I'll admit I was a bit surprised. He was fairly handsome for a Caucasian and for a man of his years. He was quite tall, over six feet I should think, dressed in dark business attire, and exhibited a somewhat angry demeanor—a real tough guy type. I thought, 'Uh oh, here's trouble.' His physical presence did not fit at all with the docile, wimpy persona of the slave I knew only through e-mail correspondence.

"Griffin swaggered into the hotel lobby like some macho John Wayne . . . until he saw me sitting in a chair, fully clothed in a conservative, but very feminine, skirt and blouse. Our eyes met and he knew immediately who I was. As I said before, it is all about attitude. I did not need to be wearing some sort of stereo-typical leather fetish outfit. My demeanor said it all. Just seeing me stopped him dead in his tracks. I ordered him to avert his eyes from my face and look at the floor. He did, instantly transforming himself from commanding to obsequious. I walked over to him, handing him my bag containing the tools of my trade—whips, handcuffs . . . the usual assortment of props—and told him to carry it as he followed meekly behind me to the hotel room.

"Once inside the room, I seated myself on the bed with my legs crossed—much like I am now. Then I told him to remove all his clothing, to fold each item neatly and place it in the bureau drawer. He did so without hesitation. Once a man stands naked and humbled with a rigid pole in the presence of a fully clothed woman, the reversal of power is clearly established. It was very apparent that he found the situation stimulating, so I continued.

"*On your knees!* was my next command, which he followed without protest. *You may crawl over and sit at my feet.* He eagerly did so." With arresting syntax, Cantu then validated the conduct she had just described, "This is exactly the sort of thing that people who like this sort of thing will more than sort of like."

"For the next hour I subjected my new slave—Griffin—to intense verbal humiliation and overall emasculating behavior. Through it all he remained fully aroused. This was precisely the scenario that turned him on, it was obvious. Griffin wasn't into torture or flogging or any of the other pain avenues associated with S&M. In fact, the entire time neither of us had any physical contact with the other. He just liked to be ordered around by a strong, beautiful, dominant woman."

Again, some misconstrued expression on my face seemed to cause her to hesitate briefly and qualify what she was saying.

"Really, Mr. Harding," she said, her tone tinged with indignation, her diction precise. "This is not so unusual as it may sound. I find that it is quite often the men who are strong, successful and domineering in their everyday lives who are secretly yearning to relinquish control to some female authority figure—what they perceive as the antithesis of the way things are in their everyday lives. They often have pudendum complex as well."

Although I had no idea what pudendum complex might be, I later looked it up. It means to be ashamed of one's external genitals. I encouraged Cantu to continue with her story and I sat nonplused as this skillful raconteur took me further into a world I barely even knew existed.

"As our first hour together was nearing its end," she went on, uncrossing and re-crossing her legs, "I figured my new slave was in need of some release. So, I ordered him to masturbate for me. For the first time, he appeared reluctant to follow my order. This surprised me, usually this is the reward my slaves yearn for. So, I insisted—with further instructions that he was not allowed to climax without first obtaining my permission. Begrudgingly he began to comply. Before long he was pleading for permission to cum. His eyes rolled upward in his head and his body appeared to be convulsing, even as his hand continued up and down like a piston. 'Please Mistress,' he pathetically implored, 'I'm *begging* for your permission.'

"I asked my groveling slave what he would do for me if I granted permission, although I already knew the answer. Whimpering men with their dicks in their hands are so predictable. He would have agreed to anything just to get permission for his sexual release. Of course, he didn't *really* need my permission. But, this was the *game* you see. He enjoyed relinquishing all control to me. I now controlled his orgasms. I owned his dick!

"I asked how much money he had in his wallet. He said a thousand dollars. He said I could have it all, if I'd just allow him to cum. True to his pledge, before he left that evening he handed me *a grand*—in cash! Quite frankly, no slave had ever given me that much money before—at least not for only one hour of my time. I knew then that Griffin was a man of means. I had discovered a gold mine!"

It felt as if she might have come to the end of her narration because several moments of silence ensued. Cantu sat staring off into space, her hands playing idly with a butane cigarette lighter. I asked a question to get her going again. "How long did you and Griffin continue with this sort of, uh . . . relationship?"

Lighting a new cigarette, she inhaled deeply before answering. "Griffin and I continued seeing each other for several months. Never once did we have what most people might consider sex, nor was I ever *paid* for having sex with him. As I said, I am *not* a hooker. But, his fetish toward female domination and to be controlled was like a drug to him. The more humiliating the task I required him to perform, the greater the high he seemed to derive from it. Each successive session became more intense than the last. To show his appreciation, he gave me cash, jewelry, clothing . . . . After one particularly intense session that lasted all weekend, he handed me the keys to a new Mercedes Benz with my name on the title. I thought for sure I'd hit the jackpot! There is no way I would ever want to see my golden goose *dead*, believe me."

I nodded. It was true, she seemed to have quite a good thing going with old Griffin the sex slave.

"After a while, Griffin begged me to leave Hawaii and move to the mainland—to California—so we could be together more often. He bought me this house where I could live and we could continue our secret relationship, away from hotel rooms, in absolute privacy. It's probably worth close to a million dollars. Would you like to see the room I made into my dungeon?"

"Maybe later," I told her.

She waved the air as if to say, "Whatever," then continued. "Not only did my slave buy this house for me, I didn't even need to *clean* the place myself. He loved coming over and having me *order* him to do all the housework! All he wanted in return was for me to abuse him and treat him like shit."

The entire scenario just seemed too bizarre to me. Cantu had spun a titillating tale, but how could I know if there was even a scintilla of truth to it. Perhaps my expression betrayed my thoughts, because she suddenly looked me squarely in the eye and said, "Before even considering relocating here to the mainland, I required he give me a written contract—making certain his offer was not merely some ruse. The contract spells it all out quite clearly. Would you care to see it?"

I nodded. This was news. No one had mentioned a contract before.

Without speaking a word, Cantu rose from her seat and exited the room, her high-heels clicking down the hallway.

Alone in the dimly lit room—the living room I would guess, but it was difficult to tell—I began to take in my surroundings for the first time. Across the room, two windows with shades pulled low, framed by a thin-line of leaked sunlight despite great effort to keep it out, likely had a view of the driveway where I'd parked. With some effort after sitting so long, I pulled myself from the big clam-chair with the intent of walking over to the windows to check on my car. In the darkness, I nearly stumbled over a small square table isolated oddly in the center of the room, surrounded by no other furniture. Its sharp corners just the right height to bang my shins, it was all I could do to not let out a yell.

The table had a single drawer. Opening it, I pulled out a sheaf of papers, four or five pages, and strained my eyes to make out what was on them. It appeared to be calligraphy. Too dark in the room to read the words. Might as well be in Chinese I was thinking, when I realized it was exactly that—Chinese writing, extending from top to bottom of the page rather than from left to right.

Paper-clipped to one of the pages, a photo of Cantu—same leather skirt, same extraordinarily high-heeled shoes—with a man, a Caucasian man. But the man did not look to be Griffin Gambil. Though I couldn't be absolutely certain, this man appeared considerably younger, and dressed in T-shirt and jeans—attire not in keeping with the sense of style Sammie attributed to her late husband. They were standing outside this very house, side-by-side, his arm draped over Cantu's shoulders. I couldn't really make out his facial features, but could see they were both smiling broadly.

What I was holding, I decided, was a letter. Either written by or to Connie Cantu, it seemed the letter was *about* the man in the photo. From the letter I discerned two things. First, Griffin Gambil was not the only Caucasian man with whom Cantu was chummy here at her Encino house. Second, the dragon lady did, surprisingly enough, have another side to her. One where she knew how to smile and look happy.

Hearing the clicking of Cantu's heels approaching, I hurriedly returned the letter and photo to the drawer and vaulted back into the over-stuffed arms of the clam.

RE-ENTERING THE ROOM WHERE I'D only barely regained my seat, Cantu stopped mid-stride, like a predator sensing prey. Had my hasty retreat from the table containing the photo and letter been detected? For a few moments I felt like some errant child worried in the presence of a feared disciplinarian. Neither of us spoke. Any words from me would have betrayed rapid nervous breath. *Her* silence bespoke a certain suspicion, but one she could not immediately identify.

Finally, she handed me the alleged contract between her and Griffin, then returned to her chair. She did not offer to turn on a lamp as I, once again, struggled without light to read words on a page. At least these words were in English.

The contract was simple and to the point, virtually absent of legalese. The gist of it was that Griffin must only concern himself with providing Mistress Cantu pleasure—his own pleasure was to be derived only from serving her. In addition, he agreed to give her complete control of his sexuality without knowing in advance what that might entail, although the contract did spell out a few examples—including but not limited to— *sexual restraint, sexual training devices—including male chastity tubes, bondage, spanking, humiliation, physical punishment, servitude* . . . . It was just as Cantu described, she owned his dick! And by extension, it seemed to me, she had laid a pretty vast claim to his mind as well.

The handwritten document went on to confirm that Griffin had voluntarily gifted the Mercedes Benz and the house—as well as various jewelry pieces, described with particularity—to his Mistress as her sole property. The final clause was especially intriguing: the contract would lapse after a trial period of six months unless Griffin made an appropriate demonstration of his devotion and submission. Mistress Cantu alone would determine what that would be.

Of course, the contract was legally unenforceable: slavery was outlawed long ago in this country. But it was drafted completely in Griffin's own hand and a legal argument might be made that it lent support to the validity of the holographic will found at the scene of his untimely demise, wherein Griffin left everything to Cantu. This was *not* going to help Samantha's case.

"Have the police seen this?" It was the first time I had spoken in a while, and my voice cracked like a boy entering puberty.

"It never came up," she said. "I didn't tell them half the things I'm telling you today. I don't like talking to badges. You don't have a badge, do you?"

I shook my head. "Like I said, I'm the probate attorney, just looking for some answers, trying to get some closure on the matter."

"Well, I really don't see how anyone could suspect me of wanting him dead. Why would I? What motive could I possibly have? At the time of his death, I didn't even know about his will leaving me everything. All I knew was that, as long as he remained alive and obsessed with me, my life was easy street." Accumulated ash fell from the tip of her cigarette onto the black lacquered table, her hand winnowing it further to the floor. "Okay, I admit I never loved him. I'm not even sure I *liked* him very much. But I know he loved me. Loved? He absolutely adored me, worshiped me!"

Though Cantu denied any knowledge of the actual will, it occurred to me that the ominous possibilities inherent in the extension clause of this so-called contract could include forcing Griffin to draft a will leaving his fortune to his mistress. But why stop there . . . maybe she would also command him to put a bullet through his brain!

"Then why did he kill himself on your front lawn?" I asked.

She displayed no reluctance at answering my question. "Several days before he died, Griffin told me he loved me. He often expressed his feelings toward me in terms of adoration, but this was the first time he ever used the word *love*. He said he loved me and never would want to live without me. He said he would do anything to prove his feelings.

"For me, this was just more of the game. I laughed at him. I taunted him. I said 'Of course you love me, I am a goddess!' I told him that he was a pathetic little worm—unworthy of a goddess' affection; that I couldn't possibly love him, that he was just one of my play-things—one of my stupid, spineless slaves! He usually got off on such debasement. That day seemed no exception. I then allowed him inside the house where he did a splendid job cleaning the kitchen for me before I sent him on his way.

"A few days later, the morning he died, Griffin came over and announced that he was going through with divorcing his wife. He said he wanted to marry me. Would I consider marrying him? Still part of the game for me, I again laughed in his face, telling him what a foolish cretin he was. I said that I was sick and tired of him and his empty promises. I told him that—because he had displeased me—I didn't want to see him anymore. I banished him from my house. We both walked outside. His car was parked on the street and I told him to get in it and leave. At that, he pleaded and groveled on his knees, right there in my driveway, for me to reconsider. I told him he was a puny man with a puny little dick and too pathetic to even look at. Knowing this is the kind of talk from me that he lives for, I turned my back on him, walked away, and went inside the house.

"What I *expected* to happen was for him to then send me some outlandish present—something even grander than anything he had previously bestowed upon me—in order to win my favor. Instead, I heard a gun shot!"

"So, you didn't actually see him shoot himself, then?" I asked.

"No. I walked out onto the front lawn and saw him lying there in a pool of blood near his car. Much of his head had been blown off. It was awful. I could tell immediately that he was dead. My first reaction was shock, of course. Then I went back inside and telephoned the police. They arrived within two minutes. I wasn't *grieving* him, but was—and am still— extremely disappointed by his death. But let me make myself perfectly clear, I am *not* responsible for what happened. We had been playing a game. There was no way I could have known he would *off* himself like that."

"Do you think he killed himself because you wouldn't marry him?"

She more or less chuckled at such a notion, sloughing it off as hardly possible. "No, no," she said. "What we had was just a fantasy for him. I've been playing this scene with male subs for quite some time and think I pretty much know what goes on in their warped little minds. If he entertained any thoughts of marrying me, it would be just to keep the game going."

"Why do you suppose he killed himself then?" I asked her.

"I don't know. Maybe this one just got away from me and I never saw it coming. But I really don't think I had anything to do with it."

Or maybe you knew about the will, I thought to myself, and wanted to speed up the game and cash in your pot of gold. As his dominatrix, maybe you even *commanded* him to write a will leaving you everything.

Perhaps anticipating my thoughts, Connie Cantu added, "I didn't know anything about the will. For all I knew, my golden goose lay bleeding and dead out on the front lawn and I was left with nothing. I had no idea he left everything to me. I was sorry to lose him . . . as a slave I mean. The last thing I wanted was for him to die. But Griffin had a lot of shit going on in his life that could have pushed him over the edge. He sure as hell didn't do it over me."

"What kind of shit?" I asked. "Do you mean like his wife leaving him for another man?"

Again she chuckled. "Not at all," she said. "Her shacking up with some old boyfriend didn't bother Griffin at all really. To a certain degree he actually enjoyed the thought of those two together."

"What . . . ?" I was dumbfounded.

"Sure," she explained. "Men with a fetish for female dominance love the idea of playing the cuckolded husband. They are addicted to experiencing shame at the hands of a woman. What's more shameful for a man than having his wife fuck some other guy, especially after she hasn't been fucking her husband in a long time? It's the ultimate psychological emasculation."

"He told you all that?" I asked.

"He didn't have to. I know how these types think. But, yes, he did tell me. A man who will crawl across the floor naked on his hands and knees and beg for the privilege to lick the bottoms of my shoes—that sort of man does not keep secrets from his Mistress."

I still had trouble envisioning Griffin Gambil as the kind of man who grovels at a woman's feet—it clearly did not fit the way Sammie described her husband at all. But the contract, in Griffin's own handwriting, was tangible proof of this sick relationship. Plus, how else would Cantu know about Griffin's lack of a sex life with his wife? It also explained why Griffin didn't put up a struggle when Samantha left. This cuckolding stuff was oddly curious. Thinking about it, a question sprang to mind.

"Do you think he had a dominatrix-style relationship with his wife, too?"

"Not likely," Cantu replied. "That's why he came to me, to live out his secret fantasy. The fact that he derived pleasure from his wife being with another man was probably something she was never even aware of."

"Well," I said, puzzled, "if it wasn't his wife leaving him for another man that drove him to commit suicide—what other kind of 'shit in his life' do you mean?"

That caustic smile reemerged, evolving into a taut sneer. With a seductive whisper, as if sharing some titillating secret, speaking so softly she caused me to lean closer in order to hear, she said, "I think you should be talking to Broadus Liberato, Griffin's ex-business partner."

With that, she again spread her legs slightly apart, making the view up her skirt more obvious. I glanced down at the dark tops of her stocking-clad thighs. She was absolutely right. I couldn't help myself. It was in my genes.

Chapter Eight

I filed the *Petition to Administer Estate* and myriad attendant documents with the California Superior Court-Probate Division. Included was a *Petition for Letters of Administration* nominating Samantha as administrator of the estate. Griffin Gambil's estate was estimated at a value of twenty million dollars—although a more accurate valuation would be forthcoming, determined by a court appointed probate referee who would perform a formal inventory and appraisal. Once issued, the Letters of Administration would authorize Samantha to conduct all business related to her husband's estate. It would be her job to delve through her husband's financial records, to send out notices to all of Griffin's potential creditors who wished to be paid, and to collect all money owing to the estate. For such services, the administrator would be paid an amount equal to that received by the attorney. Both legal and administration fees would be paid from estate assets, creditors only receive payment if there happens to be any remaining funds.

Sammie called to complain that she was having a difficult time of it, going through all her husband's *stuff*, could I please come over and help out?

I PARKED THE PORSCHE OUT front of the house, mid-point in the circular driveway, and rang the front doorbell. Sammie answered wearing a bathrobe, even though it was well past noon. The scowl on her face was instant indicia of a cranky mood.

"I'm glad you finally got here," was her sardonic greeting. "Making sense of all Griffin's shit is driving me nuts!"

"Good afternoon to you too, Sunshine," was all I could muster in response.

"Sorry, but this whole situation is really beginning to wear on me," she said without much apology in her tone. "You know, Griffin was never this disorganized. It's as if . . . I'd swear someone was here going through his papers before I got here—before I even arrived in town."

"Like who?"

"The only person I know who Griffin ever trusted with a key to his house was Gavin—his brother. Absolutely. Griffin was the most cautious, least trusting man you'd ever want to meet. He always said, 'Never let your left hand know what your right hand is doing.' And that's really how he lived, that was his motto. Griffin never trusted anyone, but he trusted his brother more than anyone else . . . except maybe for me."

"And you think maybe the brother came by and rifled through Griffin's things before you got here?" I asked.

"I don't know . . . probably not. But I haven't been able to reach Gavin to ask, either. I've left messages, but so far he hasn't returned any of my calls. Gavin worshiped Griffin and I can't imagine why he's not made himself available. It's just not like Gavin. Quite honestly, I really could use his help sorting through all this stuff. Being the grieving wife, administrator of the estate, arranging for the funeral and responsible for sorting through all Griffin's belongings —and doing it all by myself—is really getting to me."

"Maybe this will perk you up a bit," I said. "I paid a visit to Griffin's alleged 'girlfriend' the other day."

That stopped Sammie in her tracks. "And . . .?" she demanded impatiently.

Leaving out many of the more graphic details, I described Connie Cantu and related to Samantha much of what Cantu had told me about her *relationship* with Griffin. Through my entire dialogue, Samantha sat transfixed—listening to every word. When I finished, Sammie continued to sit, wide-eyed, staring at me with a look on her face of absolute incredulity.

"Does any of that fit the man you were married to?" I asked at last.

Samantha let several moments glide by before responding. "It all sounds like utter nonsense," she finally spoke, indignation setting her tone. "In my wildest imagination, I cannot picture *my* Griffin kowtowing to *anyone*, let alone some flat-chested Chinese whore!"

"Actually, I believe she's only *part* Chinese. I'm pretty sure she's part Filipino, too," I interrupted.

"I don't give a damn if she's part Martian! Pardon my French, but I think it's absolute crap! I think she made the whole thing up. You know, in my mind I pictured her to be some buxom sexpot—someone so gorgeous that, as a man, my husband just couldn't help himself. Now I find out he was cheating on me with a Chinese midget!"

"She's hardly a midget. . .," I began.

Sammie cut me off, she was becoming more and more upset. "I don't mean to sound racist, but I believe there's a word for this sort of thing. . . ." She halted, apparently trying to think of the word.

"Miscegenation?" I offered—an outdated pejorative term meaning sexual relations between persons of different races. I hadn't heard the term used in at least two decades, but it seemed like the word she was going for.

"That's it, miscegenation! See? You are not the only one around here who knows big words. But call it whatever you want, I think she made the whole thing up. Absolutely. I have no idea what Griffin's fascination was with this *slut*, but it couldn't have been the way she told you. Not Griffin, no way!"

Raising my hands in surrender, I said, "Hey, don't shoot the messenger. I'm merely repeating what she told me."

"Well . . . do *you* believe what she told you?" Sammie's tenor was downright accusatory.

"Keep in mind, I never knew Griffin," I said. "All I know about him is what you and Connie Cantu have told me. But *if* what Cantu says is true—that their role playing was an *addiction* for Griffin—it would explain a lot of things. Like why someone so in love with money, as you claim Griffin to have been, would shower a virtual stranger with outrageously expensive gifts—a damned Mercedes Benz and a house for Christ sake! You claim that such spontaneous generosity is not in keeping with Griffin's churlish nature. Maybe you need to reexamine just how well you *really* knew your husband."

If looks could kill, Samantha would have dropped me right there on the spot. She launched into a furious rebuttal, her words an unpunctuated staccato. Abruptly she stopped, as if at some mental crossroad and deciding which path to travel, cogitating a moment on what I had just told her.

In the blink of an eye, her features softening somewhat, Sammie segued from irate ranting to logical reasoning. "Assuming for a moment that everything the prostitute told you about her and Griffin was true, how does that affect us *legally*?"

I related the worst-case scenario. "The so-called contract he wrote, signed and gave to Cantu perhaps adds validity to the holographic will Griffin made . . . wherein he left everything to his mistress . . . ."

A heavy sigh from Sammie momentarily interrupting my legal analysis caused me to pause before going on.

"On the other hand," I began again, "the very nature of her relationship with him—that of dominatrix controlling his every act—might allow us to show that she exerted undue influence upon Griffin for her own personal gain . . . thereby nullifying the will and she would get nothing."

"And you think we can win a will contest on that theory?" she asked.

"No guarantees, but yes, I do believe we would prevail."

"And do you think she caused Griffin's death?" Sammie asked.

I shrugged. "Who's to say? *Cause* is open to interpretation. Cantu claims Griffin had other things going on that might have driven him to do the deed. What can you tell me about his business partner, a man with the rather odd name of Broadus Liberato?"

According to Samantha, Broadus Liberato was a "sometimes" business associate with Griffin. They had worked on certain projects together over the years and had a long standing and friendly relationship. She could think of no reason to link Liberato to Griffin's death.

"But Broadus is one of the people I need to contact regarding this probate mess," Sammie said to me. "Maybe you could speak to him in person for me and we could kill two birds with one stone."

"Two birds?" I asked. "Other than the probate matter, what other 'bird' do we need to kill?"

"I'd like your take on whether he had anything to do with Griffin's death," she informed me.

"You just told me there was nothing to link Liberato to Griffin's death," I said.

"Absolutely. But, even though I don't think it's very likely, you never know, stranger things have happened. I'd really appreciate it if you would meet with him—man to man—and see what you think."

"Sammie, for the hundredth time, I'm just the probate attorney. I keep telling you, I'm not qualified to do all this sleuthing around."

Samantha just looked at me, helplessly.

"Fine, I'll try to meet with Liberato tomorrow," I said.

Chapter Nine

Broadus Liberato's office was located among a warren of low-rise business buildings clustered to form a small complex just off Canoga Avenue near the Valley's Warner Center. Warner Center was once a huge open lot owned by Warner Brothers Studios—hence the name—until it was developed in the 1970s to become the mirrored glass office structures and upscale restaurants where the Valley's professional and business elite congregate. Warner Center is now the true business hub of the West Valley. Liberato's office was Warner Center *adjacent*.

We sat in his office, talking about Griffin Gambil. I found Broadus Liberato to be a smallish, stooped, elderly man. Sagging eyelids, throat wattle . . . the geography of an old face. Like someone from a bygone era, he was dressed in an expensive but outdated suit. The last lingering remnants of silver hair were combed straight back over his freckled pate. Looking thin and fragile, he still bore himself with the self-assuredness of a successful entrepreneur. The sort of man, I decided also, with well developed moral views and wealth of perspective and experience which can only be acquired—regrettably—by growing older.

Liberato expressed remorse over the passing of Griffin Gambil. "That boy was like a son to me for years," he said, shaking his head as if remembering some cherished long-ago time. "I taught him this business. The first property Griffin ever developed, we developed together. It was a condo project up at Mammoth Mountain. When we cashed out on that deal, Griffin was grinning ear to ear like some mischievous school boy who had just gotten away with something. For some time afterwards I think he spent every night just counting his money, over and over again. After making such a windfall on his first project, Griffin was hooked. We did lots of projects together after that. Griffin was ambitious all right."

Then, looking more solemnly pensive, Liberato added, "Maybe a bit *too* ambitious."

"What do you mean?" I asked.

"Seems Griffin never anticipated that the real estate market could ever take a dive. He lived pretty high on the hog all through the 1980s when things were really popping. He never really saved for that rainy day that, ultimately, always comes along. I tried to tell him that sooner or later the bubble was going to burst. I've been around the block a few times. I've seen it all before. The market is cyclical. When it all fell apart, around 1989, Griffin was caught unawares—despite my warnings. He lost damn near everything."

Elbows on desk, withered arthritic fingers in a steeple, Liberato stared off into space, pondering, then continued.

"When the market flattened, it went from bad to worse in this business. California was especially hard hit. You may recall, our recession here lasted a good seven years or so. That's a long time. Griffin changed during that time. He became mean—like a cornered animal. He turned on many of his longtime colleagues."

"Yourself included?" I asked, wondering just how far afield this nascent ambition of Griffin's might have led him.

Puffing his jowled cheeks with air, then slowly exhaling, he answered. "It pains me to say it, but yes. It became plain that Griffin and I could no longer work together. Quite frankly, it got to where I just couldn't trust him. He was doing some rather shady deals, and I just didn't care for the way he ran his business any longer."

"What kind of shady deals?"

"Well, I'm not going to sit here and speak unkindly of the dead. Suffice to say that our road together came to a dead end a few years ago."

"What happened?" I coaxed, hoping I wasn't pressing my luck pursuing something the old gent seemed disinclined to elaborate upon.

Broadus Liberato surveyed me with a skeptical look. "Off the record?"

"Certainly, off the record," I answered. I'm not sure just what *record* we were referring to. This was not a criminal investigation and I had no authority to be making any kind of a record regarding this questioning. I was just the probate attorney, but maybe—like Connie Cantu—Broadus Liberato thought he was somehow obligated to answer my questions and believed I was creating some sort of "record" that he did not want his next statement to be a part of.

"Griffin and I jointly held title to some real estate that we had purchased together several years back. He wanted to use these properties as collateral for a loan he needed in order to develop an entirely different parcel. In order to put up the properties as collateral he needed me to sign off on them, so it would look like he owned the collateralized properties outright, all by himself. Griffin said once he got the loan, and the separate parcel was developed, he would pay me for my half of the properties we owned together—if I would just sign off on them now. My interest in the properties had a value somewhere in the neighborhood of a million dollars—give or take a couple of bucks. That was too great a sum to entrust to a mere handshake and Griffin's verbal promise of repayment later. I refused to sign off without being bought out on the properties. Griffin became pretty irate. We had a real blowout—right here in my office—but I held firm."

Liberato sat quiescent for an hour-like moment, perhaps reliving the blowout scene of which he had just spoken. His otherwise avuncular face looking troubled. His thumb nervously burnished the white dollop at the end of a black Mont Blanc pen held in his right hand.

"What happened next?" I asked at last.

With exaggerated care, he gently set the pen down on his desktop. Then, returning his eyes to mine, he haltingly continued. "Not long after our blowout, I was working late, alone here. Griffin and that brother of his barged in—all dressed in black, like a couple of thugs from an old 'B' movie. They threatened me about signing off on the properties. To make their point, Griffin's brother pointed a gun in my direction. Million dollars or not, it wasn't worth dying for. I signed the goddamned quit claim deeds he shoved in my face. Right after I signed the documents, Griffin cozies up to me—like it's old times—and promises to repay me. His brother made me a promise, too."

"What promise?" I asked.

"His goddamned brother promised that if I made a stink about them strong-arming me, he would personally put a bullet in my head."

"And you think the brother would have actually made good on such a threat?"

"Not on his own I don't. But he really idolized Griffin. And, as I said, Griffin had turned very mean. Who knows what he might tell his brother to do? And I do believe if Griffin told him to kill me, that he just might follow through and do it. So, under the circumstances, I kept my mouth shut about the entire matter. I figured if Griffin made money on his development project I had a reasonably good chance of getting repaid. On the other hand, if I called the cops, I had a reasonably good chance of not living out the month."

Chapter Ten

"No, I still have not heard from Gavin," Sammie said in answer to my query about Griffin's brother as she let me in the front door. "I'm beginning to get a little pissed off—pardon my French—having to do all this work myself. I really would have expected him to show up voluntarily to help out. Griffin and I were Gavin's only family."

I told Samantha about my interview with Broadus Liberato. She had difficulty believing that the *boys* came on so rough with Broadus, but sloughed off such a notion as unimportant.

"Rough?" she asked. "Griffin, maybe. I told you Griffin could be a tough cookie when it came to getting what he wanted. It's conceivable that he could have gotten a little carried away. But not Gavin. Gav doesn't have a mean bone in his entire body. No way could Gavin threaten to hurt someone, much less kill them. Especially since he became religious."

"Griffin's brother is religious?" I asked.

"Extremely," Sammie responded, rolling her eyes for effect.

"Was Griffin religious?"

She laughed. "Not at all. Griffin was almost contemptuous of organized religion."

"So, why was his brother so religious then?" I wondered.

Samantha, shuffling through the stacks of paper atop Griffin's desk, pulled some pages from the bottom of a heap and handed them to me. It was a two page letter—drafted on legal sized paper—from Gavin Gambil, and typed on an old-fashioned typewriter.

"This should answer your question. Gavin wrote this a couple years ago and sent one to everyone he knew. I'm really surprised Griffin kept it. I found it in the file cabinet, filed under G for Gavin. In fact, it was the *only* thing I found under G."

I took the letter and began reading.

Dear friends in Christ,

I am writing this because I want to share with you the bliss that can be yours, if you will just believe. As you know, I have been a sinner of the worst sort for much of my miserable life. I have partied much too often and partaken of booze far too frequently. My worsening drug habit has thrown my life out of control. When I wasn't high, I found myself in the depths of depression. More than once I have seriously considered taking my own life. You all remember the automobile accident I was involved in last year that landed me in the hospital. I will confess right now that it was no accident. I intentionally drove my car off the road, hoping to end my nightmare.

But that was not the Lord's will. He had other plans for me that included leading me to salvation in order to bring even more of you to the light. This is why I am writing this letter to my family and friends. To show you the light so that you too can follow the path to Glory that I am presently on. I know many of you may be skeptical, but let me tell you my story of how I found hope in Jesus Christ. Maybe then, you will be inspired as well.

Lying in the hospital, after my car accident, a pastor from a local church visited me. He began telling me about the Lord. I told him he was wasting his time. He just smiled and gave me his card, saying that if I ever felt the need, I'd always be welcome in God's house. Several months later, feeling depressed and suicidal, I found that card in my pocket. I walked to the church and entered.

At the end of the service, the preacher asked if there was anybody present who, if they were to die tonight, knew for a fact that they would go to heaven. Several in the congregation raised their hands into the air. Then he said, if there is anybody who is not absolutely sure they will go to heaven, please raise your hand. I raised my hand because I knew I deserved to go to hell for all the drugs and partying I had done. The preacher asked me to please come forward and

You're the Only One I Can Trust

he showed me from the Bible how we could all become certain that we are on our way to heaven.

The first thing he showed me was Rom 3:23: "For all have sinned, and come short of the glory of God." This tells us that we are all sinners. The second thing he showed me was Rom 6:23: "For the wages of sin is death." This tells us that sin has a penalty and we deserve to go to hell for our sins. The next thing is Eph 2:8-9: "For by grace are ye saved through faith; and that not of yourselves . . . it is the gift of God; not of works, lest any man should boast." Now this tells me that good deeds alone won't get me into heaven. That the way to Heaven is through faith and God's grace; faith in Jesus and what He did for us.

Rom 5:8-9 says, "But God showed His love toward us in that, while we were yet sinners, His only son died for us. Being now justified by His blood, we shall be saved from wrath through Him." This tells us that through Jesus, who made the perfect sacrifice for us, we can live forever in God's Holy Kingdom. I prayed that night and invited Jesus into my heart.

The next morning the first thing I thought of was God! I was so excited. And it didn't take long before everyone noticed a big change in me. Soon I was off junk forever. To thank the Lord for what he has done, I'm happy to share this truth with you all. But just knowing the truth is not enough. You have to pray and accept salvation. If you do not accept Jesus you are rejecting Him and He will reject you when you die and cast you into hell.

Please join me in seeking the Rapture that we all can discover in our Lord. I invite each and every one of you to call me and I will be happy to bring you with me to services anytime you might want.

God Bless you and keep you,
Gavin Gilchrist Gambil

"Jesus," I muttered, handing the letter back to Sammie.
"Precisely!" Sammie laughed. "But, Gavin really believes that stuff. Who the heck are we to say he's wrong?"

She had a point.

"That's why I'm sure Mr. Liberato was exaggerating about the way the boys acted. I can't conceive of Gavin being a ruffian, he's the gentlest man you'd ever want to meet. You know, I'm actually a little concerned that Gavin has not returned my calls. He lives on his boat down in King Harbor. That's a mere hop, skip and a jump from Venice Beach. Do you think you might be able to swing on down there and check on him for me? I'd sure hate to think something has happened to him, too."

It was beginning to sound, listening to Samantha, as if everybody in this whole weird scenario was not acting like themselves. It wasn't like Griffin to become some hooker's groveling sex slave; it wasn't like holy-roller Gavin to threaten someone; and it didn't seem like the Samantha I once knew to leave her wealthy husband and run off to Arizona with a boyfriend from ancient times. The only consistent personality traits here were my own: thirty years later and I was still at the beck and call of Samantha Zimmer.

Chapter Eleven

From my house I cruised down to King Harbor on my bicycle. It was an easy pedal along the beach bike path that parallels the ocean for some thirty miles, beginning near Pacific Palisades—just north of Santa Monica—and terminating near Palos Verdes peninsula—near Point Fermin—to the south. The scenery is *un*paralleled as the path winds and twists along the ocean front. On this particular day, Santa Catalina Island sat offshore clearly visible and shining like a sparkling jewel in the Pacific—looking close enough to swim to.

It made me feel vigorous and alive to be jaunting merrily along via two-wheeled vehicle, wind in my hair and sea breeze filling my lungs, pedaling the fifteen or so miles to King Harbor. It was good exercise. Forty-eight years old and I'm still bike riding! The thought made me smile. I thought back to my own father. When he was forty-eight he already seemed an old man; his idea of vigorous exercise was climbing in and out of a golf cart, hobbling up to a tee and swinging at a tiny dimpled ball. How different we Baby Boomers are. We simply refuse to succumb to age!

Weaving in and out of the docks on my bike at King Harbor, I found the one belonging to Gavin Gambil easily enough—but it was empty. No boat occupying the narrow waterway between two concrete fingers that comprised the slip's perimeter. It was a splendid, sunny day—perhaps Gavin had taken the boat out on the ocean. But I noticed that even the dock-lines were gone. Most boaters leave their dock-lines attached to cleats on the dock when they go out for an afternoon cruise.

A few slips over from Gavin's empty one I spotted a heavy-set man, who looked to be in his late fifties, power sanding the woodwork on a pristine, but very old-looking sailboat. A classic, with teak deck, two spruce masts, and brilliantly shining bow pulpit. I wandered over to ask if he knew Gavin.

"Beautiful boat," I called out to this nautical neighbor of Gavin.

"Thank you," he replied. "They don't make 'em like this anymore. Takes a lot of work to keep her maintained, but it's a labor of love on my part and worth it."

"She looks to be a Cheoy Lee yawl," I said, drawing from a time when, as a young man, I actually knew a bit about boats. Cheoy Lee was the builder, yawl the style of rig with a smaller mizzen mast aft of the rudder. "She certainly stands out amongst all the usual floating Tupperware out here." I knew he would appreciate the perspicacious distinction between his fine old craft and the fiberglass production boats that filled most of the surrounding slips.

"You've a keen eye," he said back to me. "She's a 1964 Cheoy Lee Rhodes, forty-one feet. You a sailor?"

Thinking back to those long-ago summers when Uncle Jack taught me about boats and would take me crewing aboard the racing yachts belonging to his friends, I answered, "I've sailed some." Then added, "But not for a while. I plan to get back into it, though."

It occurred to me just then that I really *would* enjoy taking up sailing again.

"My name's Ben, Ben Harding," I told him. Casting a thumb in the direction of Gavin's empty slip I said, "I was looking for my friend who keeps his boat over there."

Reaching over the rail of his boat and extending a large ham-like hand in my direction he said, "Name's Sandy."

This salty man of the sea had a girl's name. I must have looked at him oddly because, chuckling to himself, he quickly qualified the origin of his name.

"My hair used to be a dirty blond—the color of sand—before it turned all gray, but everyone still calls me Sandy."

"Nice to meet you, Sandy," I said. "You know my buddy Gavin?"

"Sure, I know Gav. Lives on that old tub he calls *Mo Bettah*. Sweetheart of a guy. I hated to see him pull outa here, but he said he was taking his old fishing boat where it could do him some good—down where the fishing is still real sport, away from Santa Monica Bay where you never know what sort of toxic stuff the fish might be contaminated with."

"Where's that?" I asked.

"He's headed down to Mexican waters. Said he wouldn't be coming back if everything worked out for him down there."

Damn! Looked like Gavin Gambil had flown the coop. His timing seemed almost suspect to me. Why would he leave the country before his only brother who had just died was even in the ground?

"How long ago did Gavin leave?" I asked Sandy.

"Oh, maybe a week and a half ago," he replied.

That was right when Griffin committed suicide. Maybe Gavin didn't know Griffin had died.

"Of course, he isn't down in Mexico just yet," Sandy said, interrupting my thoughts. "He's spending a few weeks fishing the outside of Channel Islands before heading to southern waters. He went up to Santa Rosa Island and is working his way down to Santa Cruz and Santa Barbara Islands. In fact, he asked me to join him over at Catalina this weekend for a little bon voyage celebrating before he heads south."

This was encouraging.

"Are you sailing over there this weekend then?" I asked Sandy.

"I hate going over to Catalina on the weekends, way too crowded. I would enjoy partying with old Gavin one last time, though. One of the nicest guys I've ever had the pleasure of knowing, real salt of the earth. I hate to see him go. But no, don't believe I'll make it over there."

This was disappointing.

EVEN THOUGH HE WASN'T IN Mexican waters yet, the timing of Gavin Gambil's sudden disappearance seemed more than a little curious to me. Since I'm Samantha's friend, I made it my mission to locate Gavin—if I could—before he left the country. Besides, being the probate attorney of her late husband's estate, didn't I owe it to the *estate* to make every effort at locating the deceased's brother to give him the sad news?

I took the Catalina Flyer—a ninety-minute ride aboard this commercial ferry transport—over to Avalon, the only town on Santa Catalina Island, in the hope of locating *Mo Bettah* and its skipper. I've lived in California for nearly thirty years, but this was my first time to Catalina. Free literature about the island was the only onboard entertainment:

The Channel Islands—as this group of eight islands are collectively called—are a string of land masses sitting off the Southern California coast, stretching for 160 miles from Santa Barbara County in the north to San Diego County in the south. Santa Cruz Island is the largest in the chain. Santa Catalina Island—christened Santa Caterina because it was discovered on the name day of that early Christian martyr—is only the third largest with seventy-five square miles of terra firma. The island is twenty-one miles long with fifty-four miles of coastline, and the only one of the Channel Islands to host an actual town with year-round residents. The town of Avalon was named after an island from the King Arthur legends.

I discovered Avalon Bay to be a picturesque little harbor with sheer cliffs rising up to encircle the bay, dotted with Mediterranean-style dwellings perched precariously on stilts. It is clean and quaint, though touristy with its myriad T-shirt shops and restaurants. The main street of Crescent Avenue faces out toward the ocean with a delightful view of boats bobbing up and down on their moorings.

I popped into the first bar I passed along that main street, a place called *Luau Larry's*. I sat myself down on a bar stool and ordered a beer, looking out at the people strolling past and at the harbor beyond. I strained my eyes to read the transoms of the boats closest to shore, hoping I'd spot the *Mo Bettah*. No such luck. I flagged over the bartender and asked if he knew where I could find *Mo Bettah*.

"Mo bettah than what?" The barkeep misunderstood my question. "Something wrong with yer beer?" he asked.

The beer was fine, I assured him. "I'm not looking for something 'more better,' I'm trying to locate a fishing boat named *Mo Bettah*."

"Oh," he said, nodding his head, "why didn't ya say so? Private fishing boat or charter?"

"Private, a Bertram 37," I told him, repeating the info Sandy had given me.

"You'd have better luck asking at the Marlin Club. It's a bar just a few blocks from here, around the corner. That's where all the fishermen hang out when they come to town."

I thanked him, left a five dollar bill on the counter, and headed over to the Marlin Club Bar.

THE MARLIN CLUB WAS A tiny place tucked away on a side street. The odor of spilled beer assaulted my nostrils before I was even through the front door. It reminded me of the way our fraternity house smelled back in college. As my eyes adjusted to the darkness of a room without windows, I noticed there was an assemblage of half a dozen patrons seated around the horseshoe shaped bar made to resemble the bow of a ship. Nearly all were men, only two were female. Of the two women, one was grossly overweight and obviously drunk, with a loud obnoxious laugh that I had heard even while still outside.

The bartender was engaged in conversation with three of the male patrons—telling fish stories, I presumed—when the fat woman hollered, "Heeey! What do I need to do around here to get a damned drink?"

The barkeep, not exactly svelte himself, without even turning toward her, responded, "Just show me your tits, Darlin'!"

With that the woman leaned over the bar and raised her T-shirt up over her face, exposing two jiggling but drooping and weathered mounds. All the men "yeehawed" loudly and the bartender immediately carried a drink her way.

"See Honey? It ain't so hard to get a drink around here. You just gotta know how to ask!" he told her.

I sat down at the opposite end of the bar and waited for the bartender to notice a new customer had arrived. I sat there a long while, drumming my fingers on the bar top, before his attention was finally diverted from the two women. He walked over and asked what he could get me. I told him I was looking for the *Mo Bettah*. Once again, I had to explain myself—there was nothing wrong with his fine establishment, it was the name of a boat. I was beginning to think this was some sort of running joke amongst the boating crowd.

"Anybody here seen the *Mo Bettah?*" the barkeep shouted to the imbibing patrons.

The response was decidedly negative, except for one crusty-looking fellow sitting across from me who just stared icily in my direction. I relocated myself to the empty stool next to him.

"You know where I might find Gavin Gambil and the *Mo Bettah?*" I asked him.

Without even looking at me he grunted, "Depends who's looking fer him."

"I'm a lawyer . . .," I began.

"Wrong fuckin' answer!" he interrupted with an attitude clearly averse to being any assistance.

I began again. "Gavin's brother died. I'm the family attorney. I'm trying to find him to relay the news and get him home in time for the funeral and to help take care of loose ends."

He looked at me for the first time, as if trying to decide whether he approved of what he saw, then returned his empty gaze toward the bar.

"Sorry to hear that," he mumbled into his glass. "I've heard him talk about having a brother. Gavin's a sweet guy, this is gonna drop kick him."

"Do you know where I can find him?" I asked again.

He cast a skeptical glace my way. "You must not know Gavin or you'd know you'd never find him in a cheeseball joint like this. Gavin's one of those Bible-banging, praise the Lord types. Sloshes down a beer now and again, but hardly drinks at all."

"Good point," I told him. "You're absolutely right. I've never even met Gavin. I represent his brother's estate."

Looking away from me again, fixing his gaze back on his near empty glass of *spiritus fermenti*, he responded, "Well, I guess yer legit. Fact is, I just talked to Gav yesterday. He was holed up over at Cat Harbor. Said he was gonna hang there a few days. Said he was waiting to see if some friend of his might swing by from the mainland."

Probably his friend Sandy, I thought to myself. I thanked my crusty informer and made my way out of the bar. Just as I was stepping back out into the sunlight, I heard him holler, "Tell old Gav I'm sorry about his loss."

Back on the street once again, away from the stale stench of tobacco and beer, the world was a brighter place. Why anyone would come to this lovely little island getaway only to spend the afternoon in a stuffy and darkened bar was something beyond my grasp.

I needed to get myself over to Cat Harbor and locate Gavin Gambil. Probably not more than fifteen miles away, I was told it would take several hours to arrive there along the crude winding mountain path of a road connecting the Isthmus to Avalon. It was too late in the day to begin such a trek, so I decided to head there tomorrow. The rest of the day I'd play tourist, seeing the sights of Avalon. Grabbing a free informational pamphlet and map of the town from a roadside kiosk, off I went.

THE TOWN OF AVALON BOASTS a year round population of around 3,500, but swells to over 10,000 on any given day in summer. Renting a golf cart, seemingly the most common form of mechanized locomotion in Avalon, I drove along Pebbly Beach Road—taking in grand aquatic vistas that reminded me more of the Mediterranean than of California.

My cart chugged up a steep incline toward the ornate historical architecture of Mount Aida Inn—also known as the Wrigley Mansion because it was a summer home of chewing gum magnate William Wrigley. And Holly Hill House, an elaborate Queen Anne style dwelling with distinctive red-striped cupola—built in 1890 by a suitor bent on impressing the girl of his dreams, the pamphlet informed me. I could sympathize with his plight; we men will go to great lengths to impress the right female. The girl never married the builder, however. Legend has it that construction took so long she finally married another, but Holly Hill House remains among the oldest houses in the city.

Down the far side of the hill I continued to chug, past the golf course, riding stables, bird sanctuary, and finally out to the Wrigley Memorial—built in honor of the family that once owned this entire island. The whole city of Avalon is only one square mile in size, so even doing a slow, lingering golf cart tour, I was only able to kill a couple of hours.

The bell tower chimes from the steeple on the hill were ringing, signifying that it was now 5:30 p.m. After turning in the rented cart, I hoofed it over to the Descanso Beach Club—a short walk directly north of Avalon Harbor—and had a few beers at an outdoor bar situated on the sand as the diminishing light of the sun setting behind the mountains behind me caused the waters of the bay to sparkle like diamonds.

I marveled at what a pristine, serene place Catalina is, only twenty miles from the nearest point on the mainland. Of the enormous population of Southern Californians who live within sight of Catalina Island, I'll wager fewer than ten percent ever venture across the brief expanse of ocean to visit this island paradise so easily within their grasp. I'm happy to say that I am now among that ten percent.

That evening I dined alone at a place called The Blue Parrot, with a table overlooking the harbor. I smiled at the Polynesian motif of the place; huge wood-carved Tiki gods and paper mache tropical birds everywhere. This Southern California island, with its fusion of Mediterranean and Mexican influences, is a wonderful place on its own, no need to turn it into Polynesia. The decor caused me to think about Connie Cantu—because she was from Hawaii, I suppose. I wondered if all she had told me had been the truth. And, I wondered how a girl from such a tranquil island paradise as Hawaii finds herself in the role of harsh dominatrix looking down at men fawning at her feet. God, the world is a strange place!

After consuming my fill at The Blue Parrot, I strolled along the carless main street of downtown Avalon. The night was balmy. I paused briefly by the pristine wood-sided headquarters of the Tuna Club, reading the plaque out front of this historic dwelling: One of the most well-known private fishing clubs in the entire world, dating back to 1916, with a lengthy roster of notables over the years, including early Hollywood types. Zane Grey, Cecil B. DeMille, Errol Flynn, John Wayne, Ward Bond and a host of long ago movie people who commonly frequented the island.

I meandered over to the famous landmark Casino, located—where else?— Casino Point, of course. Nowadays, the first level of the Casino is a movie theater and an island museum. A weathered old man—looking quite the ancient mariner with white bristly beard—worked the museum entrance. He related the Casino's history to me with an enthusiasm indicative of one who had spent a lifetime in love with the place.

"This elegant circular structure was built back in the late 1920's by William Wrigley. But, don't let the name mislead you—this grand Art Deco palace was not built as a place for gambling as the name *casino* might imply, like the casinos of Las Vegas. No, no, not at all . . . it was created for ballroom dancing! You see, in the 1920's America was in the grip of dance fever, and pavilions called 'casinos' sprang up all over the country. This grand Casino Ballroom was one of the very finest, drawing thousands of nattily-dressed dancers from the mainland to perform the

Charleston . . . and later Jitterbug . . . on the huge parquet floor, fueled by the Big Band music of the era."

The old man sighed as if recalling those wonderful days of yore. I thanked him for his most informative narration and donated twenty dollars to the kitty—a basket sitting atop the counter at the museum entrance.

The theater marquee only a few steps away advertised the new and much touted film, *The Perfect Storm*—a true story about a group of fishermen lost at sea in a horrendous storm. It seemed the *perfect movie* to see on this giant rock surrounded by ocean. All alone and with nothing better to do, I bought a ticket and went in to catch a flick.

MUCH LATER, I WAS LULLED to sleep by the peaceful percussion of polite wavelets gently lapping onto the shore outside the window of my cozy—and rather pricey—hotel bedroom. Looking out at the bay from that same window the following morning, I noticed a boat making its way into the harbor. Could it be? Yes! The hairs on the back of my neck stood out in excitement. I recognized that boat!

Chapter Twelve

Gathering my things, I hastened out the hotel and down to the big Green Pier, one of the most prominent points in the entire harbor. Standing on the pier, I shouted to the skipper of the approaching Cheoy Lee yawl. Sandy spotted me and waved back. He motored the yawl over to the Green Pier, close enough for boarding, and I clambered aboard.

"I thought you weren't coming," I said, climbing into the boat's tiny cockpit.

"Well, I thought what the hell . . . so, here I am. What else have I got to do with my weekend?"

"Gavin is over in Cat Harbor," I informed Sandy.

"No problem. I'd rather drop a hook there than pick up a can in this crowded harbor. Wanna ride over with me?"

Being somewhat conversant with sailor talk, I understood. *Drop a hook* meant using the boat's anchor; as opposed to picking up *a can* which refers to attaching the boat at a permanent mooring affixed to the ocean bottom. And Sandy was correct, Avalon Harbor has over four hundred permanent moorings—every one seemed to have a boat already attached to it. Yes, a ride over would be much appreciated.

"How long's the sail over to Cat Harbor?" I asked, trying to get myself situated aboard the boat which never stopped moving.

Reaching down just below-deck and plucking a well worn, crinkled-up nautical chart from the chart table, Sandy tossed it in my direction. Unrolling the papyrus-like document, my arms outstretched, holding the expansive sea-map with both hands like a newspaper, I tried to make sense of the swirls, numbers and yellow blobs on the paper.

"It's a big ocean, a fella should always have some idea of where he is and where he's going," Sandy said authoritatively. Pointing to the foremost yellow blob, "We are right here, Avalon Bay, 33° 20.9° north-118° 19.5°

west— roughly the same latitude as Casablanca, Morocco and just two degrees south of the Greek island of Crete."

"Whoa! Seriously?" I asked with childlike incredulity, while letting out an impressed whistle.

He laughed. "Same latitude, but a few thousand miles of ocean 'tween here and those ports." His finger moved along the chart, to a place marked West End. "Here is where we're going. Cat Harbor is located approximately 33° 25′north-118° 30′ west—only twelve miles away, a distance traversed easiest by sea, but it will still take us a couple of hours to sail there."

We motored out of the harbor, past the landmark Casino where I had seen a movie the night before, and hoisted sail for the trek toward the West End of Catalina. Disengaging the noisy engine, the quiet of wind in sails was music to our ears. To escape the lee of the island we initially took a course more directed toward the mainland. Soon there was a nice breeze blowing—unusual for this early in the day—and the boat heeled over at an angle as she moved gracefully through azure seas on a port tack.

Some distance from the island, it was time to change tacks for a heading toward the West End. The yawl's deck came level under my feet as her bow passed through the wind. The jib sail fluttered from losing its wind, then swept across the foredeck in one fluid motion. The winch sang from Sandy pulling the jib sheet. The main and mizzen booms popped over on a starboard tack in unison as wind filled their sails. A spatter of sea spray wafted aft as the yawl heeled again, close hauled, back toward the island. I had forgotten how wonderful it feels to be aboard a sailing yacht in a stiff breeze. I briefly lamented declining the many invitations to join Uncle Jack as he made his way around the world under sail. What marvelous adventures I had passed up.

Sandy and I conversed as we sailed our way toward West End. I thanked him for spotting me on the pier and picking me up and told him that he was proving invaluable in my pursuit of the allusive Gavin.

Sandy laughed. "Well, Gavin oughta appreciate two buddies goin' to this much trouble just to catch up with him."

At this point, I felt the need to confess to Sandy that Gavin and I were not actually *buddies*—that I had never even met Gavin, in fact. I explained my mission and that I was the family lawyer, looking for Gavin to relay the news about his brother.

"Geez, I'm real sorry to hear that. Gavin worshiped his brother," Sandy told me, chorusing what I'd already heard from others. "This is gonna really hit him hard. Good thing I sailed over after all; best he hears it from a friend."

I agreed.

"Have you ever met Griffin Gambil?" I asked.

"Nope, never met the man. Heard a lot about him from Gav, though. He was more than a brother to Gavin. Griffin was a good deal older than Gav—by twenty years or so—and was both brother and father figures rolled into one. Gavin says Griffin is—was, I guess— a real smart businessman and the rich one in the family. Gav often jokes that God only allots a certain amount of success to any one family, and his brother got it all."

"What does Gavin do for a living?" I asked. "Is he a professional fisherman?"

Sandy chuckled. "Not hardly. Although I'm sure that's what he'd prefer to be. No, Gav is a jack of all trades . . . but a master of none, I suspect. He does some carpentry, electrical work . . . even has his own general contracting license."

"Gavin ever work with his brother on any business deals?" I asked.

"I'm afraid Gav doesn't have much of a head for business," Sandy said, shaking his head. "Gav's too trusting, too gullible . . . too easily manipulated to be much of a businessman. He did work *for* his brother sometimes, though."

"How's that?" I asked.

"His brother would buy run-down properties and Gavin would fix them up, put them in shape to be resold or to get a higher mortgage on them."

"Have you ever heard Gavin mention a man named Broadus Liberato?"

"Uh uh, don't believe so. I think I'd remember an unusual name like that. Broadus, now there's a name. And people make fun of *my* name . . . ."

Soon Ship Rock was in sight to our north. Ship Rock is a huge black boulder rising up more than sixty feet from the ocean about a mile outside the entrance to Isthmus Cove. The dark, ominous rock is covered in white seagull guano and can often be smelled long before it is seen.

"There's 'Shit Rock'," Sandy said, making a joke of the dung covered protrusion. "A reef lies between us and Ship Rock that we need to watch out for as we get closer."

"Okay," I acknowledged.

"There's also a couple of reefs to watch for as we round Bird Rock." He pointed to another, but smaller, bump on the horizon. "We'll drop a hook at Isthmus Cove and walk over to Cat Harbor on the other side, it'll be way faster than sailing all the way around the point."

According to the nautical chart, the tallest spot on Catalina Island is Mount Orizaba at 2,070 feet above sea level, the lowest point is where the Isthmus lies: right at sea level, a mere shoal separating the West End from the rest of the island. Approaching from the sea, Catalina looks almost like two separate islands since the topography at the Isthmus is so low it disappears into the sea.

We dropped anchor in Isthmus Cove and rowed the dinghy to shore. Then it was an easy walk along a dry, dusty trail traversing the low-lying plain that separates the two harbors of Isthmus Cove and Cat Harbor, not more than a mile—a distance we covered in about thirty minutes at a leisurely pace—passing an old school house and the Isthmus Yacht Club. The yacht club, Sandy informed me, was once a barracks building used to billet Union Army soldiers guarding against gunrunning during the Civil War. Catalina Island has a colorful history. Strolling past, we peered inside the club to see if any fishermen might be present who had seen Gavin, but the place was empty.

And then, a buffalo! I was startled to spot a bison crossing the dusty path ahead. It seemed completely out of place on a Pacific island. Never in my life had I been so up close and personal with one of these huge beasts, having only seen them in old cowboy movies. Yielding to the huge brown bovine, we detoured several yards as it stood its ground—defiantly blocking our way and giving a snort in our direction.

Sandy told me that herds of buffalo roam freely on the island. "Only fourteen buffalo were originally brought here way back in 1924 for the filming of a movie called *The Vanishing American*. When the film crew left, the animals were left behind. Today's population stands somewhere around 400. Prolific little bastards, aren't they? Ever had a buffalo burger?"

I shook my head, not certain if he was toying with me.

"Maybe we'll get one later, they're sold all over the island. We'll get us a few glasses of cold Buffalo Milk, too."

I looked dubious.

Sandy smiled. "Not to worry, the burgers are *really* buffalo meat but Buffalo Milk is just a booze concoction that'll knock ya on yer ass!"

Scanning Cat Harbor, there were several fishing boats anchored . . . none of them the *Mo Bettah*. I was beginning to wonder if Gavin Gambil was actually playing hide-and-seek. Our search for the allusive Gavin was effectively stalled, there was no place left to look for him.

"He'll turn up," Sandy said. The afternoon sun was just beginning its descent behind the mountainous peaks when we headed back to the yawl.

During our sojourn ashore another boat had anchored next to ours, a thirty-four foot powerboat with a yacht club burgee flying and the appropriate name of *Island Time* stenciled across the transom. On board was a couple—the guy around my own age, the girl a decade or so younger—from Laguna Beach named Mike and Laura, husband and wife lawyers I discovered. I shuddered to imagine what it might be like to live in a household of two lawyers, but they turned out to be pleasant enough. These were our only immediate neighbors, so we spent some time chatting—each of us reclined on our respective vessels. Boaters make for amiable conversationalists. Mike admired the old Cheoy Lee yawl and was apparently an accomplished sailor, swapping sea stories with Sandy.

Laura asked what I did for a living, a whistle of appreciation escaping her lips when I mentioned the firm I was with in Newport. Her husband, however, seemed more impressed by my abdication from the profession—that is, with the exception of this one final probate case—displaying genuine envy upon learning that I had turned my back on my legal brethren and walked away from such a prestigious firm.

"Wish I had the guts to do something like that," he said.

Whereupon his wife playfully punched him on the arm, chiding him, "Oh sure! You say that, but what would you do with yourself all day if you didn't have a law office to go to?"

"Maybe I'd try writing a book, a mystery novel," his insouciant response.

"We're going over to Harbor Reef later, you two should join us," Laura the lawyer said to Sandy and me, ignoring her husbands reply. A noticeable lack of understanding on my face caused her to add, "The

Harbor Reef Bar, it's a small outdoor joint right off the beach, and the sole drinking establishment at the Isthmus."

"I was at the Harbor Reef the night actress Natalie Wood died back in 1981," Mike chimed in, using a more sober voice than he'd used while sharing seafaring tales earlier. "It was Thanksgiving weekend. Sat at a table right next to Natalie and her husband, Robert Wagner. They were with some friends of theirs, partying pretty good. Too good, apparently. The Coast Guard found her floating in the water the next morning. Accidental drowning they said. What an incredible waste of beauty and talent. The saddest weekend I've ever had here."

All four of us sat silently, nodding our heads for several moments in reverence to the talented and beautiful actress. The past couple days I'd learned a lot of fascinating history about Catalina Island, not all of it ancient. This latest tidbit I could recall firsthand. Natalie Wood's death was in all the papers, and it didn't seem that long ago.

Laura's cheerful voice broke the encroaching somber moment. "The Chantays are playing at the Harbor Reef tonight!"

"*The* Chantays?" Sandy sounding instantly delighted.

"Yes, *the* Chantays. That's why we are here this weekend. My husband came to hear them play."

"Who?" I asked, still not getting it.

"The Chantays!" Sandy couldn't believe I did not recognize this band. "They are one of the premier surf bands of all time," he informed me. "Don't you remember the song 'Pipeline?'"

As a matter of fact, I did remember the song Pipeline. It was a big hit a million years ago, when I was about ten years old. I think that was their one and only hit. But Sandy was completely *stoked*, and his enthusiasm became contagious. We all agreed, going ashore later and listening to the Chantays was the order of the day.

With the night came the surf music of the Chantays. The tiny outdoor bar was jam-packed with fishermen and boaters of all types, the joint was rockin'! Sandy and I had good seats at the bar from where we could watch the band as we downed Buffalo Milk—the specialty of the house—and getting more than a bit looped in the process.

The dance floor was crowded with gyrating bodies and I spotted our newfound boating chums, Mike and his attractive wife Laura, looking slightly out of place as they did a sort of Texas Two-Step in the midst of it all. Two attorneys—firmly entrenched in that snobby stuffed-shirt world from which I had recently escaped—but, here on the island, they were just fun-loving boaters. Chances were I would never see this lawyerly dancing duo again after tonight, so it tickled me that my last image of them would be Two-Stepping at an island bar.

A middle-aged woman with salt-n-pepper hair came over and dragged Sandy away by his arm onto the dance floor. I had to smile watching these two gray-haired over-fifty folks out there shakin' and stompin' to old surf tunes—dancing the wax right off the floor! *Fifty*, the magic number that separates young from old in most people's minds. My patronizing smile faded with the realization that this "magic age" was a mere two years off in my own future. I shuddered at the thought and took another hit of Buffalo Milk.

The song ended and a stranger grabbed Sandy from behind on the dance floor, clutching him in a bear hug. Upon being released, they both laughed and high-fived it with hands in the air. Obviously they were old buddies.

The stranger looked a good bit younger than Sandy—in his late thirties, I would guess—and a typical boater, wearing jeans, Sperry Topsiders sans socks and a T-shirt with a boat logo on the back. Sandy and this new fellow were whooping it up, clapping each other on the back, laughing and yelling above the crowd into each other's ear. I saw the stranger's face suddenly go blank as his gaze followed Sandy's finger pointing in my direction. Then Sandy was leading the stranger back toward the bar where I was sitting, his friend seeming a reluctant kidnappee as they approached.

Sandy hollered, "Ben Harding, meet Gavin Gambil—fisherman extraordinaire!"

Gavin Gambil appeared flummoxed. He sheepishly extended his hand to be shaken. I took it, his palm felt clammy.

"Pleased to meet you, sir," he said.

Sir? Another reminder that fifty was looming on my horizon. I nodded at him, smiling. He looked vaguely familiar somehow, but maybe he just had that sort of face.

"Ben here has some things he wants to discuss with you," Sandy was saying to Gavin. Then looking me hard in the eye said, "But hell—it can keep for a bit, can't it Ben? The night is still young, let's just have some fun."

I looked Sandy right back in the eyes. Apparently he had not yet told Gavin about his brother and did not think this exact moment was the right time to tell him. "Sure, I guess it can wait. But just until the band takes a break and the noise dies down."

All three of us—even Gavin who normally does not drink I'd been told—shared several rounds of Buffalo Milk, as the band played "Wipeout," "Walk Don't Run," "Surfer Joe," "Penetration," "Pipeline"... all the old surf classics I had not heard since I was a kid. Under different circumstances I would've been having the time of my life, but I found myself preoccupied—focused upon this younger brother of Griffin Gambil.

This fellow standing next to me, Gavin Gilchrist Gambil—I recalled his full name from the epiphanous letter Sammie had shown me—was a handsome guy with a tanned and solid physique. I'm sure he has no trouble attracting the ladies. I didn't know what his older bro Griffin looked like, but if such good looks ran in the family, why did Griffin resort to employing a hooker and becoming her sex slave? And why did Griffin's younger brother choose this exact point in time to jump on his boat and be heading out of the country? Could that be pure coincidence?

But most immediately bothersome was that Gavin seemed so nervous about meeting me. Why would that be? I was just a stranger to him, a stranger that Sandy had undoubtedly told him was a lawyer looking for him. Did Gavin have some reason to be wary of strangers? Of people looking for him? Of lawyers? Too many things just didn't add up.

The drinks kept flowing and by the time the band took a break, the three of us were feeling no pain.

"We were looking for you earlier," Sandy told Gavin. "Didn't see yer boat out in Cat Harbor. You down at Cherry Cove?"

Gavin kept his eyes focused on me as he responded to Sandy. "No, I'm at Cat. Guess you didn't see the boat 'cuz I'm down at the end, all the way behind the point... toward Lobster Bay."

"Better shelter closer in. Why'd you pick way out there to hang a hook?" Sandy asked him.

Gavin shrugged.

I found myself wondering if he had hidden behind the point intentionally in order to avoid being found by anyone who might be looking for him.

Finally, Sandy stepped up to the plate and broached the business at hand. "Gavin, I've got some bad news to lay on ya," he said.

"What might that be, Sandy?" Gavin's words sounded forced, his eyes shifting away to some middle distance somewhere over my left shoulder, as though it might pain him to look either of us in the face.

"Bad news," Sandy began. "Very bad news. Your brother passed away last week."

Gavin continued starring blankly into space, as if not hearing him.

"Your brother is dead!" Sandy repeated.

Sadness briefly crossed Gavin's features as the hurt from Sandy's words sank in. Otherwise, Gavin showed no emotion at all—but finally spoke. "There's no denying the Lord's will," was his entire response.

Sandy continued, "Ben says you're needed back at the ranch, old buddy. Looks like you'll need to postpone that trip down Mexico way. I know how hard times like this can be. If there's anything I can do to help out, just name it."

Nodding his appreciation, Gavin hitched a shoulder—looking lost. He quietly announced, to no one in particular, "I'm going back to the boat now. I'll head back to the mainland in the morning." Then turning to me directly, "Tell Samantha I'll meet her at Griffin's house tomorrow afternoon."

With that, Gavin turned and silently left the bar—walking out into the pitch black night alone, across the flat open ground to the other side of the island . . . to Cat Harbor. It occurred to me that Gavin had not even asked how his brother died.

LATER, LYING IN A GENTLY swaying bunk aboard Sandy's yawl, I wondered—how did Gavin know Samantha was in town and staying at Griffin's house?

Chapter Thirteen

Pulling up to Griffin's house in the Valley, I parked the Boxster in the driveway right behind a big, flashy Harley-Davidson motorcycle with Arizona plates. My knock on the front door was answered by a middle-aged man with longish blond hair slicked straight back exposing gray roots, a few days worth of beard stubble—also gray—and wearing a snug fitting tank top, allowing an abundance of tattoos to be on display.

He greeted me with a discolored, yellowing, toothy grin. "Heeey! Benjamin! You haven't changed a goddamned bit, Pard!"

It was Pete Spivey, my old nemesis from high school, but I had not recognized him until he spoke; he looked entirely different. The years had not been kind—*rode hard and put up wet* as the old cowboy saying goes. Once he spoke, though, the Pete Spivey from high school reemerged to a recognizable degree.

"Hello Pete. You look good," I lied.

"Damn straight," he said. "It's all in the genes, baby!"

Samantha emerged from the back of the house, still buttoning her blouse. I got the distinct impression that I had interrupted sexplay. Jesus! Griffin wasn't even in the ground yet and they were frolicking in his bed. Maybe I'm just an old prude, but it seemed a tad kinky for my taste.

"Hi Benjamin," Samantha said, still struggling with the last button of her shirt. "You remember Pete. He's such a doll, he rode his bike all the way from Phoenix just to give me some help with all this mess."

"Can't go too long without my Sammie fix," Pete interjected, patting

Samantha on the butt. "Did'ja catch a shot of my new scoot out there?" he asked proudly. "There's nothin' like the awesome thunder of a Harley between your legs! Brand spankin' new, two-toned Softtail Springer—twin Cam 88B. Whole new generation of metal and power. Better 'n the older ones, way better engine, lots less vibration . . . ."

"Bitchin'!" I uttered the expression sardonically, just to shut him up. I could not have cared less. I didn't drive all the way out to the Valley just to hear a dissertation on motorcycle evolution.

Turning from Pete to Sammie, I shifted subjects. "Hasn't Gavin been by to help?" I asked her. Today was Monday. Gavin had said he would meet Samantha here Sunday afternoon.

"He was here yesterday for a while," Samantha answered, sighing heavily. "But Pete was already on his way by that time. Anyway, Gavin wasn't much help when he came by. Something's up with that boy. Absolutely. I realize his only brother just died, but he's acting pretty weird."

"How so?" I asked.

"He just *is*, that's all. For one thing, a lot of Griffin's papers are out of order and some seem to be missing. I asked Gavin about it and he got really defensive about the whole thing. Gavin has never been a very good liar, especially since finding the Lord and all. I know he's covering up something. I think he may have gone through Griffin's things before I got here."

"What types of documents are missing?" I asked.

"I can't really be sure yet, but I found bills, notes, and architectural drawings for properties that Griffin does not seem to own. The deeds are nowhere to be found. Then there's the bank accounts showing deposits and withdrawals, but no explanation of where the money came from or went to."

"And you think it was Gavin who went through the papers, " I reconfirmed.

"Unless it was that hooker—Cantu. Maybe she went through Griffin's papers, looking to remove anything that might conflict with the will?" Samantha suggested.

I took a moment to consider that possibility. "Cantu might've had a key, I suppose. She might have come in search of anything that would bolster the holographic will or to destroy anything that might hurt her chances. But it seems awfully risky for her to come by here, considering the man died right in her front yard and she's likely under some suspicion—especially in her dubious line of work and all. If she had gotten caught, the police would have been all over her."

"Do you think I should tell the police about the missing documents?"

"I suppose you should," I told her, "although I don't think they will do anything with such information, other than merely note it in the file."

I had intended to stick around a few hours and help sort through Griffin's legal documents while Sammie concentrated on his personal effects, but my desire to assist was quickly diminished. Spivey mostly stood around, consuming beer and lending his crass comments to the situation, the running commentary often punctuated by loud belches. I never met Griffin, but it was hard to believe that my sweet Sammie from high school had left her husband for someone like this. I would have continued helping, sorting through the piles of documents, but after the first three quarters of an hour it became readily apparent that these two wanted to be alone together—perhaps to finish what I had previously interrupted or to begin anew, who knows?

I was happy to leave. Utilizing all the gears of my little sports car, I zoomed through the winding and twisting curves of Topanga Canyon like a kid in a hot rod. This heavily wooded canyon that connects the Valley to the ocean had once been a hotbed of hippie high-life in the late 1960s and early '70s. Uncle Jack once remarked that if Topanga Canyon ever caught fire, the smoke would get the entire San Fernando Valley stoned to their gills! The area still retains a natural, rustic appearance, but no anti-capitalist, free-loving hippie would be able to afford that real estate today. The place is filled with multi-million dollar "cottages" tucked away in the woods.

Making my descent down the canyon and turning left onto Pacific

Coast Highway, the scenery abruptly changed; the Ozark-like tree-studded hills were replaced by modern high-rises along the sandy waterfront. The salt air stung my eyes a little as I continued homeward—toward Ocean Front Walk—in my topless chariot. Breathing deep the ocean's aroma, I was more than happy to escape the aura of death that I associated with each trip to Griffin's house. Tomorrow he would be laid to rest at Forest Lawn Cemetery. I was ready to put the entire matter to rest along with him. Let it remain a suicide, let the chips fall where they may. Let Samantha live happily ever after with her tattooed, biker lover. Let Gavin cruise down to Mexico, and let Connie Cantu find a new slave. Let's all get through the business of probate and let poor old Griffin rest for eternity in peace.

AMONG THE JUNK MAIL WAITING in my mailbox were two pieces that caught my attention. The letter from the State Bar I opened first. Good news. The answer I'd filed in response to Ara Ratono's complaint against me had convinced the Bar that no ethical rules of conduct had been violated and the Bar was closing the matter *without prejudice*. That should have been a relief, but the whole Bar thing had not really occupied much space in my brain. Still, it was one less thing to be concerned about and was the conclusion I hoped the Bar would reach concerning such a frivolous claim. Now all that remained of Ari's ridiculous allegations was the actual malpractice claim filed with the court.

The second letter was from an attorney regarding the Griffin Gambil estate. I wasn't at all surprised that Connie Cantu had hired a lawyer to protect her interests regarding the estate. The letter was putting us on notice regarding her claim pursuant to the holographic will found at the scene of Griffin's death, which they intended to submit to probate. Litigation was being initiated. It was the beginning of a contest of wills ... in more ways than one.

There was no point putting off breaking this new development to Samantha. It was my legal obligation to keep her informed. I picked up the wall phone in the kitchen and dialed her number. She answered breathless; either she had run to answer or I had, yet again, interrupted something I'd already grown tired of imagining.

I quickly updated her about the will contest. The shrillness of her response to my news caused me to involuntarily drop the phone. It went clattering down onto the hardwood floor, the handset *bungee jumping* up and down, suspended from the wall by the coiled telephone cord. I let the phone remain there, bobbing up and down. No need to pick it back up, I could hear every irate word Samantha was screaming from three feet away.

Chapter Fourteen

The month of June usually signifies the beginning of things—for students, the toil of studying is over and summer begins; most weddings are planned for June, the beginning of a new life together as husband and wife. For Griffin Gambil, however, June signified his *end*. Perhaps someone like Griffin's good Christian brother, Gavin, might argue that June was the beginning of eternal life in heaven for dearly departed Griffin. Far be it for me to take issue with such sentiment.

Like everything else associated with Griffin Gambil, his funeral held a few surprises. For one thing, considering Griffin Gambil was a man worth twenty million dollars, the funeral was surprisingly short of mourners. Fewer than ten people by my count. Another surprise, Samantha showed up alone, without Pete Spivey in tow.

"Where's Pete?" I asked her, not really caring.

"We didn't think it was proper for him to come," she said. Then added, "Besides, Pete hates funerals."

"I see," I said, unable to hide a tone of sarcasm.

Her eyes glared at me from under her black widow's veil. "No, you don't see. So don't use that tone with me, Benjamin! I love Pete. Pete is the only man I have ever truly loved, the only one I ever wanted to be with. I never should have married Griffin. I never should have *settled*. But this is my final tribute to Griffin and that's why I came alone. I didn't think I should show up at his funeral on the arm of the man who took me away from him. It just didn't seem . . . respectful."

"I see," I said again, but differently this time.

With that, she completely changed the subject. "Benjamin, I'd like you to handle putting my estate into a living trust for me. Can you do that?"

I nodded.

"When I die, I don't want there to be any confusion regarding the extent of my estate or my wishes as to the distribution of my assets. I don't want anyone to have to go through the chaos that I am with Griffin's affairs. For such a smart businessman, he certainly dropped the ball when it came to passing on his estate."

"Sometimes even smart businessmen don't like to think about dying, and procrastinate when it comes to protecting their estates for their heirs," I told her.

"I want everything spelled out, plain and simple. And I do *not* want to procrastinate," she said.

"I'll take care of it for you, Samantha. Don't worry about it," I assured her.

"I don't have any children or other family," she went on. "So, I want everything to be placed in trust and passed to Pete when I die."

I was stunned.

"Samantha, I don't think that's such a good idea . . .," I began.

"It's what I want, Benjamin. It's what I *truly* want. Will you do this for me?"

"This isn't the time or place to discuss it," I told her. "Come by the beach house tomorrow and we can talk about it."

"I could use a break. A day at the beach sounds nice. But I won't be changing my mind about the trust."

Broadus Liberato, Griffin's sometime business partner, was present to bid a final farewell. He was accompanied by an elderly woman—who I assumed to be Mrs. Liberato—and a small retinue of middle-aged men all dressed in appropriately dark suits, business associates perhaps. They all made the sign of the cross with their hands across their chests and bowed their heads in unison as the eulogy was read. The Liberatos gazed mournfully at the casket, poised on its runners, surrounded by Astro-turf. I wondered what Broadus was mourning more: the passing of his old (former) friend or the unlikelihood of his ever seeing the money from the properties he was coerced into signing over to Griffin with only a verbal promise in return. A verbal promise that had died with Griffin.

There was another man, all alone, standing in the general vicinity of the Liberato group, but seemingly not a part of them. A solitary figure of substantial physical stature, heft of muscle and fat in seemingly equal measure, under-dressed: no suit, clad in blue-jeans and a too snug T-shirt stretched over a buttery belly. A huge bulbous nose and red veins spidering through his severely pock-marked flesh made his visage unfriendly, almost menacing. At no point in the ceremony had he come by to condole Samantha, and now his was one of the only heads not bowed as prayers were being recited. In fact, my scrutiny of him, I noticed, was being returned with an arrogant stare. Beyond arrogant, almost challenging somehow. It was a downright evil look.

I caught his eyes and held them, but he never blinked. If looks could kill I was being bludgeoned to death with daggers. It was unnerving. It was I who first looked away, nudging Samantha to ask if she knew him. But as I attempted to point him out to her, he was gone. I couldn't imagine how someone so large could vanish so suddenly in these open surroundings, but he was nowhere to be seen. Strange. I tried to slough it off as probably no big deal, but the memory of that intensity with which he'd been staring caused a slight shiver up my spine.

NEAR THE END OF THE ceremony I noticed a distinctly non-family member standing respectfully off in the distance, several feet away. It was Connie Cantu. Apparently, Griffin meant more to her than she'd led me to believe. She'd come to pay her respects to this man; a man who'd paid *her* to display a complete absence of respect while he was still alive. I looked to Samantha, but she had already spotted Cantu as well and was delivering an icy glare her way.

"Do something," Samantha whispered to me out of the corner of her mouth, seething. "That *whore* should not be here today."

I walked casually over to Connie Cantu. She recognized me from our earlier interview.

"It's commendable that you came to say a final good-bye to Griffin, but your presence is upsetting Mrs. Gambil," I told Cantu.

"That was not my intent," she began somberly with head bowed, "but if my presence displeases the widow . . . ." She paused, that certain curl of her lips I remembered from our last meeting reemerging to form a sarcastic smile. Then looking up at me, she completed her thought. "If my presence displeases the widow . . . that's just too fucking bad, isn't it!"

Thinking she might cause a scene, I started to walk away from her. Then, deciding otherwise, turned back to face her. There was a question I wanted answered. "Do you happen to have a key to Griffin's house?"

"Which one? Griffin owned many houses." She spoke this in what I took for a mocking tone.

"His residence," I answered calmly.

Her eyes never left mine as she reached into her purse and handed me a key, saying "I shan't be needing this any longer, I suppose."

I took the key and left her there as I returned to Samantha's side. Opening my palm to show the key to Samantha, I told her, "Looks like you might have guessed correct. Perhaps it *was* Cantu who went through Griffin's belongings. Cantu had her own key."

"I need to have a word with that slut," Samantha sputtered as she bustled in Cantu's direction. I tried to grab Samantha's arm, but she shook me off and made a beeline for Cantu.

The two women spoke in hushed tones for several moments. There was no arm waving, finger jabbing or shoving, as two men might in a similar confrontation. They just stood there, face-to-face, talking. Finally Cantu nodded her head in seeming defeat, walked away and left. Samantha had been able to accomplish what I had not, getting Cantu to leave without causing a scene.

"Nice work," I told Sammie as she rejoined me. "What did you say to her?"

"I asked her to please leave."

My look of disbelief caused Samantha to more fully explain.

"I asked her to walk away right now—away from this ceremony and out of my life entirely. I told her that if she gave up all claims to Griffin's alleged will, she could keep the Mercedes, the house in Encino, and anything else given to her by Griffin—even though it was *all* community property and under the laws of California I could take it all away from her. I told her that I was certain she had deliberately driven Griffin to take his own life, but I would not pursue any criminal complaint against her if she would just do as I asked. And then . . . I told her that I knew all about her police record in Honolulu."

"She has a criminal record in Hawaii?" I was amazed.

"Who knows?" Sammie answered. "Judging by the way she responded, my guess would be that she does."

GAVIN ARRIVED AT HIS BROTHER's funeral . . . late. The eulogy completed and the body being lowered into the ground when I spotted him on the far side of the plat. Dressed in khaki slacks, dark tie and dark blue blazer with gold buttons, and still shod in scuffed, salt-stained Sperrys—with socks this time, though—tears were streaming down his tanned cheeks. I watched his shoulders shake as he quietly sobbed. He made eye contact with Samantha, and I saw them mutually nod, but neither approached the other.

When the dismal ceremony had ended, Samantha and Gavin entered the limo together, the only two family members. The short procession of four automobiles proceeded from the cemetery. I followed directly behind the long black limousine in my tiny blue sports-car. As bright sunlight pierced the tinted rear window of the limo, I could barely discern what looked to be Gavin sobbing heavily on the shoulder of a more stoic Samantha.

I realized then that not a single tear had I witnessed from Samantha. Not during the funeral and not even that first night at my house, after I picked her up at the airport and she told me about her husband's death. Was she just hard as nails, or what? How well did I really know this new, middle-aged Samantha Zimmer? She certainly seemed far different from the sweet high-schooler of my memories. Then again, how well had I *ever* known Samantha Zimmer?

As the little cortege proceeded along the sloping, tree-lined cemetery road, a *fifth* car joined the procession. It was pretty hard not to notice: a huge white, late model Dodge Ram pickup truck, riding high off the ground atop enormous ballooned tires. Far longer than even the stretch limo, my tiny auto could easily fit within the truck-bed of this four-wheel-drive monster. As we rounded a gentle curving bend I looked back and could plainly make out the features of the driver through the expansive windshield. It was the incredible disappearing man with the large nose who'd been giving me such a stink-eye earlier. The shiver re-emerged along my spinal column.

But upon exiting the cemetery and turning left onto the highway, the pickup turned right, in the opposite direction. The huge truck quickly dwindling into nothingness in my rear-view mirror, I felt silly for my paranoia and decided it must have been the eerie setting itself—a funeral, standing amongst a vast orchard of headstones—that caused my fervid imagination to get the better of me. Likely the fellow hadn't been staring at me at all, much less evilly. I laughed at my foolishness, while taking another check in the rear-view just to be sure.

Chapter Fifteen

The past week I had worn shoes and long pants two times. Once when I visited the office of Broadus Liberato and once at Griffin's funeral. That was twice more than I ever thought I would in a single week after turning my back on the practice of law to live out my life as a beach bum. After not wearing such regalia for a couple of months, long pants made my legs itch and shoes felt very heavy and hard on my feet. With any luck at all, those items of clothing could be sentenced to solitary confinement in my closet for a long time.

The usual morning beach fog—"June Gloom" we locals call it—was just burning off, yielding to a warm sunny day more typical of July or August, when Samantha showed up around noon. What a pleasant surprise; she arrived alone, without Pete Spivey.

"Where's Pete?" I asked, hoping she would confirm that he would not be joining us.

"Pete doesn't really do the beach scene." Sammie's words were music to my ears. "He rode the Harley down to Orange County to hook up with some biker buddies of his."

"Orange County? That's hardly biker territory," I told her. Orange County is generally considered conservative, white bread, pristine suburbia.

"They're all meeting at a spot called *Cook's Corners* for a ride through some place that's supposed to be just beautiful . . . Trabuco Canyon. Pete says it's really spectacular and damn near had me talked into going with him."

Pete was correct. Trabuco Canyon was a scenic expanse of two-lane pavement that wove for several miles along the southern extremity of Orange County, so densely tree-lined that headlights were often a necessity even in broad daylight. I had often enjoyed testing the traction of my mid-engine, road hugging Porsche along this bucolic stretch of road.

"But you didn't go with Pete," I said, "you came here instead and I'm glad."

"I needed a day at the beach, plus it's hotter than hell in the Valley," Sammie said, smiling. "Besides, we need to talk about drafting my will and setting up a trust."

"How about a bike ride and a little fun first, we can discuss the trust later . . . maybe over dinner," I suggested.

"All right, as long as we get it done," she said. "I don't want to put it off."

I RENTED A BICYCLE FROM the corner bike shop for Samantha and we pedaled our way along the beach bike path, into the thick of the Venice carnival area. The carnival is an ongoing event in Venice; 365 days a year one can find jugglers, people walking on stilts and all sorts of carnival-like entertainers gathered to entertain along the beach boardwalk. Sammie talked me into getting a henna tattoo, a temporary tattoo that looks like the real thing. I got a tribal armband tattooed across my left bicep. Sammie said it made me look sexy and dangerous—an image I rather liked for her to have of me.

Leaving the carnival area, we rode over toward Manhattan Beach to watch a volleyball tournament. Manhattan Beach lays claim to being the beach volleyball capital of the world, there are matches in progress on nearly any given weekend. Standing on the Manhattan Pier watching the brown and fit young athletes leaping and spiking on the sand below, I recalled long-ago volleyball games with Uncle Jack. I missed those days and the times spent with my uncle.

Volleyball is fun to *play*, but I can only *watch* it for so long. I was soon ready to move on. King Harbor marina was only a few more miles down the bike path, so I suggested we ride in that direction. I was hoping Sandy might be out and about so I could thank him for all his help last weekend with locating Gavin. Sammie admitted she had not ridden a bike in years, but was up for continuing our pedal along the beach.

Sandy was on the deck of his boat, attending to the bright-work. He put down his tools and stood up to wave us over as he saw the two of us approach. Even in her mid-forties, Sammie still had a girlish figure and looked damn good wearing shorts and a bikini top bent over those handlebars; no wonder Sandy spotted us riding by.

I returned his wave as our bikes noisily clattered down the metal gang-ramp and along the dock to his boat. I introduced him to Sammie, he invited us aboard and we all sat around chatting. I thanked Sandy for all his help regarding Gavin.

He waved it off, saying, "You know, it's the darndest thing, but Gavin asked me if I knew anybody wanting to buy his boat, the *Mo Bettah*. Said he wouldn't be needing it any longer."

"Why's that?" I asked.

"That's exactly what *I* asked him," Sandy said. "Gavin says he's in need of a change—especially since losing his brother and all—but has decided against going to Mexico. Says he's found someplace better. Says he's moving where the weather suits his clothes and the fishing is great."

"Where's the weather and fishing better than California or Mexico?" I challenged.

Scratching his scruffy chin, Sandy again chorused with, "That's what *I* asked him."

"And?" I asked again.

"Says he's had it with L.A. and is moving out to the land of Aloha . . . Hawaii. Says if he can get a decent dollar for his boat, he's gonna buy a newer one in Hawaii and spend the rest of his days fishing those clear blue tropical waters."

I looked over at the *Mo Bettah* floating calmly in her slip. "Well, she's a fine-looking vessel. Gavin should be able to sell it without much trouble."

"Maybe *you* should buy her," Sandy suggested, raising an eyebrow at me.

"Too rich for my blood," I told him.

LATER, BACK AT THE BEACH house, Sammie and I collapsed exhaustedly into lounge chairs on the sun deck after our nearly four hour bike ride.

But we had not rested long when she rousted me out of a perfectly comfortable position to begin work on her will and trust instrument.

"You promised . . . bike ride first, then you'd start working on it," Sammie whined lightheartedly.

We left the sun and went inside where I sat at my desk in front of the computer and pulled up the necessary format. Once again I strongly advised against leaving everything to Pete Spivey. Once again Sammie told me to mind my own business and just do the legal work.

"Can you finish it today?" she asked.

"I think so. Drafting a trust is not a particularly time consuming project, *if* you know what you're doing. But don't try this at home kids," I joked. "For those who aren't well versed in this specific area of law it can be very risky. A little like brain surgery, one mistake and the whole thing might be considered null and void."

Even though estate planning was not my specialized area of practice, I had completed several hours of study on the subject as part of the mandatory continuing legal education required to keep my license active, and I'd done some estate work for certain clients over the years. I had the forms on my computer and Sammie had a list of all her assets that she wanted included in the trust, so we were ready to roll. I spent several hours whittling away at creating a proper trust instrument for her estate while she returned to sun herself on the outside deck overlooking the ocean.

I JOINED HER OUT ON the deck as the sun was sinking into the Pacific. Without the sun for warmth, it quickly turned chilly. Samantha moved from her lounge chair to squeeze in next to me on mine. She snuggled against me, resting her head on my shoulder as the sky turned from blue to brilliant orange. It felt nice, like we were kids again, the girl beside me the same sweet Sammie I remembered. But I knew enough now not to allow myself to be pulled into Sammie's web, just as I'd been so many times as a lovesick teen. This was pure Samantha: lying here with me, romantic innuendo, even though she'd made it clear her heart belonged to Pete Spivey. Still, it sure did feel nice.

"I really appreciate all you have done for me," she whispered.

"*De nada*," I answered as casually as I could muster.

"But I intend to pay you for drafting the will and creating the trust for me. What do you charge?"

"Thirty-five thousand dollars," I said, straight faced.

She laughed, "Such a bargain!"

"Hungry?" I asked.

"Um huh." She was hungry.

WE STROLLED OVER TO ONE of my favorite haunts, the Baja Cantina, and ordered margaritas and dinner. The restaurant, stretching from the banks of the Venice Canal, was nearly a block long and housed a labyrinth of eating areas—some inside, some out in the open air—with firepits and several bars where throngs of patrons sat chatting and consuming spicy fare. The decor was old Mexico, with fading yellowed photographs of donkeys and long-ago people clad in Spanish outfits.

"Cool place," Samantha remarked. "I've never been here before, but for some reason the name rings a bell."

"Baja Cantina? Could be you heard it mentioned during incessant television coverage of the O.J. Simpson trial a few years ago," I suggested. "Baja Cantina was where Ronald Goldman was headed to meet some friends on the night he was killed—murdered along with Nicole Brown-Simpson, O.J.'s wife. Unfortunately for Goldman, he never made it here."

"That was such a sad ordeal," Sammie responded, nodding her head, recalling the trial of the century.

I agreed, then shifted in a more lighthearted direction. "The first time I ever came here was way back in the 1970s with my Uncle Jack," I told her. "It was much smaller then, a real hole in the wall. Only consisted of those few tables over there." I pointed to a row of five tables on the far side of the room. "Back then it was a hangout frequented only by locals and the truly hip of L.A. My Uncle Jack knew everybody. Each time we came here friends would join us. I remember one time, Louise Lasser—one of the actresses from the TV show *Mary Hartman, Mary Hartman*—joined us for dinner. Do you remember that show?"

Sammie laughed. "I think I remember. Wasn't it on late at night and involved some quirky woman and her neighbors? The woman always wore her hair in pigtails, right? Kind of a soap opera spoof, as I recall."

"Absolutely right," I laughed. "As a young guy I loved that show. My buddies and I would sit around watching it, laughing hysterically at the droll humor of Dabney Coleman, Mary Kay Place, Graham Jarvis, Martin Mull, and Lasser . . . it was the kind of show that drew a sort of cult audience. So, when one of its main stars joined us for dinner and was chummy with my uncle, I was incredibly impressed.

"Anyway, each year more and more people heard about the Baja Cantina and it kept expanding . . . ."

"And now it takes up nearly the whole block!" she finished my thought for me. "I can see why, it's a cool place."

Drinks arrived. Looking at her over my salt-rimmed glass, the years had been neither kind nor unkind to Samantha. She was still wildly attractive to be sure, but time had changed her. In school, Sammie possessed a wholesome innocence—the personification of some Rockwellian all-American girl next door—with an understated beauty that went largely unappreciated by many of the hormonally rabid boys of that age. But her sweet, Doris Day good looks did not go unnoticed by me. To my boyhood sensibilities, Sammie had seemed the essence of beauty, femininity and grace.

That, however, was in a time long ago. Now there was a camouflaged hard edge to her; difficult to pinpoint, but it was there. Perhaps she acquired it during her years living and working in dog-eat-dog New York City, or maybe it just attached itself as life happened. It occurred to me that, as a woman in her mid-forties with no children and a deceased husband, Samantha had arrived at a difficult stage of her existence— probably too old to bear children and certainly too young to be a widow. Standing at such a precipice of mid-life might just engender some degree of hard edginess.

Samantha sat across from me making small talk that was hardly registering in my already overcrowded stream of thought. Her were lips moving, but I heard naught. I was engulfed in my perplexity over her and why she decided to leave her husband for someone like Pete Spivey. A final reach for the brass ring? The desire for an abrupt and definite change from the life she had known might be expected at this juncture, I suppose—much like my own leap at the metaphoric brass ring as I turned my back on a lifetime of lawyering and trundled off to the beach.

Her brass ring was Pete Spivey. This lovely woman who spent her procreative prime in a passionless coupling, had at long last rediscovered the lost love of her youth—however crass and tattooed he may be. As her friend, I knew I should feel nothing but happiness for Sammie—that she had rekindled her relationship with Pete. It struck me as uniquely unfair, however, that she be seated across from a friend who secretly longed for the termination of her newfound joy . . . who wished—still—that it was *he* who could be the object of her affection.

"Tell me about Pete Spivey," I said at last.

Sammie looked taken aback. "What do you want to know?"

"Well, for starters, what does he do for a living?"

"He's more or less retired," she told me. "He sold his automobile upholstering business back in the Midwest and mainly lives off the proceeds. He also got a bit of insurance money when his wife died. His needs . . . our needs . . . are simple. We don't require all that much money. Actually, one of the things I like *most* about Pete is his ambivalence toward money. Completely unlike Griffin who was always wheeling and dealing. Griffin lived for the art of the deal . . . and look where it got him: a professional whore for a girlfriend, and a bullet in the head."

"You said Pete had a wife who died. What was her name? How did she die?" I asked.

"Her name was Jennifer. She died in a skiing accident up in Michigan or someplace. Smashed into a tree. You know, like Sonny Bono. Only in this case she *fell* from the ski lift and landed on top of a tree. Her back and neck were broken. Jennifer's death devastated Pete for a long time."

"When did this happen?"

"It was two years ago. To this day Pete can't bring himself to talk much about it."

"Understandable," I said. Then changing tacks, "What about all those tattoos Pete has? Don't they bother you?" I was curious.

"You know, you really need to get more *hep*, Benjamin." Due, perhaps, from being with her much older husband all those years, she oddly used the outdated terminology from an era of hep-cats and daddy-os to admonish me for not being *with it*. "Tattoos are quite fashionable these days, in case you didn't know. Besides, I told you, *I* think tattoos are sexy! In fact, I've been kinda turned on all afternoon since seeing that band on your arm."

She was joking, of course, and we both laughed. But her comment caused a flushing from my forehead to my neck.

"I'm sorry, Sammie. I have nothing against Pete. It's just that I have a hard time picturing you leaving your husband for a guy like him. In high school you seemed so . . . ."

"So cute, sweet, precious and adorable?" she joked. "Look, Benjamin, we have all changed since high school. The one thing that never changed for me, however, was my passion for Pete. Even when I look at him today, all these years later, to me he's the same handsome, athletic teenage boy he was thirty years ago. I don't expect you to understand, but I never stopped caring for him."

Oh, I understood all right, believe me. Thirty years later I'm still carrying a torch for Samantha Zimmer, that cute little co-ed. Also thirty years later, I'm still running in second place to Pete Spivey. But, I didn't tell any of this to Samantha. Changing the subject, the rest of dinner was spent going over her will and the trust document I had just drafted.

AFTER DINNER WE WALKED ALONG Venice Pier and watched fishermen casting their lines out into the ocean to catch night fish. We could feel the power of the Pacific, surf pounding against the pilings on which we stood, sending shudders through the long concrete structure. The night was still young and warm, so we put the top down on the Porsche and cruised on over to King Harbor, stopping at Sandy's boat for a nightcap.

I brought Sammie's trust instrument with me and Sandy acted as one of two witnesses necessary for the instrument to become fully executed. The way it was set up, all Samantha's property—both personalty and real estate—would now be owned by the trust. As soon as probate on Griffin's estate was completed, the assets passing to Samantha would transfer into the trust as well. All that was well and good. What troubled me was that if Sammie should die, Pete Spivey would automatically get everything in the trust.

Sandy pointed out the FOR SALE sign placed by a local yacht brokerage firm on the *Mo Bettah*, Gavin's fishing boat.

"Looks like Gavin is really serious," I commented.

"Looks that way," Sandy concurred. "Can't say as I blame him really. With his brother gone, Gav has no family or obligations to keep him here in California. And Hawaii truly *is* a fisherman's paradise."

"Most folks in the world would give their left nut to live in sunny Southern California," I argued.

"Maybe so, but any fisherman who ever pulled a big feisty rainbow-colored Dorado out of the water—Mahi Mahi they call it over there—develops tropical dreams in a hurry. And Hawaii often beckons anglers with such dreams," Sandy concluded.

"Ironic in a way," I mused.

"What is?" Sandy asked.

"Just that Griffin's girlfriend is *from* Hawaii. It was Griffin who brought her to California in the first place. So she's here, and now Griffin's brother wants to move *to* Hawaii. Just strikes me as a bit ironic."

"Hey," Sammie chimed in, "people move all the time. No big deal. The grass is always greener someplace else. Look at you and me, we both started in the Midwest and now—here we are—sitting on a sailboat in a yacht harbor two thousand miles away in California."

"Well, *this* grass clearly *is* greener than my suburban Chicago roots," I remarked.

"No argument from me," Sammie agreed, and we all three laughed.

Just then Sandy spotted Gavin boarding the *Mo Bettah* and called to him. Gavin looked up and—it seemed to me—ducked quickly below upon seeing Sammie and me on Sandy's boat.

"That little snot," Sammie said of Gavin. "Let's pop over there and make a nuisance of ourselves."

"Oh, leave the poor guy alone," I retorted. "His brother just died. He probably just wants to be by himself."

But Samantha was already jumping ship and heading in the direction of the *Mo Bettah*. Sandy and I shrugged to each other and followed her. As long as we were here, I might as well get Gavin to act as secondary witness to Sammie's trust.

Rapping her knuckles on the side of the hull, Sammie began calling Gavin's name. The margaritas earlier and nightcap moments ago with Sandy apparently making her oblivious to how obnoxious her conduct might be perceived. Gavin had little choice but to appear and confront us, but it was clear he resented this intrusion.

"Gavin," Sammie began, "will you be coming over to the house tomorrow?"

Before Gavin could answer, Samantha continued. "I really could use your help. It seems your brother's *whore* had a key to the house and rummaged around in his personal effects. Lord knows what she probably ripped off before I arrived in town. She also made a mess of Griffin's financial records. You worked with him, I could really use your help trying to piece everything together and make some sense of the chaos your brother left me with. I'd like to get this stupid probate over with as soon as possible and your help might speed things along."

Gavin silently nodded his assent to help Sammie.

I showed Gavin the trust instrument and he apathetically attached his name as witness, *Gavin Gilchrist Gambil*. Being a notary, I would place my stamp on the document myself when we returned to the beach house later.

"I see you have the boat up for sale." I pointed to the broker's sign, making small talk as I carefully stashed the trust document back in its envelope.

Another silent nod from Gavin.

"Sandy tells me you're moving to Hawaii," I continued. "Gonna get a new one there?"

Yet another nod.

"Lucky you," I said. "All right if I come visit sometime? It'd be nice knowing someone in Hawaii with a fishing boat."

Gavin shrugged like a small child reluctantly responding to a grown-up.

Sensing Gavin's discomfort at conversing with Sammie and me, Sandy jumped in, changing the subject. "Where you been all evening, Gav?" he asked.

Gavin shrugged again. Like someone doing a sulking James Dean impersonation, he mumbled, "Been with my girlfriend. She lives out in the Valley."

"Shit man," Sandy was grinning with delight, "first time I ever heard of any girlfriend. This serious?"

Gavin grinned back sheepishly, not answering.

The irony I mentioned earlier resurfaced. Gavin was moving to Hawaii, but had a girlfriend in the Valley. Gavin's deceased brother had a girlfriend in the Valley who had moved *from* Hawaii. Suddenly a most implausible thought struck me.

"Did you ever meet your brother's girlfriend?" I asked. "She lives in the Valley, too."

Gavin, who had been contemplating his feet, still in James Dean mode, suddenly looked up. A deer caught in car headlights look of stunned fear shone on his face.

"Wha... what are you talking about?" he stammered. Then adding indignantly, "My brother didn't have any girlfriend. Griffin had a wife!" His eyes focused on Samantha, for the first time glaring angrily at her. "Just because his *wife* proved to be unfaithful doesn't mean Griffin didn't take his vows as a husband any less seriously."

To have a girlfriend while still married would be adultery, something unthinkable in Gavin's opinion. But how could it be that Gavin was so unaware of his brother's mistress and the circumstances of his death? I would have assumed that Samantha had given him the details by now. I wondered only briefly about all this before Samantha chimed in to address Gavin's assessment of his brother and her.

"You are absolutely right, Gavin," Samantha responded with deliberate cadence. "Griffin had a wife. Griffin did *not* have a girlfriend. He did *not* cut you—his only living blood relative—and me—his legal spouse—out of his will by leaving his entire estate to a *girlfriend*. He wouldn't do that, would he Gavin?"

Gavin slowly shook his head, fixing her with a look that burned in silence.

"And if Griffin wouldn't do that, he sure as hell wouldn't have left his entire estate to a *stranger*, would he Gavin? I may not have been a loyal wife, but Griffin would certainly never leave everything to a stranger. Right, Gavin?"

Gavin haltingly responded with a mumbled, "No, my brother would never do something so stupid. Griffin was the smart one in our family."

"I know," Samantha agreed with emphasis. "And I know he had far too much regard for you, his only brother . . . as well as for me. But you know what I am the most sure of, Gavin?"

Gavin's continuing glare was his only response.

Samantha's voice, gradually growing more shrill with each word, carried a menacing tone of which I had not thought her capable.

"What I know with absolute certainty, with every fiber of my being, is that Griffin had waaay too high a regard for M-O-N-E-Y to ever leave it to some fucking, worthless whore! And that's what Griffin had in the Valley, Gavin, not a girlfriend he cared about—he had a *whore*! Did you know about Griffin's whore, Gavin?"

I could tell the image of his dear departed brother being with a prostitute was more than Gavin could take. He looked briefly as if he might burst into tears from Samantha's verbal assault. But it was anger, rather than tears, that filled his eyes. There was a moment when he looked as if he might actually take a swing at Samantha. I stepped in closer, ready to block him if necessary. Then, slowly and reluctantly, Gavin nodded his head. He knew about his brother's mistress. How he knew wasn't clear, but I found myself wondering if he also was aware of the kinky relationship they engaged in.

I realized that we had now established that Gavin was aware of his brother's prostitute, but that my original question had gone unanswered.

"Did you ever meet her?" I reiterated.

Gavin just stood there on his boat, the picture of indignation, defiantly refusing to answer.

Samantha answered for him. "I don't think the type of woman Griffin was seeing before he died is anyone Gavin would ever want to meet. It would violate Gavin's sense of ethics. It would be completely out of character for him."

Indeed, it *would* be out of character for someone like Gavin—a born-again Christian who doesn't drink, curse or fornicate—to want to meet his brother's prostitute. But I found myself once again contemplating how nearly every person I'd met thus far throughout this bizarre case seemed to be *out of character*: tall, handsome, tough-guy millionaire Griffin Gambil didn't have much of a sex-life with his curvaceous wife, but enjoyed groveling at the feet of an under-endowed hooker; sweet

Samantha from high school had left her wealthy husband of fifteen years to shack up with a tattooed, motorcycle-riding cretin—merely because he *made her juices flow*; a not particularly attractive, diminutive Asian prostitute was able to command a high price—cars and houses—for her services; the hooker suggests it was Broadus Liberato who was in some way responsible for Griffin's death, but Liberato turns out to be a withered old man seemingly incapable of harming anyone.

And let's not forget me, a recent retrograde beach bum who, forsaking lawyering, gave up a partnership with an established law firm in order to pursue the fine art of doing nothing. And somehow I now found myself tackling the strangest probate case I've ever heard of—a case that probably should be investigated by the police as a potential murder. None of the people or events I'd encountered recently were as they should have been.

Chapter Sixteen

A month after Griffin died the probate process was still in its infancy, but Samantha was finally making some headway sifting through her late husband's papers. She called me over to the house one day, only telling me she'd figured out something important. When I got there, I found her sitting on the floor of Griffin's former home office, surrounded by piles of neatly staked manila folders and papers.

"Finally I'm beginning to make some sense of this hodge-podge filing and accounting system Griffin left for me to unravel," Samantha said. "The key was figuring out that Gavin is holding title to several properties that were really owned by Griffin."

"I don't understand," I replied.

"It's like this," she explained, "remember I told you that Griffin trusted nobody except for his little brother?"

I nodded.

"Well, it seems that my darling late husband had a couple of lawsuits pending against him. In fact, among the people suing him was his former partner in crime, Broadus Liberato. Anyway, in order to avoid getting liens placed against his properties and to keep certain properties out of litigation, title was held by Gavin. Gav owned the properties on paper, but Griffin was the true owner."

"Gavin was Griffin's straw man," I interjected.

"Exactly," she replied. "The way it worked, Griffin would purchase the property in Gavin's name, so that Gavin's name appeared in the chain of title. Gavin would then immediately sign a Quit Claim Deed to Griffin, transferring full ownership *back* to Griffin. But instead of recording the Quit Claim Deed, Griffin would hold on to it, leaving Gavin as the owner of record. That way, if anyone came after Griffin with a lawsuit or tried to put a lien on the property they would discover that Griffin owned no interest in the property. When the time came to sell the property, Griffin would then record his deed, establishing his legal right to sell it. This was the little monopoly game Griffin and Gavin played, it was them against the world."

"So, how did you discover this bit of mad genius?" I asked, facetiously. "You found the Quit Claim Deeds?"

"Not exactly," Sammie replied. "What I found was a lot of things that just didn't seem right. So, I forced myself to try and think like Griffin in order to make some sense of it all. That's when I decided he and Gavin must be playing fast and loose with some of this stuff. I confronted Gavin with my suspicions and he fervently denied everything. But, like I told you before, Gavin is not a very good liar. I *shamed* him into spilling his guts to me about the whole thing." Samantha could not repress a chuckle, recalling how she manipulated poor Gavin into telling her the truth.

"So, where are the Quit Claim deeds then?" I inquired.

"I'm glad you asked," Sammie spoke lightheartedly, "because that clears up yet another mystery. It was *Gavin* who rummaged through Griffin's things before I arrived. Remember me telling you I suspected someone had been in here?"

"Right," I nodded. "I thought we decided it was Connie Cantu."

"Wrong, moose breath!" Sammie laughed. "It was Gavin. Absolutely. He admitted the whole thing to me. He has his own key to the house of course, and he came in one night looking for the Quit Claims so he could remove them—hoping nobody would ever be the wiser. Unless the Quit Claim deeds get recorded, the property remains in Gavin's name."

"So, what are you going to do about it?" I asked.

"Nothing," was her curt reply.

I stared at her dumbly.

"Let him keep the deeds," she went on. "According to Griffin's *true* will—not that handwritten thing the police found in his car, the formal will he drafted years ago—Griffin left damn near everything to me. At first I didn't understand why Griffin didn't provide better for his brother, why Gavin got the short end of the stick. But now I think Griffin left it all to me knowing I would take care of his poor baby brother. Gavin just doesn't have a head for money. He would blow his entire inheritance on something stupid, like a million-dollar fishing boat or some such nonsense. Griffin knew that. Gavin is entitled to more than Griffin actually left to him, let Gavin keep the properties. Plus, this way those properties can stay out of probate."

"What are the properties worth?" I asked.

"Best guess . . . around three million dollars," she answered nonchalantly.

Legal fees in probate matters are determined by a percentage of the estate value being probated. Involuntarily, my mind quickly computed how much my fees had just been reduced. I was also mentally sorting through all that Sammie had just laid on me. Much of it didn't really sit too well—not that my opinion matters.

I wondered why, if Griffin and Gavin were such tight brothers, Griffin had not specifically provided for Gavin in his will, rather than trusting Samantha to take care of him. And, speaking of Gavin, it almost seemed as if there were two Gavins; the Bible quoting, non-drinking, non-fornicating, non-cursing nice-guy that so many people describe . . . and the moody, elusive, Mexico or Hawaii-bound, intimidating, gun-toting (according to Broadus Liberato) fellow who steals deeds from his brother. Will the real Gavin Gambil please stand up!

And Sammie's casual attitude toward Gavin stealing the deeds. It was difficult for me to accept the cavalier manner that Samantha had so generously *given* three million dollars in real estate to a man who had just tried his best to *cheat* her out of it by *stealing* the Quit Claim deeds. Is anybody really that kind, generous and forgiving? I have a real soft spot for Sammie I admit, but the lawyer in me questioned the efficaciousness of such generosity.

Also, though it was quite true that Griffin's first will left nearly the entirety of his twenty-million-dollar estate to his wife, the glaring fact that the will was drafted *before* Samantha took up with good old Pete Spivey caused me to wonder if that was still Griffin's intent at the time of his death. Poor bastard likely just never got around to changing that first will after he and Samantha parted ways.

Or did he? Maybe that's why he wrote the holographic will found in his car. Maybe Griffin's death truly was a suicide—just as the police contended—and this was Griffin's last-ditch attempt to make those long overdue changes to his will. Perhaps the holographic will did, in fact, express his true intent . . . that he wanted his mistress to get everything. Doubtful he wanted his entire estate to go to the wife who left him for another man. And, horror of horrors, Griffin would certainly be rolling over in his grave if he knew all that money he loved so much was now being left in trust to Pete Spivey!

But what troubled me more than anything was that Gavin Gambil must have gone through Griffin's papers in the aftermath of Griffin's death, before I'd gone to Catalina to find him. Therefore, Gavin *knew* his brother had died. If so, then why was Gavin leaving the country—heading for Mexico on his boat—before his brother was even buried? And why did he feign ignorance about Griffin's death when Sandy related the sad news to him at Catalina Island?

I also recalled that the letter Gavin wrote extolling Christian exuberance was the only thing Sammie said she found in Griffin's file cabinet under "G" and wondered what else Gavin might have extracted from among Griffin's documents. Perhaps the "G for Gavin" file contained some written document that might explain why Gavin had been specifically excluded from his brother's will. Perhaps Gavin lifted such a document from the file along with the deeds he stole. Far too many unanswered questions, if you ask me.

Chapter Seventeen

The attorney representing me in the malpractice claim, and paid by my insurance carrier, filed a motion for summary judgment in the matter. Such a motion is often an effective strategy in very weak cases, like the one Ari Ratono had leveled against me, because, if successful, it allows the moving party to avoid going through a costly trial. A motion for summary judgement argues that the plaintiff cannot win the case because, even if the facts supporting the plaintiff's claim are undisputed, they do not, as a matter of law, rise to the level of the negligence alleged in the plaintiff's complaint. A summary judgment motion, therefore, asks the court to dismiss the claim without proceeding through an actual trial. In other words, it points out to the judge just how full of crap the plaintiff is in his allegations and that it would be a waste of the court's time to even hear such a bullshit claim.

Our motion was granted. I couldn't help shooting a triumphant smirk at Ratono the arrogant lawyer basher as I exited the courtroom. Not that I'd been losing any sleep over Ara Ratono and his dross allegations of malpractice, but my overtaxed brain felt lighter with that entire matter behind me, resolved in my favor.

Now each day I got up, did my morning run on the beach and tried to divorce myself from Griffin and Samantha and that whole miscast set of characters as well. I tried my best to settle into the role I had recently chosen for myself—that of middle-aged beach bum. I rode my bike along the beach bike path, sat under the California sun—prematurely aging my body to an enviable shade of brown—and even tried to revive long-forgotten surfing skills on a used board I bought from the surf shop around the corner, but it was just no use. Call it a case of misguided loyalty to a teen infatuation or a lawyerly sense of duty to seek out justice

. . . or merely old fashioned curiosity, but I just couldn't stop cogitating on the people and events surrounding the death of Griffin Gambil.

More than a week had gone by since I last saw or spoke to Samantha, so I jumped in the Porsche and, with top down, cruised up Pacific Coast Highway toward Topanga Canyon. Turning right onto Topanga Canyon Boulevard, the salt air soon became replaced by the scent of heated pine needles as the tree-lined canyon walls engulfed me. Winding, curving, climbing and gearing my way through the canyon, I turned off at the crest near Mulholland and pulled over to the side, into a small parking area overlooking the vast San Fernando Valley below. It was a reasonably clear day and the hills of Chatsworth at the farthest edge of the Valley were readily visible. Some days, that entire mountain range disappeared into the murky brown air below. But, when the air was clean and clear—on days such as this one—the Valley was a rather glorious sight from atop Topanga Canyon.

Looking down, the San Fernando Valley was an enormous topography come to life. The major thoroughfares cut and sliced the Valley with clear straight precision. All the various townships below—independent, yet all a part of the expansive megalopolis known as Los Angeles—were clearly discernable: Canoga Park directly below with Topanga Canyon Boulevard running straight as an arrow all the way to Chatsworth; Van Nuys Boulevard farther to my right, earmarking the more eastern portion of the Valley; and Ventura Boulevard disappearing into those distant brown hills without woods called Woodland Hills . . . where Samantha and the late Griffin's house lay.

Somewhere between Woodland Hills and Van Nuys, nestled midway between the bisecting asphalt of Winnetka and Reseda Boulevards, was the town of Encino. I got the urge to drive in that direction first.

Descending the canyon and officially entering the Valley, I merged onto the Ventura Freeway only to exit a few miles later at Balboa Boulevard. Why was there a street way out here in the dusty Valley—far from the ocean—named after the man who discovered the Pacific Ocean? No matter. I turned onto Balboa going south, crossing Ventura Boulevard and made a few turns onto lesser streets until I was sitting out front of Connie Cantu's house.

There was a real estate company's FOR SALE sign stuck in her front lawn. Speaking of lawn, it was in desperate need of mowing. I turned into the long, winding driveway and stopped in front of the garage. No sign of life was apparent. I sat there for a few moments, contemplating what to do next. Then the automatic garage door swung open and the Mercedes began backing out.

My car blocked the Mercedes from getting more than a few feet out of the garage. The big sedan stopped its egress and Connie Cantu exited from the driver's side —all 5'2" of her, elevated to about 5' 7" by super-high platform heels. She stood with her hands on her hips, glaring in my direction. I got out of the Boxster and walked a few steps toward her.

"I no gotta talk to you!" she said.

I stopped dead in my tracks, stunned by the strange manner she spoke, sounding the way Asians are often stereo-typed in the movies. Pidgin English, so in contrast with her previous loquacious eloquence. I struggled for something to say.

"You're selling the house?" Not much of a question, that the house was for sale was obvious.

"It my house. I sell if I want," she answered, hands still on hips. "Now get outa my way, I need get to Matson on time."

"Matson?" I asked. "Where the heck is Matson?"

"Not where . . . what," she barked. "Matson Lines in San Pedro. I shipping my car home to Hawaii. I had enough of California."

"You're selling the house and shipping your car. You moving back to Hawaii?" I asked, realizing that was obvious, too.

"I can do that, no law says I can't."

"What about your inheritance from Griffin Gambil? What about probate? What about the will contest?" I asked her.

Cantu whirled her index finger in a lazy gyre as if to indicate she couldn't care less. "No care about that stuff now. Griffin's wife can have it all. I already tell my lawyer to drop lawsuit. I don't want anything, just to be left alone."

She was sure making this easy all of a sudden. With Cantu out of the picture there would be no litigation to determine which will governed the distribution of Griffin's estate. With no will contest and Griffin's death deemed a suicide by the police, this might just end up being your standard garden-variety probate case after all. How did I get so lucky?

I should have felt relieved, but I didn't. *Why* was Cantu dropping her claim . . . and why was she talking so strangely in that pidgin jargon? This whole thing just *smelled* bad to me.

"When you finally find a buyer, your broker will have you fill out a full disclosure form regarding this property," I told her. "Don't forget to disclose the bloody suicide that took place right here in the front yard. It's the law!"

I turned to leave, climbing back into the little blue Porsche and starting the engine. I looked back at Connie Cantu. I caught her in mid-stroke of making a hand gesture. I couldn't tell if she was blowing me a kiss or giving me the finger—maybe she was doing both, Chinese style.

I GOT BACK ON THE freeway, north toward Woodland Hills. I wanted to deliver this bit of good news to Samantha in person. She would be happy to learn Cantu dropped the will contest.

It took a while for Samantha to answer the doorbell. When she did, it was obvious that I had once again interrupted her and Pete Spivey in their latest rendition of the horizontal hula. Jesus! Didn't they ever get tired? These two are middle-aged for Christ sake! As a middle-aged man myself, however, I had to admire Spivey's stamina.

"Sorry," Sammie said, anticipating my thoughts, "Pete is leaving tomorrow for a biker rally. We'll be apart for more than two weeks."

"Two whole weeks!" I said, feigning exhaustion. "Whew! That's one mighty long rally."

"It's all the way up in South Dakota, a little town called Sturgis. Pete says it'll take at least three days just to get there on his bike, an 'ass buster' he calls it. But it's a really big deal. Half a million bikers from all over the world meet up there each year during the first full week of August. Pete really wants me to go with him, but I've got so darn much to do here with this probate stuff, I just can't get away. Pete's riding in caravan with a bunch of guys he met a few weeks ago at Cook's Corners."

"Well, that's just great for good old Pete, isn't it?" I said sardonically, but happy to hear Spivey was leaving town, even if only for two weeks. "You must be sad he's leaving, but I've got some news that might make your day a little brighter."

I told Samantha about Cantu abandoning her litigation and moving back to Hawaii. Samantha did not seem all that surprised. It was as if she already knew all about it. Disappointed at this lackluster response to my big news, and feeling like a third wheel preventing Sammie and Spivey from consummating their farewells, I left.

BACK ON THE VENTURA FREEWAY, Highway 101, and exiting at Las Virgenes Road/Malibu Canyon, I decided to cruise my way home through a different canyon this time—not Topanga. The drive through the green and rocky hills of Malibu Canyon was a pleasant one. Approaching Pacific Coast Highway once again, instead of turning left toward Venice Beach I turned right and took a quick detour over to Pepperdine University Law Center.

Stopping at the security gate, I informed the guard that I was an attorney headed for the law library and showed him my Bar card. The drive up the steep hill that leads to the law center offered awesome views of the blue Pacific Ocean with Catalina Island clearly visible floating on the horizon. The law library is perched high upon a cliff overlooking the infinite expanse of sea below, hardly offering incentive for industrious law students to abandon play on the beach in exchange for arduous pursuit of the voluminous legal tomes contained within.

I got on the school's computer and researched a question that had been plaguing me as I traversed the scenic canyon in my convertible. What I discovered made me catch my breath.

I knew this whole Cantu situation smelled bad. It now became clear why Connie Cantu was so willing to drop any interest she had in Griffin Gambil's estate once Sammie threatened to expose her police record. I wondered if Samantha could somehow have already known what I had just discovered when she confronted Cantu at the funeral.

What I read on the computer screen also explained why Cantu was getting the hell *out of Dodge*—leaving California—before Samantha changed her mind. What I didn't understand was, if Samantha knew what I had just now discovered, why was she willing to let Cantu leave at all?

I printed out the information and sat for several minutes, just staring at the paper in my hand. Connie Cantu had been charged only two years ago by the State of Hawaii . . . with attempted murder. The alleged victim was a former lover—but that may be a misnomer. Probably he was another of her sex slaves—just as Griffin had been. According to the report, Cantu was acquitted after the alleged victim refused to testify against her. She probably *commanded* him not to testify. The power this diminutive dominatrix held over her slaves seemed boundless.

I suddenly felt the clammy certainty that Griffin's death was no suicide. Cantu must have commanded Griffin to draft a new will and then put a bullet through his own skull. Damn! She was a murderer!

The notion that Samantha would allow Connie Cantu to flee California if Cantu had been responsible for Griffin's death was deeply troubling to me. So, I confronted Sammie with it right away, telephoning her from a pay phone at the law library.

I told her, "There's a damn good chance that if she attempted to murder some guy back in Hawaii, she might have tried it again here in California . . . only this time she was successful!"

Samantha denied knowing about Cantu's prior arrest. "I was only bluffing about a police record," she explained. "I just assumed someone in her line of work would have had run-ins with the law. But, surely the LAPD ran a check on her. Surely they know about her past violence."

"Maybe not if she was acquitted. But let's make sure," I said. "I'll contact the fuzz and tell them what I know about her."

"No," Sammie interrupted. "I'll do it. He was *my* husband after all. I'll call the police as soon as we hang up."

But, Samantha never did call the police with this new information.

As I left Pepperdine, turning left onto Pacific Coast Highway, I never even noticed the large white pickup truck that would have filled my rearview mirror had I taken the time to glance at it. The entire drive home I was preoccupied with thoughts of Connie Cantu, the devious world she occupied and the way she must have manipulated poor Griffin Gambil to draft that bogus will . . . and finally to kill himself. Oblivious to the truck dogging me all the way home, I finally spotted it as I was approaching my garage.

I pushed the button on my car's visor and the overhead door began opening. A nervous glimpse in the mirror revealed the same large, menacing, pock-marked fellow from the funeral was now out of the truck and shambling in my direction. I peeled into the garage, hoping to close the door and shut him out, but he was already inside with me, opening my car door and yanking me out of my seat with pasty white meat-hook hands that were ripping my shirt.

Raising me to where I was poised on my toes like a ballet dancer, pulling me so close that I could feel his breath in my face and practically see the blood coursing through the veins in his wide flaring nostrils, his guttural bellow escaped from behind tobacco-stained clenched teeth. "You little puke! You fuckin' little candy-ass lawyer puke! You think yer so goddam smart? Well, you ain't! Now yer gonna pay the tab. Time yer got what's comin'!"

Shit! Cantu knows I'm onto her and has sent one her sex minions to rough me up. And this was one very big boy she had under her spell, even larger than he appeared at Griffin's funeral—or had I suddenly shrunk within his vise-like grip? "Look," I somehow managed to sputter, "I know all about your weird little fetishes and why you're here."

He looked blank, but momentarily loosened his grip, which encouraged me to continue. "You're her sex slave. She's controlling you. But think, man! The jig is up, she's a murderer and she's about to get busted. No need for you to go down with her. Just leave right now and we can pretend this never even happened."

A two-handed shove sent me spiraling across the garage, landing flat on my back looking up at him. He stood glowering down at me for what seemed an eternity, then came a hard kick to my ribs, sending spikes of pain through my entire chest and an involuntary bleat from my lips.

"Yer some kinda whack job, asshole! But don't think this is over, cuz it ain't. Big shot fuckin' lawyer. You don't know fuckin' shit. Ain't nobody gettin' *busted* but you, shithead! Remember, I know where you fuckin' live now," his finger stabbing the air in my direction for emphasis. "The law or nothin' ain't gonna protect you. You just think about that!"

With that, he turned and strode victoriously out of the garage. The truck peeled out, rubber burning tread marks onto the pavement. A bumper sticker with an angry rams-head characterization of the Dodge logo framed by the words THIS TRUCK EATS CHEVYS—SHITS FORDS! Damn. I should've focused on the license plate number instead of reading redneck bumper stickers.

Chapter Eighteen

Nearly a month went by. Being attacked in my own garage had taken me from frightened, to seething, to humiliated, to just plain bruised and sore. For a while I'd considered buying a gun for protection, but settled on keeping a baseball bat behind the seat of my car. Next time, I told myself, I'd be ready. But the pocked brute in the white truck had not reappeared, and for that much I was thankful.

The police, I presumed, were now well aware of Connie Cantu's violent past. I was convinced that Cantu caused Griffin's death—either directly or, at least, indirectly—so no further sleuthing was required on my part. I had my answers, it was a police matter now.

Pete Spivey rode his motorcycle up to South Dakota to attend the biker rally. He would be gone a couple of weeks, minimum. Gavin promised to look in on Samantha each day and help out with all the administrative work that needed to be done to complete probate.

Everything seemed to be finally coming under control. The probate of Griffin's estate was my one and only case, so my lawyer duties were at a minimum. I could now settle back and live out my beach bum daydreams as per my original plan—before hooking up with Samantha and being dragged off on this bizarre tangent.

ROUGHLY THREE MONTHS AFTER POOR old Griffin Gambil died, there was one particular morning that seemed to culminate all that I had hoped life might be after walking out on my law partners to embrace beach life. To my great delight, the ocean water was unusually warm—allowing me to spend the morning surfing the nicely breaking sets of waves, sans wetsuit. Invigorated and exhausted after nearly two hours frolicking in the Pacific, I left the water and, carrying my board under my arm, began trudging through the warm, soft sand toward my little house on the beach.

Passing by two rather attractive girls seated on beach towels (in their early thirties I would guess, so *girls* is most assuredly not the politically correct word), they both smiled a friendly hello to which I responded in kind.

"We were watching you surf," one of them spoke up. "Sure looks like fun."

"It definitely is," I assured her. Wet, chilled and tired, I continued walking to my house a few yards away, adding over my shoulder in passing, "Hope I didn't embarrass myself too much out there."

The breeze carried her response. "It was lots more fun watching you than reading my book."

Smiling sheepishly, not at all sure if that meant my aquatic antics had appeared skillful or merely amusingly goofy, I continued trekking my way across the sand.

Arriving at my little beachfront bungalow and beginning to open the front gate, one of the girls, getting up and moving in my direction, asked, "Oh my, do you live here?"

I replied in the affirmative, to which the other girl, also on the rise, remarked, "Wow, you really *are* living the true California Dream. Surfing and living right here on the beach. Do you know how lucky you are? It's amazing." Nodding, I gave silent thanks to good old Uncle Jack.

"You two aren't from California?" I asked, thinking perhaps they were tourists.

"Oh yes, we've lived in California several years," the first one responded. "But, I'm afraid the California Dream gets a bit diluted the farther inland you live." Translation: They lived in the Valley, twenty miles and a universe removed from beach life. A place, by the way, where I'd been spending far too much time lately.

"We like coming to the beach as often as we can, though," the second one added. "This is where the truly *hunky* guys are—athletic, tanned, sexy men!" She looked coyly at me, her words like music to a concert-starved man. "That's why we were watching you. Looks like our morning is starting off pretty good."

Clearly they were flirting with me, not something I'd encountered in a while, and I found myself enjoying it. The longer we engaged in conversation, the more overtly flirtatious these two young bikini-clad beach bunnies became. My mind drifted off for a moment as I began imagining myself involved in a threesome: discarded bikini tops cast upon the floor, two topless girls giggling and jiggling as they nibbled on my ears and rubbed my shoulders—every guy's fantasy!

The ringing of the telephone in my house jarred me back to earth. Pretending to ignore it at first, the ringing persisted.

"I'll be right back," I assured the girls as I sprang up the stairs, entered my house and grabbed for the phone.

"What is it?" I barked into the speaker.

"Mr. Harding?" It was Gavin Gambil. I recognized the voice, and detected a slight tremble in it.

"Yeah, Gavin," I said, softening. "Everything okay?"

"Mr. Harding, I'm at Valley Hospital. Someone tried to kill Samantha. She's still in a coma. No one knows for sure if she will make it. She's in the hands of our Lord now."

Shit! "I'm on my way," I told him and hung up.

Chapter Nineteen

The events following Gavin's call are now a blur to me. Seeing Sammie, my beautiful former high school heartthrob, lying in a hospital bed, suddenly looking like a pale old woman waiting for death to claim her, deeply saddened me. But, learning how such a fate befell her filled me with uncontrollable anger!

Apparently, Gavin arrived at the house in Woodland Hills the previous afternoon to help Samantha, as he had each day for a week. Except that this time, the smell of gas permeated the house and he found Sammie collapsed on the floor of the kitchen. The tiny window of the adjoining bathroom was open, allowing a slight bit of fresh air to enter the room, and the air conditioning was on. It seems that was just enough to keep Sammie breathing. Another hour though, and she would have succumbed to the noxious fumes of the gas.

Gavin carried her from the house and placed her on a deck chair by the pool as he returned inside to open all the windows and doors and turn off the gas, for fear the house might explode. Administering mouth-to-mouth, Sammie did not respond. Gavin rushed her to the hospital and sat with her all night. In the morning he called me. While I was out riding waves and flirting with girls far too young for me, Samantha was lying in a hospital bed fighting for her life. I chastised myself, although without good reason—there was no way I could have known what happened. What I did know, however, was that Connie Cantu was responsible. She had to be!

In a rage, I sprinted from the hospital room and raced the Porsche to Cantu's house. A SOLD banner was added to the broker's sign in the front lawn. The house was empty.

I drove to the office of the broker named on the sign and demanded to talk to the agent handling the sale. The agent was an older woman wearing far too much make-up and with too many rings on her fingers for good taste. I told her that I was the probate attorney for the prior owner of the property and convinced her that if she did not supply the information I was seeking, I could gum up the current sale of the property for years and she could kiss her real estate commission goodbye. My intimidation worked and I left her office with the Hawaii address for Connie Cantu—the address where the proceeds from the sale were to be sent at the close of escrow.

That's how I found myself on an Aloha Airlines flight making its descent into Honolulu International Airport. I wasn't waiting for the LAPD or even Steve McGarrett of *Hawaii Five-O* to book 'em Danno on this one. I intended to track down Cantu and . . . and what? I wasn't quite sure, but I was all fired up to *personally* bring about justice on behalf of both Griffin and Samantha.

DEPLANING, I WALKED OUT ONTO the concourse, tasted my first breath of fragrant, humid, tropical air—August, I discovered, is the hottest, most muggy month of the year in Hawaii—and flagged down a cab.

"Where to, Brah?" my Polynesian cabbie asked. He kept both his enormous brown hands on the wheel. Attached to the hands were mutton-like forearms. Connie Cantu notwithstanding, Hawaiians, it seems, are not a diminutive people.

I handed him the address written on a yellow Post-It. It was a street I couldn't pronounce, a Hawaiian name.

"777 Kapiolani," the name easily rolled off the cabbie's tongue, not mine.

I nodded to him in the rear-view mirror.

"Dat be down near Waikiki, but it's not a hotel, Brah," the cabbie informed me.

"Just take me there, please," I told him.

"Sure ting, Brah. Here we go." With that, the cabbie hammered down the meter flag, spoke something completely unintelligible into his Motorola microphone, and sped away from the airport at a good clip.

I had never been to Hawaii before. What I saw from the windows of the cab was not too impressive: old buildings in various stages of disrepair, some nearly falling down, and a super highway system eight lanes across, complete with huge concrete overpasses and the attendant traffic. But no sashaying hula girls, no sandy beaches or turquoise ocean waters as I might have expected. First blush impression was that of an improbable city hybrid composed of Hong Kong, New York and South Central Los Angeles . . . with a smattering of rural Georgia thrown in for good measure, I thought as a flock of chickens crossed the busy street in front of the cab.

Passing a giant Pineapple-shaped water tower looming up in the sky, the pungent, sickly-sweet scent of millions of that same fruit at a processing plant we were passing assaulted my nostrils. I was hoping this twenty-minute cab ride was not the scenic tour. Crossing over what appeared to be the same canal several times in order to navigate numerous one-way city streets, my driver made a final quick turn and abruptly stopped at the curb.

"Dis be da place, Brah," he said as the meter continued running.

"Can you wait for me a moment?" I asked, exiting the cab.

"Sure Brah, meter still going, yeah? Ca-ching, ca-ching!" He laughed a hearty Hawaiian laugh.

I HAD ASSUMED THE ADDRESS would be Cantu's residence in Honolulu. But, Kapiolani Boulevard was a bustling commercial street, filled with shops and various business establishments. I checked the number on my Post-It, 777, and located the storefront that matched those numbers. Damn! It was a mail drop. I should have known. Probably the same one she told me about using for her slaves to contact her.

Climbing back into the cab, I wasn't quite sure what to do next. I was a stranger in a strange land. I asked the cabbie if there were any hotels nearby. He looked at me like I was completely insane.

"Sure Brah. Dare be lots hotels here. Dis is Waikiki . . . hotel capital of the world!"

"Well, take me to one," I said.

"Nice one or so-so?" he asked.

"Nice, I guess."

"Beach or no beach?"

This was getting to be too many choices.

"Beach, I suppose." Maybe I'd feel more at home that way.
"You got it, Brah!" And off we sped.

THE DRIVER DEPOSITED ME AT the Ilikai Hotel. It was right on Waikiki Beach, overlooking the ocean and marina. It looked nice enough, perhaps a tad dated—vintage 1960s but well maintained. The cabbie pointed out that the Ilikai was used a lot in the old *Hawaii Five-O* and *Magnum, P.I.* television shows. Sure enough, the place did look vaguely familiar.

I checked in at the registration desk, declined a bellman's offer of assistance with my single overnight bag, rode a dark Koa-wood paneled elevator up sixteen floors and plopped down on the bed in my room.

My body was ready to sleep for the night, but because of the time change it was only 7:30 in Hawaii. I knew I should force myself to adjust to local time, so I went for a walk. On the corner across the street was a coffee shop called Wailana's where I had my first Hawaiian meal: cheeseburger with fries and a Diet Coke—a slice of papaya on the side. Then I strolled Ala Moana Boulevard all the way to Kalakaua Boulevard into the heart of the Waikiki marketplace area—a thousand shops all selling the same T-shirts proclaiming, "HANG LOOSE." A light drizzle began to fall from the sky. Welcome to paradise!

I ended my first day in "the Islands" reclined outside on the 16th floor balcony of my room at the Ilikai Hotel. The air smelled fragrant from the rain that had ended only a short while before. I watched clouds racing across the blackened Hawaiian sky and thousands of twinkling lights on the distant hillsides shimmering in the dampness. The white-noise hum of traffic along nearby Ala Moana Boulevard was continuous, as were the boats in Ala Wai Yacht Basin—Hawaii's largest marina—all lined up in symmetrical fashion. So, this was Waikiki . . . Honolulu . . . Hawaii . . . paradise.

I drifted off to sleep right there on the balcony, sixteen floors up.

THE NEXT DAY I CALLED the hospital to inquire about Samantha. Her condition remains unchanged, they said. Then I contacted the real estate agent in California. She told me the proceeds from the sale would be delivered to Cantu any day now. I gave her my phone number and she agreed to let me know when the check was actually in the mail.

My coming to Hawaii was a stupid move. You'd think all those years thinking like a lawyer might have caused me to slow down and forge a better game plan, but instead I rushed off to be the conquering hero and bring justice to a situation that seemed to have none. Now I had to just sit and wait for the check to arrive and hope I could nab Cantu when she picked it up at her mail drop.

I ran a brisk four and a half miles through Ala Moana Park followed by a refreshing swim in the ocean. What a treat! The ocean water here was as warm as a heated swimming pool and, I had to admit, much more to my liking than the frigid ocean back home that seldom reaches above seventy degrees, even in summer.

Strolling along Waikiki Beach, wavelets lapping at my ankles, tourists were setting up for their day in the sun. The most beautiful beach in America they say, and "they" may be right. Notwithstanding the high-rise hotels springing from the sand and crowds of tourists from every part of the world, it was a lovely stretch of sand, with the famous Diamond Head crater off in the distance marking the extreme opposite end.

A real majority of the tourists appeared to be Asian: Chinese, Japanese, Korean . . . I'm sorry, but they all looked alike to me. I mean no disrespect and realize how politically incorrect such a statement might be, but that makes it no less true. I found myself wondering if even a Chinese person could tell another Chinese from the hordes of Asian nationalities. I'm of German and Italian descent, but am not sure I could tell an Irish Caucasian from a Swedish or German Caucasian. I'm not even sure if I could tell an Italian from an Eastern European or a Jewish person just by looking at them. With all due respect, most Italians, Eastern Europeans and Jewish people tend to have dark hair and olive skin—if there's some particular physical trait that sets them all apart, I'm not aware of it.

Suddenly it occurred to me, I might not be able to recognize Connie Cantu. Sure, I could probably spot her in a crowd in Encino where she might be the only Asian. But here in Honolulu, where the various Asian nationalities comprise eighty percent of the population, Cantu might just blend in with the scenery and go unnoticed to my uncultured *haole* eye. (Haole, I quickly learned, is what Caucasians are called in this mostly brown or yellow-skinned 50th state of ours. What I didn't learn until much later is that haole actually means foreigner. It wouldn't matter if you were third generation born in Hawaii, if you were Caucasian you were a haole. This must be the only state in the union where native white people are openly called foreigners.)

Returning to my hotel room, the red message light on the telephone was lit up. It was the realtor. Her message said this was the fastest escrow of her career, the check to Cantu had been mailed two days ago. Shit!

I HUSTLED VIA CAB DOWN to the mail drop on Kapiolani Boulevard. The good news, I was told, is that mail generally takes three days or more to arrive from the mainland. Good, there was still hope of catching Cantu picking up her check.

I tried to solicit further information about Ms. Cantu from the Asian gentleman who operated the place—Korean, I learned he was—by fabricating a story about a letter wrongly mailed from California to Connie Cantu. I told him the letter contained highly classified information that could seriously jeopardize an ongoing criminal case on the mainland. I said I was a lawyer from California and my office was responsible for mailing the letter by mistake. I showed him my Bar card to add veracity to the story.

"If she opens that letter, I'm in big trouble!" I lied to him. "That's why I came here in person to retrieve the letter from Ms. Cantu before it reaches her."

He said he was very sorry, but it was a federal offense to interfere with the delivery of mail. I couldn't argue with that. However, if I made it worth his while, he would check her slot to see if the letter in question had indeed arrived. I laid a ten dollar bill on him, but his palm remained open. I landed a second ten spot on top of the first and he disappeared into the back of the establishment, returning a brief moment later.

"Today's mail still being sorted," he told me. "You wait and I'll see for you if letter is here."

I waited, and it wasn't. I planted a hundred dollar bill on him and he promised to call me at the hotel the moment the letter arrived.

"I'm staying at the Ilikai," I said. "Ever heard of it?"

He looked at me as if I was the stupidest haole he had ever seen.

Chapter Twenty

I was sunning myself on the outside balcony when the phone rang. The letter had arrived!

I took a cab down to Kapiolani Boulevard and tried to remain inconspicuous as I hung around waiting for Cantu to show up. I was hoping such a large sum of money arriving in the mail would inspire her to check for it daily. The wait lasted several hours, with me strolling furtively up and down Kapiolani, keeping the mail drop in sight all the while. And then, I saw her.

I had worried that I wouldn't recognize Cantu, but she was actually quite easy to spot. Her mark of distinction was the way she walked and moved. Ever the dominatrix, she walked with an attitude not in common with most of the Asians who came and went. She strutted into the mail drop like she owned the place.

But now that I had found her, what was my next move? I had not choreographed that far in advance. When she came out, I followed her around the corner and watched her climb into the Mercedes, still displaying the California license plates. Spotting a cab dropping a fare on the opposite side of the street, I sprinted to catch it. Luckily, Cantu was rifling through her mail, seated behind the wheel of her car still parked at the curb. This bought me a few moments.

Hurling myself into the rear seat of the cab, I pointed to the Mercedes as it pulled away, shouting to the driver, "Follow that car!"

The cabbie spied me in the rear-view mirror with a look of disbelief. "You got it, Brah! I bin waiting all my life to hear a passenger say those words to me."

It was the same huge kanaka who had been my driver from the

airport when I first arrived. Pleasantly surprised, I pointed this out to him. What are the odds? But it was clear he did not remember me.

"Sorry Brah, no offense but all you haole tourists look da same to me, ya know?" he said over his beefy shoulder as he sped in hot pursuit after the cream-colored sedan.

WE FOLLOWED THE MERCEDES ONTO the H-1 freeway, away from the city and toward the ritzy suburb of Kahala.

"Only rich people live in dis part o town, Brah," the cabbie told me.

But Kahala was not Cantu's destination, she kept going. At some point, just past a huge department store called Liberty House, the freeway ended and became several lanes of stop-and-go traffic called Kalanianiole Highway—try saying that five times fast!

We stayed on her tail as Cantu proceeded through several different townships, marked by signs along the highway identifying them with Polynesian-sounding names like Aina Haina and Hawaii Kai.

At Hawaii Kai, Cantu turned left into a shopping center where a bank was located. She made a stop there, presumably depositing the escrow check. Then it was back to the highway, up a steep incline toward a sign that read "Hanauma Bay."

My driver joked, "Look like she maybe going snorkeling, Brah!" He let out a hearty laugh and told me Hanauma Bay was a marine sanctuary open to the public for snorkeling and communing with myriad colorful tropical fish. But Connie Cantu kept on going, past Hanauma Bay.

We continued on and the road narrowed along a cliff drive that offered the most beautiful view of turquoise water as far as the eye could see. This was what people raved about when they spoke of Hawaii, but you'd never know it from the sights an arriving tourist is subjected to on the drive from the airport to Waikiki. A volcanic blowhole was shooting geysers skyward as I spotted Cantu turning left onto a road just beyond a wide expanse of beach.

"That's Sandy Beach," my driver pointed out. "Da kine body surfing. No ka 'oi, yeah?"

He was trying to be an informative tour guide, pointing out that this beach was excellent for body surfing, but it was difficult to follow the Hawaiian expressions, so I asked him to please just concentrate on the Mercedes—thank you very much.

We stuck to Cantu like glue until she pulled up to a residential area closed to the public by a set of iron gates inscribed with the word *Queensgate*. How appropriate for this woman who so enjoyed male adoration and ruled over them like some sort of demented royalty to live in an area called Queensgate.

"Shit!" I exclaimed unabashedly. "Now what?"

"Don' know, Boss," my driver said, adding in Hawaiian, *Pau'Oia ho'I bā*, which—after I asked—he translated to, *We're finished, that's all she wrote*.

We pulled over on the side of the road and watched as Cantu inserted some sort of card into a slot, causing the gates to open. She drove through and I wondered what to do next. Suddenly I was thrown back in my seat as the cabbie accelerated and the taxi lurched forward, speeding toward the gates. Amazingly, we made it through before the gates re-closed.

"So much for security gates, huh Brah?" the driver chortled.

Inside the gates was a community of tan stucco houses nestled up to a golf course. With a golf course for a backyard and the ocean in the distance, each house enjoyed a beautiful view. Cantu pulled up to one of the houses, the overhead garage door magically opened and the Mercedes disappeared inside.

"Stop here," I instructed my driver. "I'd like you to wait for me. I may be a while."

"No problem, Brah. The meter keeps on running. Ca-ching, ca-ching. I'm gonna be able to send my kid to Punaho on dis fare, Bruddah!"

I STOOD OUTSIDE HER HOUSE for several minutes, trying to calculate my next move. Then, throwing caution to the wind, I figured I'd come here for answers and, damn it, I intended to get answers! The direct approach would yield the most immediate results. Walking up to the door, I knocked . . . loudly.

My knock was answered. Barefooted, without the usual elevation of her high heels, Connie Cantu was a truly tiny creature. Like a giant Gulliver in the presence of a Lilliputian, I stood towering over her with only the threshold between us. Seeing me at her front door, she began swearing in Chinese. At least I think that's what language she used. She did not, however, slam the door in my face as I might have anticipated and, once she regained her composure, allowed me to state my business . . . though she did not invite the giant in.

I wasn't particularly tactful and immediately accused her of *murdering* Griffin as well as attempting to murder Samantha. Gentle, rhythmic ukelele music could be heard in the background as the cabbie listened to the car radio while he waited. It somehow diffused the intensity I'd intended by such accusations.

Cantu responded with words spoken spare and deliberate. Gone was the Chinese as well as the pidgin that was prominent when we spoke last.

"Is this why you came all the way to Hawaii? To accuse me of horrible crimes? I can assure you, Mr. Harding, that I have absolutely nothing to hide. I will answer any question you may have, even though I am certain any authority to ask such questions was left behind in California. Go ahead, ask me anything about these terrible crimes that you want. I will give you an honest answer. We will clear this up right now . . . then don't you ever bother me again!"

I was stunned by her candor. "If you did not have anything to do with Griffin's death, then why did you drop your claim to his estate and flee back to Hawaii?"

She glared up at me from within the doorway. "I did not *flee*, as you put it. Hawaii is my home. I only lived in California at Griffin's request. As long as he was paying the bills, I stayed. With him gone, I returned to my home here in the Islands.

"Besides, his widow threatened to disclose to the Los Angeles police my prior . . . altercation with the Honolulu authorities. Even though I was acquitted of any wrongdoing here in Hawaii, I was concerned that the police in L.A. might make a big deal of it. In light of all the circumstances, I decided it was prudent to leave."

"And you didn't care that you were giving up any rights to the Gambil estate from the holographic will Griffin left?" I asked.

"Of course I *cared*. I found the idea of inheriting all that money most appealing. But I'm not really as greedy as you might assume, Mr. Harding. After discussing it with my attorney, he thought my chances were slim for prevailing over the rights of a long-time spouse and that it would cost a small fortune to even pursue. It was a simple balancing act; a slim chance at inheriting a fortune versus a reasonably good chance that Griffin's death would be blamed on me because of who I am and my prior arrest for essentially the same thing."

"You were arrested? For what?" I played dumb.

"I don't think I want to talk about it," she responded, but I prompted her to tell me about it anyway—assuring her that it would remain *off the record*, just our little secret.

It was my lucky day, Cantu was in a talking mood. She sighed and held the door open wider, instructing me to remove my shoes first—in customary Asian fashion—before motioning me inside.

The interior was rich, dark wood and Oriental rugs. Sunlight streaming in from skylights in the roof gave a bright, cheery feeling to the place. Very different from the Encino house where we'd first met, and not at all the sort of place I'd picture a dominatrix to reside.

From the entry I could see clear through to the far side of the house where a wall of glass offered an unobstructed view of the golf course and lush hillside beyond. I followed in that direction as her bare feet padded along the parquet wood floor. We sat in opposite chairs, looking out at the view. A bamboo coffee table separated us. On it was a copy of *Honolulu* magazine and a box of Sherman cigarettes.

"Beautiful view," I remarked.

"Yes, yes. I know. Do you want to discuss the view? I would prefer to tell you what you came here to find out— about my arrest. Then you can leave and I never have to see you again, if you don't mind."

I nodded.

"Well," she began, "a couple of years ago I agreed to meet with one of my cyber-slaves. You remember, I told you about my S&M website?"

Again I nodded.

"This slave had been corresponding with me and sending me money for several months. He had become one of my regulars. He pleaded for a chance to meet with me in person. He filled out my standard online questionnaire form—an application for an *in-person* meeting. One of the things a slave must do on the application is to supply a safe-word."

"Safe-word?" I asked.

"A safe-word is any word a slave chooses that will signal me that I have gone too far—that I have crossed that fine line between *pleasure-pain* and *real* pain. A word that clearly conveys the message that he would like me to stop," she explained. "This is particularly important in sessions where corporal punishment is being employed. I have no way to judge a slave's tolerance for pain. He may be screaming for me to stop whipping him, but all the while enjoying it and wanting me to continue. This is typical of S&M games. So telling me to stop is *not* going to get me to stop. What is needed is some different palliative word, one that we both know means to stop. This particular slave chose the word *mambo*."

Cantu looked me in the eye, apparently waiting for some inappropriate comment from me regarding such an odd choice for a safe-word. I offered no commentary and she continued.

"This guy was into CBT, flogging and all sorts of punitive pain . . . ."

"CBT, what's that?" I'm no prude, but had never heard such a term.

"Cock and ball torture," she informed me in a purely matter-of-fact tone.

I let out an involuntary moan just imagining such a thing.

"I'm sure you don't want me to go into the specifics, but he was really *into* pain. I had been beating and torturing him for the better part of an hour and was really admiring his threshold for tolerance when I noticed that he had lost consciousness. It scared the hell out of me. I thought maybe he was dead! I called the police and he was rushed to the hospital. He nearly died. The State of Hawaii charged me with attempted murder! Do you know why all that happened? Because my stupid slave forgot his damned safe-word! I never wanted to actually hurt the poor bastard, it was just a game. Fortunately for me, the slave refused to testify against me or to help the police in any way. He was too embarrassed about the whole thing and just wanted it to all go away.

"But it didn't go away. We actually went to trial and it was the most horrible experience I have ever endured. I cannot understand how you lawyers do your jobs. You may think what I do for a living is low, but I think what you do is the lowest. Anyway, with no testimony from the alleged victim and no proof that I intended to hurt him, I was acquitted.

"I never want to go through such an ordeal again. This is why I don't care to fight with Griffin's widow, I don't want to be in court. And, even though I'm not responsible for Griffin's death, I am afraid of being charged with a crime. I just couldn't stand to go through it all again."

"Are you telling me that you had absolutely nothing to do with Griffin's death?" I asked her.

"I don't know if that would be completely accurate. I suppose I did play some *small* part. But I certainly never believed he would kill himself over it."

She paused as a small contingent of golfers passed by the window. I was at the edge of my seat, anxious for her to continue. At length, she did.

"You see, often when Griffin and I were playing our little game and my pathetic little sex-toy was out of his mind in blissful agony, he would swear undying allegiance to me and promise to do absolutely anything I asked. So, one such day I told him, 'Fine. Divorce that wife for whom you are nothing but a cuckold and sign everything you own over to me!'

"I never for one moment thought he would do it. You must remember, this was but a *game* we were playing. Griffin was a sniveling wimp of a man only while we were engaged in play; this was the antithesis of his true self. The rest of the time he was his usual self-serving, bullying, boorish self. He was a man who loved money. Giving me gifts—even extravagant gifts like cars and real estate—was one thing, handing *everything* over to me just because I told him to was quite another matter."

Cantu sighed, as if relating all this information was boring her. Then, lifting the box of cigarettes from the coffee table and lighting one of the brown sticks, she continued.

"On the particular morning that he died, Griffin told me he was actually going to follow through with a divorce that he filed sometime ago but never actively pursued. I reminded him that this was only *half* what I commanded him to do. I reminded him that he must sign over *everything* he owns to me as well. I told him that it wasn't enough to own him sexually, I wanted to own him *completely*—lock, stock and barrel!

"The next thing I knew, he was a bloody mess lying dead on my front lawn. I never told him to kill himself and had no idea he actually drafted a will leaving everything to me. I only found out after the fact. I am sorry that he died, but I feel no remorse, I feel no guilt. This was merely a *game*.

Never in my wildest imagination did I think Griffin would kill himself. And I still don't think I was the reason he did it."

Connie Cantu's garrulous openness was very convincing. She nearly had me believing it truly was a suicide and, although she played a role in it, she could not be held liable for Griffin's death.

"And what about the attempt on Samantha's life?" I demanded, a little less vigorously than in my earlier accusations.

Cantu just looked at me for several moments. "I already dropped my lawsuit over the wills," she finally said. "What possible motive could I have for wanting to see her dead?"

This was true, Cantu would seemingly have nothing to gain by killing Samantha. I was beginning to feel somewhat foolish for flying off the handle and coming all the way to Hawaii without more to substantiate my hunches.

"Tell me, when did this attempted murder occur?" Cantu asked cautiously.

I told her the date and she disappeared into another room, asking me to wait a moment. She reappeared, handing me a narrow piece of paper, delivering it into my hands delicately as if it were a fragile Faberge´ egg.

Cantu stood by silently as I remained seated, inspecting the paper. It was her ticket stub from the flight that took her from LAX to Honolulu. According to the ticket, Cantu was already back in Honolulu before the attempt on Samantha's life took place. She was offering this as her alibi.

"One more thing," I said, handing the ticket stub back to her. "Are you acquainted with Griffin's brother?"

"His brother?" she replied, reclaiming her place on the chair facing me. "I know he had one, but have never met him. Why do you ask?"

"No reason, really. It's just that the brother was seeing someone who lived in the San Fernando Valley and now has suddenly decided to move to Hawaii. Pretty big coincidence, don't you think?"

"Well," she said, picking up her cigarette and taking another long drag, "it's a big Valley. How would I know who some brother of Griffin's might be seeing? As far as him moving to Hawaii . . . a thousand of you haoles move here every week. It's like some sort of infestation. But if he really does move here, and he's anything like his brother, tell him to look me up. I have an opening for a new slave, since my last one died . . . as long as he can remember his safe-word."

My cab was still waiting and returned me to the Ilikai. The tally was greater than the cost of the airfare to the Islands.

"I hope your kid enjoys Punaho," I told the big kanaka, as I forked over a thick wad of cash. Punaho, I learned, is a very expensive private school in Hawaii.

"Hey, here's my card, Brah. Anytime you need cab ride, call me! Aloha nui loa."

He drove off and I took the outdoor elevator to the sixteenth floor. Rising up in the glass enclosure, I could see all of Ala Wai Yacht Basin and the blue Pacific stretching out clear to the horizon. It was easy to understand why this was the honeymoon capital of the world; Hawaii truly was beautiful, if you discounted the scenery between the airport and Waikiki. I wished my visit here had been under more pleasant circumstances. Shared with the right woman, this tropical paradise with gentle sea breezes would be amazingly romantic.

But romance was the farthest thing from my mind—Cantu's descriptions of sexual sadism and manipulation were more than enough to quash such notions. Besides, my brain was reeling, sorting through the amalgam of conflicting information surrounding Griffin and the attempt on Samantha. Cantu had been convincing, but I remained dubious.

The really frightening part, though, was, if Cantu truly was innocent, then who did try to kill Samantha . . . and who sent the thug with the large nose to beat me up? These were my thoughts as I exited the elevator and walked alone down an empty hallway, a renewed sense of danger my only companion.

Entering my room, the message light was on. It was the hospital. Samantha was conscious and asking for me.

Chapter Twenty-One

The red-eye flew me back to California and I made a beeline for the hospital, but at six o'clock in the morning it was too early for visiting hours. I found my way down to the hospital cafeteria where I nursed a cup of coffee for an hour, killing time. Seven was still too early for visitors, but I was able to convince the nurse to let me into Samantha's room.

Sammie smiled up at me, looking nearly her old self again. "Benjamin, thank God," she said.

Smiling back down at her, I was flattered that on her hospital sickbed it was me, her old high school admirer, whom she was asking to see. I was very touched.

"You're the only lawyer I know," her words stabbed me in the heart and my smile faded.

"You wanted to see me because I'm a lawyer?" I asked incredulously, my heart once again shattered by this old high school flame. When would I ever learn? "Why do you need a lawyer?"

"I'm not sure, Benjamin. I told the police what happened to me and, for some reason, I think they now suspect me of killing my husband. So I clammed up and refused to answer their questions until you got here. Benjamin, what the heck is going on? I didn't kill anyone. I'm the damn victim here! Absolutely. I'm the victim twice over—hell, three times over! First my husband dies, then I discover he left everything to a prostitute and then I'm nearly murdered!"

Her voice rose an octave with each sentence. She was becoming so excitable that I considered calling a nurse.

"Calm down," I told her. "I'm confused. Why are the police suddenly considering you a suspect in a death they have already written off as a suicide?"

"Because of Pete," Sammie told me. "They think he killed Griffin and that I was in on it with him."

"Pete killed Griffin?" I was becoming even more confused. "Let's back up," I told her. "Start at the very beginning."

Sammie took a deep breath before speaking again.

"I was sitting at Griffin's old desk, sorting through the stacks of papers piled there. I didn't hear anyone enter the house, but suddenly there were fingers wrapped around my neck—strong fingers—and I was being choked." She wrapped her own fingers about her neck as illustration.

"Could you see who it was?" I asked.

"No, he came from behind as I was sitting in the chair hunched over the desk. I gasped for air, and felt myself beginning to lose consciousness. I may have actually *lost* consciousness for a few moments, I can't be sure. When I stopped fighting it and my body slumped, I guess he figured I was dead because the choking stopped."

"What happened next?" I was riveted.

"I sat there slumped over in the desk chair, but alert enough to realize my best chance at survival was to continue playing dead. His hands moved from my throat to my blouse, sliding under it and down the front to feel my breasts. Still standing behind me, both his hands cupped both my breasts. I was only half-conscious but remember thinking, 'What kind of a sick-o strangles a woman and cops a feel after she's dead?' I became terrified he might want to rape me—what he believed to be my corpse— but that never happened." Samantha emitted a sigh of relief, followed by a long pause, as if purging the unthinkable from her mind.

"Instead, he walked away, leaving me in the chair while he turned on the gas jets in the kitchen. I could smell the gas right away. Then he walked around the house closing all the windows, I could hear him.

"Finally he returned to me, I could feel him standing behind me. I continued to play dead, scared to open my eyes or move a muscle lest he begin choking me again." Samantha laid rigid in her hospital bed, her eyes shut tightly as she recounted the horrific events. "And then, from somewhere behind me in the room, I heard him speak. I could barely contain my horror at the sound of his voice. Of course, I recognized the voice instantly."

Samantha, opening her eyes and looking up at me, said, "It was Pete."

Chapter Twenty-Two

"Pete Spivey is the one who tried to kill me," she said.

My mouth fell open. I was stunned.

"Thinking I was already dead, slumped over the desk, he told me he was sorry. Can you believe it? He apologized to my dead body for killing me! He said he was sorry, but money is warmer than love . . . then he actually laughed. I heard him. With me dead, the estate I inherited from Griffin would now be his. God! Benjamin, you were so right about Pete. Absolutely. How could I have been so stupid to leave everything to that *asshole!*"

"Well," I added, "Pete Spivey is no Einstein, either. He kills you to inherit a fortune before Griffin's body is even cold in the ground? Jesus! Couldn't he have at least waited a while? Didn't it ever occur to him that the police would do the math and the answer to that equation leads right straight to Pete Spivey?"

"And I'm not the first person he has murdered," Samantha gasped. "Pete murdered his wife, too. Absolutely. He told me."

"You knew he murdered his wife!" I was beside myself.

"No, he confessed to the back of my head . . . after he thought I was dead. He told me that he pushed her from the ski-lift onto the trees below. He did it for the insurance money."

"Jesus!" was all I could muster.

"Pete confided the whole story to me, thinking my stone dead ears could not actually hear him. And the whole time he was rambling on about killing his wife and being sorry about doing me in, the house was filling up with gas fumes. I felt myself losing consciousness again, but was too scared to move. His last words to me were, ' Really gonna miss ya, Kiddo', before he walked out the front door.

"I waited for the sound of his motorcycle to rev up, to be sure he was actually gone. But I never heard that sound. Finally, I struggled to push myself away from the desk and get on my feet. My legs wouldn't support me and I tumbled to the floor. I could feel myself passing out from the gas and did my best to crawl into the kitchen to shut it off. I probably should have crawled out the front door, outside to the fresh air, but I never heard Pete's motorcycle leave and was afraid he might still be out there. Plus, my brain wasn't operating on all cylinders, all I could think of was turning off that gas. The next thing I knew, I woke up here in the hospital.

"Apparently, the house heated up pretty quickly with all the windows closed and caused the air conditioning system to kick on. There was one small bathroom window that Pete missed closing. That one window and the A/C created just enough ventilation to keep the gas from doing me in, otherwise I would never have lasted until Gavin arrived. Gavin came by to help with the probate paperwork and found me lying on the kitchen floor. He turned off the gas and rushed me to the emergency room. The doctors placed me in a hyperbaric chamber filled with pure oxygen, it cleared the gas from my lungs. Lucky I guess."

Sammie was sobbing. Her story was appalling, but did not keep me from asking my next question. "What does an attempt on *your* life have to do with Griffin's death?" I asked. "Why are you now a suspect in *his* death?"

"The police think that Pete and I *conspired*—I'm pretty sure that's the word they used—to kill Griffin. And then my co-conspirator decided he didn't want to share the twenty million with anyone, so in a double-cross he tried to kill me."

I had just recently begun to think that Griffin's death was a suicide. Suddenly it was being investigated as a murder again. This was all making my head spin. "But, why do the police suspect you as an accomplice in Griffin's murder ... if indeed he even was murdered?"

"Because I left Griffin to go live with Pete. I had what they call 'motive' because Griffin filed for divorce and I would get almost nothing if we divorced."

"Wait a minute here," I chimed in. "I don't presume to know the law in Arizona where you and Pete were ... uh, *shacking up*. But Griffin filed for divorce in California and I do have an understanding of the law in this state. Under California law you would have received one half of all the community property assets. That may not be quite the whole enchilada, but certainly enough so that you wouldn't need to kill him."

"Believe me, if Griffin and I divorced I would get very little . . . ."

"But . . .," I tried to interject my superior legal knowledge until she held up a hand, gesturing a plea for my continued silence until she was through speaking.

And then Samantha dropped the bomb on my theory.

"I would get very little because we entered into a prenuptial agreement. You see, when Griffin and I married, he was already a rather wealthy man. It was only *after* we married that he lost everything and had to earn it all back again. I agreed to sign the agreement because it actually seemed fair to me at the time. He had earned all that money on his own, who the heck was I to be entitled to it if our marriage fell apart? Under the terms of the prenup, I would still be fairly well provided for . . . but hardly what anyone might call wealthy."

"Apparently, the police think money was important to you . . . important enough to kill your husband for it," I jumped in.

"Maybe that's true for most people, but not for this girl. If money was what I was after, I'd have stayed with Griffin. Absolutely. Not only was he rich, but he was a good husband—treated me with kindness and respect—and wasn't too bad-looking, either. The only thing wrong with our marriage was that I still carried a torch for Pete. When Pete came back into my life, I left to be with him. Money never entered into the picture."

"Do *you* think Spivey killed Griffin?" I asked Samantha.

She hesitated. "Well, he's certainly capable of it. I think he's proven that. He killed his wife for money and tried to kill me for money as well. But there's only one thing I know for absolutely certain."

"What's that?" I asked.

"That torch I had for Pete? Its flame is completely extinguished, I can assure you. It makes me sad, though. Now I really wish I could have my old Griffin back. Our life together really was pretty darned good. How could I have screwed up so badly?"

Samantha began to sob once again. I felt terrible for her. She had lost her husband and she had lost the love of her life . . . too bad they weren't both the same person.

I WAS DOG-TIRED FROM AN all-night flight across the ocean and an entire morning spent absorbing the horrifying tale and emotional discharge from Samantha. All I wanted was to go home and crawl into bed. Pulling into the garage and turning off the engine, I trudged over to the mailbox to collect the accumulation of bills and advertisements, climbed the six steps to the front door, absently fingering the correct key to push into the lock, when . . . .

The door was ajar. The brass door handle lay on the ground nearby, completely sheared off from the door itself. An old Bob Dylan lyric quickly flashed across my tired brain: *The pump won't work because the vandals took the handles.* Sleep deprived and more puzzled than frightened, I stood on the porch a minute or two foggily calculating what to do next, determining whether it was even prudent to enter my own house under such dubious circumstances. Had it been nighttime I might have retreated without entering. But it was broad daylight, the ocean to my immediate left teeming with beach-goers and people all around.

Retracing my steps to the garage, I grabbed the baseball bat kept hidden behind the seat of my car, then returned to the front porch and swallowed hard before slowly pushing open the door and peering cautiously into the living room.

The place had been ransacked: furniture overturned, books and magazines strewn all over the floor—the ocean breeze from the open door causing pages to flutter and turn. Stepping inside, anger quickly replaced trepidation as I looked around. The place was a mess, not at all the way I'd left it. I may be a bachelor, but I'm not *that* messy.

In the kitchen someone had maliciously taken dishes from cupboards and smashed them onto the floor, creating shattered fragments that had once been the carefully selected china pattern my long-gone ex-wife had requested an eternity ago as wedding gifts, and which she, for some reason unbeknownst to me, graciously left behind on her way out of our marriage, even knowing such culinary finery meant virtually nothing to me. And there among the shards of fine bone dinnerware was the dented carcass of the dishwasher door, which—it looked to me—someone had destroyed by lowering the door, then jumping on it with all their weight until it broke off.

I made my way upstairs to inspect the bedrooms and found them, in stark contrast to downstairs, untouched—which caused me to wonder whether I had interrupted the vandal before he'd made his way upstairs . . . and whether the perpetrator might still be inside. Holding the bat firmly with both hands, ready to swing at anything that moved, I began looking in closets and under the bed just in case.

I decided, after finding no lingering culprit, that it seemed an unlikely coincidence to arrive home, after being away the last several days, at the precise moment a burglary or vandalism was taking place. Besides, what sort of idiotic vandal picks the middle of a bright sunny day with hordes of people all around for breaking and entering?

The vandal *had* made it to the upstairs part of the house, however. Walking into the master bathroom I saw the evidence, glaring evidence, that this was not some random break in—this was personal.

Taped to the mirror at eye level was an 8"x10" black-and-white photograph . . . an extreme close-up of female genitalia. Scribbled in red Magic Marker the words: *What a pussy lawyer sees when he looks in the mirror!* It might have been perversely laughable, a lawyer joke made in extremely poor taste, had the circumstances been different. As it was, there was nothing humorous about it. This had to be the work of the same pock-marked lunatic from Griffin's funeral who'd accosted me in my own garage. I thought I'd seen the last of him.

Why Connie Cantu would send her goon after me again, especially since Cantu now appeared to be in the clear, with Pete Spivey as the prime suspect in Griffin's murder, was beyond me. Perhaps she was regretting dropping her claim to Griffin's millions and this was her retribution. And, if so, how far might she go? How long must I continue looking over my shoulder, on guard for the maniac in the white truck? Unconsciously, I put a hand to my ribs, recalling the pain from the kick received during the last encounter with him.

The sounding of the car alarm from the Porsche in the garage quickly jolted me from such musing. I raced downstairs, out the door and around to the garage. Lights flashing, horn blasting, siren blaring: something had set off the automatic alarm on my car. Yanking keys from my pocket, they slipped through my butterfingers and clanged onto the concrete floor, somehow landing slightly under the car and in front of the rear wheel. On my hands and knees, fumbling to retrieve them from beneath the chassis as the shrillness of the alarm deafeningly continued in my ears, I clicked the key-chain button and turned off the alarm.

Silence.

Then the squealing of tires on pavement. I jumped up and spun around to spot the white Dodge Ram pickup speeding by the alleyway behind the garage. As the truck flew by, an arm extended out the driver's-side window with the hand's middle finger pointing skyward. The driver shouting "GET THE MESSAGE, ASSHOLE?" as he disappeared around a corner.

Unfortunately, I could think of no good reason why Cantu—or anyone else for that matter—would be sending this guy to mess with me. So, no . . . I guess I wasn't getting the message! Unless, of course, the message was just to scare the bejesus out of me. Then yes, message received loud and clear. But I was at a loss for what to do to end the terror.

Chapter Twenty-Three

It was a hot August day when the police apprehended Pete Spivey. He was returning from the big rally in South Dakota, doing an *Easy Rider* on his Harley with a small group of fellow bikers, the wind whistling in his ears and the sun darkening the skin around his tattoos. The rear tire of his bike barely completing a single revolution atop California pavement before the flashing sign at the border Agricultural Inspection Station brought them all to a grinding halt.

Forewarned to be on the lookout for someone on a two-toned Harley-Davidson matching Spivey's description, the Agricultural Agent waved the entire bunch of motorcycle cowboys over to the secondary inspection station immediately adjacent. Armed with weaponry as well as a Grand Jury Indictment, a squadron of patrol cars surrounded the group of riders as they entered the secondary area.

The way I heard the story is that these disgruntled bikers almost seemed to relish the gendarme intrusion, as if a fitting conclusion to a week of playing Hells Angel wannabes. One fellow dressed in leather chaps, with a very long, graying beard extending nearly to his belt buckle á la ZZ Top, and riding a *rat bike* with what looked to be everything he owned attached to it, started getting belligerent with the arresting officer. The officer informed the bearded biker that it was Spivey they were authorized to apprehend and cart back to Los Angeles, but there was certainly room in the squad car for him, too . . . and that his bike with attendant personalty could 'just sit here in the desert for a week or so' until the local authorities got around to retrieving it . . . if there was anything left of it by that time. Spivey's bearded compadre backed off; his entire world was that bike and the things attached to it. He couldn't afford to risk someone looting his property while he sat in a jail cell.

Still, it was very nearly a hero's sendoff that Pete Spivey received from his chums as he was placed, handcuffed, in the back of the patrol car. Sometime later, a local towing company arrived with a trailer and impounded Spivey's beloved two-wheeled chariot.

In clear contrast from the recalcitrant swaggering bravado on display just a few miles back, it was a different, more humble, Pete Spivey who emerged as the miles separated him from his friends. Pete tried speaking politely from the back seat to the officers occupying the car with him, trying to find out what all the fuss was about, but—other than reading him his rights—the officers remained stoically silent. There would be a time for proper police interrogation of Pete Spivey, but not now.

FORMALLY CHARGED AND INCARCERATED IN Los Angeles County, Pete Spivey adamantly denied any involvement in the murder of Griffin Gambil or the attempted murder of Samantha Gambil.

"Jesus! I was in freakin' Sturgis, South Dakota. Best estimate, seven hundred and fifty thousand people were there with me at the rally! I wasn't even *in* California when this happened to Sammie. Besides, I love her! Why would I want to kill her?"

"I can give ya twenty million reasons why, wise guy," the investigating detective shot right back at Spivey. "Twenty million dollars might be adequate incentive to kill someone . . . even if you did *love* her. With Samantha Gambil out of the way, you were probably drooling all over yourself anticipating the fortune coming your way."

Spivey's attorney tried to argue that it was Griffin's brother—Gavin Gambil—or the relatives of Samantha who would inherit the fortune, not his client. That's when the police detective told him about the trust instrument Samantha had created—the one I, as her attorney, begrudgingly drafted—leaving everything to Spivey. This was new information to Spivey's attorney, who had been given the case less than an hour prior.

The attorney looked at his client incredulously as if considering employing the *stupidity defense*, i.e. nobody would be so stupid as to commit murder with such an obvious motive. Spivey's attorney started to speak to the detective in rebuttal, apparently thought better of it and remained silent . . . something he strongly advised his client to do as well.

But Pete Spivey was not the type to remain silent. He was an emotional sort of fellow, passionate in his love-making—as Samantha could, unfortunately, attest—and easily excitable under stressful situations, such as the one in which he presently found himself.

He continued to voice his denials, but upon learning that it was Samantha herself who had testified against him to the Grand Jury, Pete knew the jig was up. He had to do something bold to save himself. In a bungled attempt to vindicate himself of the charges, Pete Spivey—completely contrary to his lawyer's advice—blurted the truth about killing his own wife, Jennifer Spivey, in Michigan two years prior.

"Why would I admit killing Jennifer and not Griffin?" he rationalized. "That should *prove* I'm not lying when I say I had nothin' to do with Griffin's death or hurting Samantha."

His confession to killing Jennifer Spivey—obviously intended to be exculpatory—was the lynch pin that would ultimately convict Pete Spivey before a California jury for the death of Griffin and the attempted murder of Samantha. Most assuredly the state of Michigan will want to try him for spousal murder as well.

Chapter Twenty-Four

By law, a trial date must be set within sixty days of being arraigned on indictment. Spivey's was set for January 2001. It couldn't come quick enough as far as I was concerned.

Both the trial and jury deliberations were completed expeditiously. The clear and convincing evidence listened to and absorbed by the group of a dozen peers left no reasonable doubt as to the Defendant's guilt. I was present for much of the trial, there was no reasonable doubt in my mind either.

Relevant to the charge of murdering Griffin Gambil were Spivey's fingerprints on the gun. This alone, however, would not be enough to convict, since the gun belonged to his live-in lover, Samantha, and he *admitted* handling the gun on numerous occasions. His prints would naturally appear on the weapon.

"It was Samantha's gun. Her husband bought it for her years ago, for protection. Protection from *what*, she never told me. When she moved in with me in Phoenix, Samantha brought the gun with her," Defendant Spivey explained under oath.

"Do you know how the gun came to be in the possession of Griffin Gambil?" Spivey's lawyer asked his client on the stand.

"Yes, I do," Pete answered.

"Would you tell the court, in your own words then, how a gun went from your household in Arizona to the possession of the deceased in California?"

Spivey testified that the gun came to be in the deceased's possession because Griffin *borrowed* the gun from him and Samantha.

"Did Griffin Gambil give any reason *why* he wanted to borrow the gun?" the attorney asked.

With a quick, rapid-fire flow of words, Spivey answered the attorney's question.

"Griffin told us he used the same gun once before a few years back to scare his old business partner and it worked so well he wanted to borrow it again for some new deal he was working on."

"Objection! Hearsay, your Honor!" the prosecutor was on his feet. But the jury had already heard Pete Spivey's rapid-fire testimony about the gun, it was a bell too late to unring.

By his testimony, Spivey had attempted to shift culpability from himself to the victim. As damage control, the prosecution later called to the stand Broadus Liberato. As Griffin Gambil's oldest and most consistent business partner, Liberato testified that *he'd* never seen a gun in Griffin's possession.

"It just wouldn't be Griffin's style to carry a weapon," Broadus Liberato concluded.

No testimony was given as to whether Griffin's brother *Gavin* had ever brandished a gun in Broadus's presence, however. No one thought to ask such a question, since Gavin Gambil's prints were not on the gun and no one but Liberato . . . and myself . . . knew Broadus's statement—although technically truthful—was misleading. While it might not have been 'Griffin's style' to carry a weapon, it *had* been his style to bring along his gun-toting brother on at least one occasion.

Samantha's testimony was a double-edged sword for Spivey. Samantha corroborated Spivey's claim that Griffin *borrowed* the weapon, although—according to her sworn testimony—she had no recollection of Griffin ever saying he'd used a gun in the past, or that he needed it for a "business deal." Also, she was quite certain that Griffin had returned the gun *prior* to his death. She offered a detailed description of the evening Griffin visited them in Phoenix, the visit wherein the borrowed gun was returned. She was quite clear in her recollection, she said, because Griffin had arrived by automobile—rather than by airplane, his usual mode of transportation—since he would not have been able to carry a gun aboard an aircraft.

"Griffin returned the gun to me and I immediately placed it in a drawer in the bedroom," Samantha testified.

"And this would be the very same bedroom that you shared with the Defendant, would it not?" the prosecutor asked.

"Absolutely. That's correct, Pete and I lived together and shared the same bedroom." According to this testimony, Spivey had easy access to the gun any time he chose to remove it from the drawer.

Notwithstanding all evidence presented, Spivey contended he could not have committed the crime because he was in Phoenix, Arizona at the time Griffin was killed. He was with his live-in girlfriend, Samantha Gambil, on the day in question. Samantha, however, tearfully clarified for the jury that Pete was *not* at home in Phoenix that *day*, but arrived home quite late that *night*. Although there was nothing to prove Spivey was even in Los Angeles at the time of Griffin's death, the circumstantial evidence that Spivey *could* have been in Los Angeles on the day Griffin Gambil was killed was all the jury needed to convict.

"It would be an easy six-hour drive from Phoenix to Los Angeles," the prosecutor told the jury. "Ample time to commit the crime and return home to Arizona late the same evening."

Based upon the evidence presented, the jury found the Defendant had motive to kill Griffin Gambil: since the Defendant openly admitted killing his own wife for money, it seemed logical he might kill Griffin Gambil for money as well—killing Griffin was the first step in a master plan to get the Gambil's fortune.

And they found the Defendant had opportunity: Spivey was not in Phoenix, his alibi witness denied being with him and Phoenix was only a few hours away by automobile. Also Spivey had fluid access to the gun that killed Griffin Gambil—a gun that had the Defendant's fingerprints all over it.

Pete Spivey was convicted of Second Degree Murder in the killing of Griffin Gambil.

As to the charge of the attempted murder of Samantha Gambil, there was the evidence of Samantha's own first-hand sworn testimony that Defendant Spivey was her assailant. Though she admitted never actually seeing her assailant's face, since she was attacked from behind, she clearly recognized his voice as that of her lover, Pete Spivey.

The prosecution's theory was simple: although Spivey was, indeed, in South Dakota for the motorcycle rally, he had left the rally, flown to L.A., stolen a car at the airport, drove to Woodland Hills, and attempted to kill Samantha. After the attempted murder, he returned to LAX, whereupon he ditched the car and flew back to South Dakota.

Offered as corroborating proof were airline records showing that a round trip ticket in Spivey's name for travel from Rapid City, South Dakota to LAX had been issued, also Spivey's own credit card receipt as payment for this travel. Arrival in L.A. coincided with the very day the attempt took place.

Samantha's testimony that she never heard Spivey's Harley-Davidson arrive or leave on the day the attack took place supported the theory that Spivey arrived at the Gambil home via automobile, rather than his customary motorcycle; that the Defendant drove a stolen car from LAX to the San Fernando Valley. This was further supported by a police report that a car was stolen from the airport on the same day that Spivey arrived and was found abandoned right back at the airport sometime later. There was even further evidence linking the auto theft to Spivey: part of a used ticket stub for air travel from Rapid City, South Dakota to Los Angeles was discovered inside the stolen vehicle.

Defense argued that, although there appeared to be proof that Spivey may have, in fact, traveled by commercial airline from South Dakota to California, there was no proof offered by the prosecution that he made the *return* flight to Rapid City, and therefore the prosecution's theory was flawed.

The prosecutor addressed this issue, rather brilliantly I thought, in closing argument. "Ladies and gentlemen of the jury, it has been said that circumstantial evidence is like a chain, each piece of evidence is as a link in the chain. But that is not so, because if a single link breaks the entire chain would fail, and justice would fail. No, no. It is more like a rope, composed of many strands and cords. One strand might be insufficient to sustain the weight, but several stranded together may be of sufficient strength. I believe what we have presented are strands and cords more than sufficient to sustain a conviction. But that is, ultimately, for you good people of the jury to decide."

Pete Spivey was convicted of attempting to murder Samantha Gambil and for Grand Theft Auto. Once again, the jury found motive: killing Samantha was step two in the Defendant's plan to get Griffin Gambil's fortune—by killing the widow who had left everything to Spivey in a trust instrument; and opportunity: evidence tended to prove that Spivey had flown from South Dakota to Los Angeles, stolen a car and arrived at Samantha's house to commit the crime. It appeared that Pete Spivey was not particularly clever about covering his tracks; he left plenty upon which to convict.

FOR A WHILE AFTER THE trial, the police further pursued their investigation of Samantha as a possible co-conspirator with Spivey in the death of Griffin Gambil. Against all my admonishments to the contrary, Sammie insisted that I act as her defense attorney—even though I am not, nor have ever been, a criminal defense lawyer.

But—other than the most feckless circumstantial fact that she had left wealthy, smart, handsome Griffin to take up residence with the slovenly, unemployed Spivey in the Arizona desert—there was little else linking her to any conspiratorial theory. Pete Spivey, himself, even denied any conspiracy involving Samantha.

No charges were ever formally filed against Samantha due to lack of direct evidence connecting her to any crime. Sammie attributed this good fortune to my brilliant legal expertise, but I know the truth—the police dropped the case of their own accord; not much lawyering was involved.

Samantha had really been through a lot—her husband dying, her former lover convicted of murder . . . and almost being murdered herself—which explained the deep post-trial depression that engulfed her. But, as I pointed out to her, there was a bright part. Sammie had been right all along; her husband did *not* commit suicide. Apparently, it was not in Griffin Gambil's nature to kill himself, just as Sammie had known all along. Had it not been for Samantha's ardent belief that her husband's death could not have been by his own hand, and her soliciting me to investigate the matter—thereby keeping the issue alive—Griffin's killer might never have been apprehended.

Further, Samantha herself might have fallen victim to Spivey's treacherous plan to enrich himself at the expense of her and Griffin. Without Sammie convincing me to intervene, Gavin would have gone on to Mexico and not been available to rescue Sammie from the noxious gas.

Funny how life is, one small thing can put into motion so many other events—the absence of which might yield an entirely different outcome. Had Samantha and I not re-connected on the internet after thirty years in response to a high school reunion e-mail, everything might be quite different.

Sammie continues to beat herself up over what she refers to as her incredibly bad character judgment and decision making: leaving her husband for another man, then making his murderer the beneficiary to a trust containing his fortune. But I keep assuring her that we *all* make mistakes. Spivey made a felonious and deadly mistake. Griffin made a mistake in taking up with a prostitute. Both of us—Sammie and me—were mistaken in our belief that it was Connie Cantu who was involved in Griffin's death. *My* mistaken notions were compounded—I had even suspected good old Gavin for a while. And I'm supposed to have a trained legal mind!

"You just can't keep chastising yourself for past mistakes," I advised her. "For all good things there is a reason and all's well that ends well." Okay, so I'm the king of understated platitudinal clichés. I could think of nothing better to offer.

Chapter Twenty-Five

The court-appointed appraiser inspected all the real property owned by Griffin Gambil at the time of his death as well as the cars, jewelry, clothing and other personalty of the deceased. A final Inventory and Appraisement was filed with the Probate Court. As the dust was beginning to settle on this matter—February, a full eight months after Griffin died—it turned out the Estate of Griffin Gambil fell substantially below the twenty million dollar mark of the original value estimation. Five million of the decline in the estate's value was due to the generosity of Samantha Gambil, who removed several properties from probate because title was held by Gavin Gambil, as well as the Encino house given to Connie Cantu.

Another culprit in the devaluation of the estate was Griffin Gambil himself. Apparently the late Mr. Gambil had defrauded a few of the local lending institutions before his untimely demise and restitution was necessary in order to avoid costly and time-consuming lawsuits against the estate.

Of the remaining properties in the estate, several did not appraise for anywhere near what we anticipated. Several were discovered to be *upside down* with respect to the loans on them —that is, the loan was greater than the value of the property. Such properties added zero value to the estate and a few of the properties actually diminished the overall value.

The estate was now determined to be worth a little more than two and a half million dollars. In line with the devaluation of the estate, my anticipated fees had been dramatically reduced as well.

Whoever sang "It never rains in Southern California" must not have lived here in winter. From January through mid-March, it rains what seems like every day. Here it was February, my tan was fading and I felt like I was beginning to *rust*.

With reduced attorney fees and cloudy skies, I needed a break. So, I decided to catch a jet to Hawaii and cash in on a few days of sunshine. On my last visit to the Aloha State, I never really got a chance to explore the island much. But I remembered the wonderfully warm ocean water, so this time I lugged along my surfboard.

CHECKING IN AT THE HILTON Hawaiian Village, located directly next door to the Ilikai—my former home base as I searched for Connie Cantu the one and only other time I've been to Hawaii—I psyched myself up for a few days of doing nothing but relaxing and allowing the spirit of Aloha to envelope me.

Beautiful, sun-drenched day after sun-drenched day at Waikiki Beach! Ah, the piped-in ukelele music and smell of suntan lotion were sweet. As long as I kept pouring out money, my every need would be taken care of here at this perfectly lovely garden spot of the world. Smiling Polynesian ladies (probably from Southern California) would serve me lunch right on the sand if I so desired. The sun in Hawaii always seems to be shining, a breeze just cool enough for complete comfort always blowing. Too good to be true? Just phony tourist bullshit? It didn't matter, at least not to me. I was just there to relax, soak up the sun, people watch, and fill my head with visions of sashaying hula girls!

Catching a giant wave in the winter surf on the North Shore is every surfer's fantasy, so I made the trek over to Waimea Bay to watch the pros. It was awesome: waves big as mountains rising up in the ocean as fearless surfriders on fiberglass boards paddled out into them.

But *watch* was all I did. Those liquid mountains were clearly out of my league. It did inspire me to use my board on the more timid waves of Waikiki, however. Beautiful sets, two to four feet high, kept rolling in day after day. I just couldn't get enough of it. It set me to thinking, maybe I should sell the Venice Beach house and move to Hawaii. I could operate a hot dog cart on the beach right next to those waves, selling junk food to tourists and meeting interesting folks from all over the world. I could just spend the rest of my days enjoying the sun and fabulous surf!

Those were my thoughts—carefree, happy thoughts—as I finished a delightful afternoon of frolicking in the ocean and climbed over the rocks, carrying my surfboard in the direction of the Ala Wai Marina parking lot.

Then I spied something that stopped me right in my tracks! At first I was unable to comprehend what my salt-stinging eyes were showing me.

A car was pulling into a parking spot at the far end of the lot, near the Hawaii Yacht Club. It was a late model, cream-colored Mercedes Benz—still bearing California license plates. I recognized the car instantly.

Connie Cantu climbed gracefully from the automobile and began crossing the blacktop parking area with tiny but brisk steps. Approaching her from the opposite direction, strolling at a more leisurely pace, was... Gavin Gambil! Cantu raced in his direction and threw herself into his arms, both of them laughing as they walked hand-in-hand along the docks.

I stood motionless, watching the two of them until they disappeared from sight. Then, setting my surfboard down on the grass that borders the blacktopped marina parking lot, I silently padded along after them in my bare feet.

Cantu and Gavin boarded a yacht tied in a slip. I lost sight of them again as they disappeared below in fifty-six feet of floating fiberglass that reeked of money.

I snooped alongside the boat and inched my way aft until the name painted on the transom came into view, *Waay Mo' Bettah!* it read.

On davits extended above the name dangled a smaller Grady-White center console boat outfitted for fishing. The name on the smaller vessel was *Bite Me!* Well, bite me indeed! What the hell was going on?

Retrieving my surfboard, I returned to the hotel on the opposite side of the marina and placed a call to the mainland, to California... to Samantha Zimmer-Gambil.

My mind was clouded with the implications of what I had just witnessed down at the docks. There had to be some logical explanation for Griffin's ex-lover/hooker/dominatrix and his beloved, Bible-quoting younger brother being together aboard a million-dollar luxury yacht in paradise. But none of the explanations I could conjure-up bode well.

"Benjamin!" Sammie's voice was jubilant. "Long time no hear. You sound far away. Where are you?"

"In Honolulu," I told her. "I'm here for some sun and surf—got tired of watching the L.A. rain fall—but need to ask you a question. It's . . . uh, related to probate."

"Ask away." Sammie finally sounded in excellent spirits. I was glad for her, the probate of her late husband's estate was nearly completed, and she was moving on with her life after a very messy past eight months.

"The properties that you excluded from probate . . . the ones that Gavin held the deeds to, do you have copies of those deeds?"

"Uh huh, I have photocopies in the file," she answered. "Once I busted him, Gavin gave me copies of the deeds."

"How about the property that Griffin deeded to Cantu, do you have a copy of that as well?"

She did.

"Would you please pull them from the file and fax them to me?"

"What's this all about, Benjamin?" She sounded merely curious, not overly concerned. That was good, because I still wasn't quite sure what to make of this new development and didn't want her asking a thousand questions.

"Nothing earth shattering," I said, trying to sound reassuring. "I brought along the probate file—just for something to do with my idle time here in paradise—and noticed that I have no documentation in it regarding those properties. No big deal, but if you could fax them to me it would complete the file."

I gave her the hotel fax number, we chatted a few more minutes, then hung up. I did not tell her about Gavin and Cantu. I decided to keep what I had seen to myself until I could make some sense of it.

THE FAX FROM SAMANTHA ARRIVED within the hour. I took the pages with me to dinner, something to peruse as I sat alone at a restaurant in the Ward Center overlooking Ala Moana Park. I wasn't even half through my salad when I noticed something on one of the deeds. It jumped right off the page at me, screaming *Look at this!*

It was the deed transferring the Encino house to Connie Cantu. The *gift* Griffin gave her, the little something to nudge her from paradise and relocate her—and her services—closer to Griffin's own turf in the San Fernando Valley. The grant was dated several months before his death. Only the grantor was not Griffin . . . it was Gavin Gambil. *Gavin* deeded the property over to Cantu. Cantu had told me that she never met Gavin. Now that I had seen the two of them together, and discovering it was Gavin who, in fact, conveyed the property to Cantu, I wondered how much—if anything—that Connie Cantu ever said to me should be believed.

Still, I wasn't sure just what the relevance of all this might be. Any mystery surrounding the entire Griffin Gambil matter had been solved—I hated to be making a mountain out of a molehill.

Pete Spivey had been convicted of Griffin's death. Spivey confessed to killing his wife, and Samantha testified that it was Pete who tried to kill *her*. The man was clearly guilty of tampering with the lives of three people and was now justifiably behind bars.

Liberato had miraculously dropped his lawsuit to reclaim the money Griffin cheated him out of. Cantu had relinquished any claim she might have had on Griffin's estate and Gavin had already come clean regarding taking the Quit Claim deeds.

Although Griffin's estate had diminished in value—along with my fees—probate was moving along nicely and nearing completion.

Everything was all wrapped up nicely, *finito*.

So then, what was it I found so unsettling about discovering Gavin Gambil and Connie Cantu living in the lap of luxury here in paradise? Something about it just didn't seem right. It threw the whole equation off. 2 + 2 equals 4 . . . unless there are other numbers involved, in which case it would be folly to stick with 4 as an answer.

I wrestled with this problem all evening. That night even the restful Hawaiian surf lapping onto the sandy shore of Waikiki Beach outside my window did not easily lull me to sleep.

Chapter Twenty-Six

I needed to make some sense of this Gavin/Cantu business, if for no other reason than my own peace of mind. So, I decided to confront Cantu with the facts in hope of soliciting a few answers—just as I had done before.

I drove my rented car toward the Windward Side of Oahu, hoping I might be able to once again locate Cantu's home. Making a left turn just past Sandy Beach, I found the gated community of *Queensgate*, waited for a car to enter through the security gates, and followed closely behind to gain entry, just as my cabbie had done the last time I was here.

Once inside the gates, however, the sea of tan stucco houses all looked alike; I wasn't certain which belonged to Connie Cantu. Parking on a street I thought could be hers, I wondered what to do next. It must have been close to an hour, sitting in that hot car watching as people came and went. Then I spotted her walking out to the mailbox located curbside in the middle of a block of houses.

"Aloha Miss Cantu," I said with false cheerfulness, pulling alongside her in my car.

"Wha! You again. Why you no can leave me alone?" The odd pidgin patois was back.

"I'm sorry to be a bother," I spoke with polite muster, stopping the car next to where she was extracting mail from the box. "The probate of Griffin's estate is nearly completed and the criminal matters surrounding his death have all been dealt with in a court of law . . . you did hear about the criminal trial, didn't you?"

She nodded. "Yes, I had to fill out papers with my testimony about it and told I might could be subpoenaed. That why you here?"

"No, not really," I answered. "There are just a few remaining loose ends, minor things really, and you were so helpful during my last visit here that I wondered if I might prevail upon you again."

"Quit pushing my leg, Mistah Lawyer. What you really need from Connie Cantu?" she asked with unguarded suspicion as she finished collecting the few items of mail from the box and turned in the direction of her house. I paced alongside her, still in my car.

I noticed that Cantu was wearing a large gold crucifix on a chain around her neck. It seemed an odd choice of jewelry for someone in her line of work. As we approached her house, I saw a small metal emblem of a fish fastened to the front door. This had nothing to do with a love for fishing, it was a Christian symbol. Had this admitted dominatrix who used sex to bring strong men to their knees found religion? I'd seen her in the company of Gavin Gambil—a self-professed man of God. Was she a recent convert? I wondered, but kept that question to myself—at least for now.

"I'd like to ask you about your house in California, the one in Encino," I told her.

"Oh dat," she interrupted. "It not mine no more, I sold it to nice haole family. But you already know dat."

"Yes, yes I do," I agreed. "What I'd like to ask has nothing to do with you *selling* the house."

"What then?" she asked.

"When Griffin Gambil deeded the house to you, did you see him do it? Did you actually see him sign the deed?"

Gone was the haughty dominatrix attitude of my previous encounters with Connie Cantu. She seemed subdued, almost docile this time around.

"No," she told me. "I not see him sign deed. He just hand deed to me and say, 'Here Mistress, this house yours forever.' I took deed and gave it to lawyer for recording before Griffin could change mind. Some-ting wrong wit dat?"

"No, nothing wrong with recording a validly executed and delivered deed," I told her. "Did Griffin mention the house was actually owned by his brother? Did you know that it was Griffin's brother who actually signed his interest in the property over to you?"

"Bruddah?" she asked, tilting her head curiously. "He say nothing about bruddah to me."

"But, you knew he had a brother," she had already confessed this the last time.

She nodded, confirming that she knew *of* Gavin.

"But you never met Griffin's brother? His brother was not present when Griffin gave you the deed?"

"No, did not meet bruddah!" She sounded certain and final. Then, fingering the gold cross that adorned her throat, she added, "Not 'til later."

"So you do know the brother now, is that correct?" I asked in my lawyer's voice.

She hesitated, then nodded defeatedly. Walking around to the passenger side of my rented car, Cantu opened the door and sat down next to me. The car was a compact, only inches separating us in our seats. When next she spoke, the pidgin vernacular vanished and a dramatically different Connie Cantu emerged: poised and self-confident like the first time we had met, but far short of the dominatrix bitch we both knew she could be.

"Look," she said directly into my face, "I do know Gavin Gambil, okay? I never knew it was Gavin who actually owned the house. I assumed it was owned by Griffin. It makes sense now, though. That must be how Gavin discovered my relationship with Griffin, when Griffin asked Gavin to sign over the deed.

"Gavin came over to the house in Encino, shortly after I moved in. That was the very first time we met. Gavin tried to convince me to stop seeing his brother. He really loved his brother and told me that I was the instrument of the devil, leading Griffin down the path to hell!

"At first I thought this fellow was some sort of lunatic, spouting off all this religious mumbo jumbo at me. I found it all to be rather laughable, actually. My own credo had always been *believe nothing, dare all*. I mean, one person's theology is another person's belly laugh as far as I was concerned. But this brother of Griffin's kept hammering away at me and the more I listened to him, I found myself drawn to him."

"Sexually?" I asked, immediately regretting my own question.

"No, not really. At least not immediately. I think at first I just found him interesting somehow. I know you must think this whole dominatrix stuff is pretty weird, right?"

I shrugged indifference, but she was right.

"Maybe it *is* weird," she continued. "But when the going gets weird…

the weird turn pro! And that's what I did. I decided if men wanted to adore me from afar and worship the ground I walked upon, I would *charge* them for the privilege. But Gavin was different. He made me realize I'm a switch hitter."

"Huh? You mean you like women? You're a lesbian?" I asked.

"You would like to picture me making love with another woman, wouldn't you, Mr. Harding? Sorry to disappoint you, but no, nothing like that. What I meant is that for years I have been exclusively a *topper*, now I enjoy being a *bottom*."

"Huh?" Redundancy had taken over my line of questioning. "A topper? A bottom?"

A sigh of impatience passed her lips. "A topper is the person in control, the dominant one. A bottom is the subservient one, a *subbie*. I switched from being dominant to being submissive. Gavin showed me that side of myself."

"Sexually?" I asked, still redundantly.

"Yes, sexually. Totally sexually! It was our very first time together and I suddenly found myself *enjoying* taking orders from a man. It was all very new and arousing for me. Humbling myself, kissing his feet, obeying his every command . . . it was indescribably delicious. I'd be on my knees licking Gavin's feet—sucking each of his perfectly delectable toes—and really getting off. It was the biggest turn-on—the most intense sexual charge—I've felt in years!"

She stopped and looked at me, seeming to expect a response. I could only sit there, stunned at this revelation. After several moments of me saying nothing, she continued. "In fact, it was the most *completely erotic* experience of my entire life, prostrating myself at his feet, lavishing his feet with my tongue!"

"And Gavin was receptive to that?" I asked, finally finding words. Knowing Gavin's reputation as a man of deep religious convictions, it seemed unlikely he would embrace such deviant behavior.

"You'd be amazed how fast he took to it," Cantu said. "I think he enjoyed having a beautiful woman humble herself at his feet. As far as I could tell, he really seemed into it!"

"Well, if what you have is purely sexual, then why the religious trappings—the cross around your neck and the fish emblem on your door?" I asked with impertinence.

"You ask a lot of very personal questions, Mr. Harding. But I have no problem with answering. At first it *was* purely sensual. I enjoyed Gavin playing the part of the vengeful master with me as his worthless wench. Part of our early role-playing included him hurling Bible verses at me like they were thunderbolts from on high as I groveled at his feet—but a few of those verses must have penetrated my soul because it has become much more than just sex now. Now it is spiritual as well."

Cantu stopped a moment, staring blankly straight ahead, then raising her eyes to the heavens and crossing both hands across her small breasts as if having some sort of rapturous experience right there in the seat next to me. I swear, if we'd been seated in a convertible she just might have levitated right out of the car.

"Gavin brought me to the Lord," she announced at last, her gaze still upward. "Instead of traveling toward eternal damnation, I now anticipate communing with God in the Kingdom of Heaven one day. I have taken Jesus into my heart." Then, lowering her eyes back to my level, she turned her face in my direction and continued. "The Bible says that women should be subservient toward men and that wives shall obey their husbands. But I don't need to wait until we are married, I *already* obey Gavin as if he were my husband."

"What do you mean by that?" I asked, glad she had returned to earth.

"Just what it sounds like. I do whatever Gavin asks of me. To humble myself in any way he wishes. I try to be whatever he wants me to be. For example, I am an intelligent woman and have always prided myself on being well-read and speaking articulately. But Gavin sees this as exemplary of prideful arrogance, which stands in the way of my salvation. He prefers that I humble myself by speaking in the fractured English of my forebears, so I mostly speak pidgin these days."

So that was the reason she spoke differently—sometimes articulate and other times not. Gavin was making her speak in the pidgin dialect as a way of humbling her and exercising his dominance over her.

"Also, there is a passage in the Bible forbidding women from cutting their hair, and Gavin has asked me to let my hair grow long. It's from the book of Corinthians, written by Paul: *But woman, if she have long hair, it is glory to her; for the long hair is given to her in lieu of a veil.* It pleases me to obey. I have not cut it for several months."

Now that she mentioned it, her hair had grown noticeably since we'd first met. She has the sort of ultra-healthy, beautifully thick dark hair common among Asian women. Just another way for Gavin to control her—like forcing her to speak pidgin—but the longer length was actually flattering on Connie Cantu.

Suddenly it occurred to me, the photograph I'd stumbled upon at the Encino house that first day—the one of her with some unidentified Caucasian man—must have been Cantu and Gavin. In the photo they were both smiling happily, perhaps still flush with the joy of newfound salvation. Still, I couldn't help wondering if her alleged conversion and obeisant behavior was truly religious or just an extension of some new kinky sex kick.

"Perhaps you find it difficult to believe someone like me has found salvation," she went on, apparently able to read minds now as well. "I'll admit, at first I wasn't receptive to Gavin's preaching, it was just a kick to play the subbie for a change. I was really getting off on it—it was great sex. But, after a while, his words struck a chord. I accepted Jesus and my life has changed. It was a miracle, it truly was. I saw the error of my ways and that my *arrangement* with Griffin was both sinful and immoral. It had to end—Gavin said so.

"And then, as if it was a sign from on High, the Lord claimed Griffin's life. I might never have had the strength to cut loose my golden goose, so the Lord did it for me. God took Griffin from me because I was not strong enough to do it on my own. Griffin's death was a gift to me from God."

"Does that make Pete Spivey an instrument of the Lord for murdering Griffin?" I was curious how far this strained logic might stretch.

"Who can say?" Connie Cantu answered, shaking her head from side to side. "The Lord works in strange and mysterious ways, doesn't he?"

"He surely does," I agreed. "How about that pock-faced goon you sent over to vandalize my house and rough me up, he a servant of the Lord as well?"

"I don't know anything about goons." She sounded indignant. "And I'm sure I don't know what you are talking about when you say someone roughed you up."

Not believing her for a minute, but playing along, I said, "So, you promise there won't be any future visits from the dude in the pickup truck? I can count on the fact that you have called off the dogs?"

Perhaps humoring me, she responded, "Whatever you say, Mr. Harding. I promise. No dogs from Connie Cantu."

I decided to take her at her word, let such sleeping dogs lie. Besides, what reason would she have at this point for the guy to continue harassing me? Sure, I could've harangued her for messing up my house and for that kick, which badly bruised my ribs, but I decided there was no point in it. To forgive is divine, or so they say.

CANTU COMING CLEAN ABOUT HER relationship with Gavin, and her assurances that there would be no further visits from the pick-up truck goon, seemed to finally clear the air between us. So a few days later, as I was once again emerging from the frothy surf near the marina, I didn't hesitate to wave hello to Connie Cantu as I spotted her strolling the docks near the Hawaii Yacht Club. She returned the wave, and even motioned me over—inviting me to check out the new boat and say hello to Gavin. I took her up on this invitation and sauntered over to the *Waay Mo' Bettah*.

Gavin seemed somewhat less than thrilled to see me, but invited me aboard at Connie's prompting. The boat was spectacular. It must have cost the earth—certainly more than a million dollars, anyway.

Not one to mince words, I came right out and asked Gavin how he could afford such a vessel. Without missing a beat he told me that he sold most of his California properties to Broadus Liberato and used the proceeds to purchase the vessel.

In my mind I skeptically responded, "You mean you sold the properties *back* to Liberato that you and your brother stole *from* Liberato. The same properties that *you* later stole from your own brother, but only after he was too dead to do anything about it."

As if he somehow heard my sarcastic musings, Gavin qualified his conduct. "I sold them back to Broadus for half their worth, half what I could have gotten on the open market . . . to make amends for the money my brother owed when he died. Otherwise, Mr. Liberato would have been out the money—unless he sued the estate—and I didn't want for Samantha to have to go through all that ugly litigation. This way

Mr. Liberato got his properties and I got enough money to purchase my dream boat. It seemed fair all the way around . . . and the right thing to do."

From the start, there had been something about Gavin Gilchrist Gambil that I found mistrustful. Maybe it was his holier-than-thou attitude. Now I was rethinking that position; perhaps I had misjudged him. Perhaps he really *was* holier-than-thou. After all, he was the one who saved Samantha's life. Then he rescued Connie Cantu from the gates of hell. And now it appeared that he'd done right by Broadus Liberato as well.

"Good for you!" I told Gavin, meaning it. Extending my hand for him to shake as a gesture of newfound respect, he knocked it away and embraced me with both arms in a sort of bear hug. This took me quite by surprise, I am not often hugged by men. But it forged a bond well in excess of a simple handshake. I was truly beginning to like Gavin Gambil.

By the time I left Hawaii, my belief in human nature had been greatly restored. I was convinced that Gavin was a good man and a good brother to Griffin, and that Gavin deserved to own his *dream boat*. I was happy that Connie Cantu had found the Lord, and that Gavin and Connie had found each other. It was good *karma* all the way around. The frosting on the cake was that my surfing skills had improved considerably and my tan was back.

I arrived back in Los Angeles to pouring rain, but it's still always nice to return home. The gray surf pounding angrily upon the shore in front of my house was in stark contrast to the gentle blue Pacific I had enjoyed in Hawaii. No matter, the ocean held many moods, today it was angry . . . but I wasn't. Even with the rain pummeling down, all seemed right with the world.

A message from my realtor awaited me. My big Tudor house to the south had finally sold. This meant I was completely free at last of that conservative mecca called Orange County . . . and a sizeable chunk of change would soon be coming my way. I could use it. Griffin's probate could continue a few more months before I would see any fees for my efforts. But that would ultimately yield a handsome—though less than originally anticipated—sum as well. If I just did one simple little probate case like this a year, I could earn enough money to support my beach bum lifestyle indefinitely and those years of law school would not fall completely by the wayside.

I smiled to myself—one simple little probate case like this? Benjamin, be careful what you wish for . . . .

Chapter Twenty-Seven

In April I talked Samantha into attending our high school reunion.

"It's our thirtieth," I said. "Chances are this will be the last opportunity for all of us to get together."

"It's not *my* thirtieth reunion," she correctly reminded me. "I was two years behind you, remember? I only knew about the reunion because of Pete."

"Still," I said, "it was this reunion that got us together in the first place and I think you should go . . . as my date. You'll know everyone and it might be a nice break from all the stuff that's happened this past year."

ARRIVING BACK IN THE OLD hometown was like strolling about a field of dreams and memories. And the reunion was a truly terrific event. Sure, it was a room filled with middle-aged people—wrinkled women sporting ersatz coifs and fashion in a futile attempt to look eternally sexy and youthful; accompanied by paunchy, balding men holding in their stomachs, feigning fitness that abandoned most of them more than a decade ago—but, after absorbing the initial shock of changes inflicted upon us all by the aging process, we were—each and every one of us— eighteen again!

Setting eyes on people I had not seen in thirty years, I felt an instantaneous bond that transcended the years. It resurrected a part of me that had long lain dormant, some ancient Midwestern former self that had all but been eliminated, burned away from years in the California sun. It was as if I was suddenly a high school boy once again, back in Illinois. I had forgotten what it felt like to be that boy, but allowing the teenager in me to resurface was a liberating experience. Time had stopped, the clock turned back.

Wendy Fredenthall, with no escort to divert her attention from the crowd, greeted each and every person who entered the reunion hall with a big hug and a squeal of delight. Laugh lines she had in high school were now deeply etched furrows, but she was still an attractive woman. Her effervescence remained intact, and being greeted by a shouting and leaping Wendy quickly set the mood for us all.

I danced with Doris Lund. This time I was not wearing a powder blue tux, but she was still taller than me. Any self-consciousness had evaporated with the years for both of us. Doris's husband was a bean-pole of a man with thick glasses and four strands of hair carefully plastered across his pate, but *he* was taller than Doris. Doris Lund-Blumberg, as anyone could tell, was every inch a happy woman—a marital success story.

With Samantha on my arm much of the evening, I finally had the date that was denied me at Senior Prom. Albeit thirty years after the fact, it was almost as good. But that bastard Pete Spivey, even in absentia, was still able to horn his way into the limelight. Spivey and his sordid crimes against Samantha became the prime topic of conversation much of the evening.

Most high school classes have their rags-to-riches success story or class celebrity; ours was a felon . . . a murderer. Having already lived through it once, I did not relish hashing through the intricate details yet again. But, because of my personal involvement—and the fact that I'm a lawyer, so everyone wanted to pick my brain about the legal aspects of it all—I was drawn inescapably into the Spivey dialogue.

Although, perhaps that was somewhat preferable to some of the other topics batted around that evening: sad and morbid revelations about those classmates who were not with us on this night because they had already gone on to meet their maker. Such tales sharpened my already keen awareness of mortality. I recalled the beautifully youthful faces of a few and shuddered to imagine their corporeal remains smouldering in some grave.

Discussion about Spivey also saved me from enduring more than I could bear of the more ordinary reunion topics: mundane droning about children—offspring of our generation who are now in high school or college . . . still preferable, however, to those involving grandchildren! Good God, grandchildren? At our age? How could this be? But, do the math: we are clearly of an age to be grandpas and grandmas. I found this most unsettling. In the end, I took solace in the escape that conversation involving Pete Spivey afforded.

WHEN THE REUNION WAS OVER, there was much handshaking and group hugging as we bid our fond farewells with promises of staying connected. We all knew it was merely empty sentiment, however. Other than the long-expired commonality of attending the same high school—our former kinship—what did any of us really share at this stage of life? It was pleasant enough reuniting with so many aged faces from the past, but I was good now for another thirty years.

Samantha, on the other hand, who I nearly had to drag to the event, was downright weepy by evening's end. Her tears caused me to recall the lack thereof over the death of her husband, and I casually mentioned this to her on the airplane as we headed back to California.

Samantha, seated right next to me with her tray table up and seat still in a full upright position, turned her head to stare with uncommon intensity at my face—as if considering some deep and important revelation to bestow upon me. But she did not speak.

"What's the matter?" I broke the sudden silence.

"Benjamin," she spoke hoarsely, perhaps the aftermath of our long night of intense partying, "You have been in love with me for a very long time, haven't you?"

Her question startled me.

"I suppose I have," I replied, smiling, trying to make light of it.

But Samantha did not smile back. She sat staring, her eyes boring into me—penetrating a part of me that she had never probed before. She seemed in search of something, I don't know what.

"I love you too," she spoke softly. "Did you know that?"

I sat dumbfounded, unspeaking, unblinking.

She continued. "I think I've always loved you, Benjamin. Absolutely. But I may not have realized it until just now. You've always been there for me, Benjamin. Like my knight in shining armor, you've always been someone I could rely on . . . the only person I could truly trust. You have never let me down. You would *never* let me down, would you, Benjamin?"

Slowly I shook my head. I could think of no circumstance wherein I would intentionally let this woman down. She was my first great love, and perhaps the person I *should* have married. But I was wondering where this was all going. The boyhood girl of my dreams had just told me that she loves me. Thirty years of pent up emotion began gurgling to the surface, clouding my sensibilities.

She continued. "Besides being my most trusted friend, someone I deeply love, you are also my lawyer. That's correct, isn't it? You *are* still my lawyer?"

I nodded, confused as to what being her lawyer had to do with anything. I took on that role by defending her in the pending criminal proceeding, not as a probate lawyer, wherein the *estate* was technically my client.

"I have a confession to make, Benjamin. I am not the fine, upright good-girl you have always imagined me to be," she said. "Your concept of me has always been skewed. I think I was always afraid to let you too close, for fear of shattering that sweet, misguided perception you held of me."

She continued staring deeply into my eyes, my soul. I sat, quietly listening.

"You're the only one I can trust, Benjamin. The only person to whom I can confess my darkest secrets. I have used people all my life, Benjamin. I don't deserve a trusting friend like you. I have used people, so many people . . . Pete, Griffin, Gavin . . . I even used you."

Her words surprised me and took a moment to digest. I certainly didn't feel used. Where this revelation was leading was impossible to tell.

"You asked why I didn't shed tears for my dear departed husband? I'll tell you. When I discovered Griffin's infidelity, I was livid that someone might use me like that—misuse me—and I decided to get even. That's why I moved in with Pete. Sure, I had feelings for Pete, but the main reason I moved in with him was because he was the complete opposite of my husband. Absolutely. I wanted Griffin to hurt—to feel like there was no part of him that I was attracted to, that my *ideal* man was different from him in every way. But, Griffin took my leaving in stride. That made me more furious than ever! Griffin wanted to remain friends, and that pissed me off—pardon the French—even more.

"Griffin would come and visit us in Phoenix, can you imagine? I went out of my way to punish him by letting him know that I was having the best sex of my life and that money—that almighty dollar that Griffin revered so devoutly—meant absolutely nothing to me. He responded by bringing his whore to California and buying her a house with money that was lawfully half mine.

"Each step of the way he took my jabs and counter-punched with devastating blows of his own. Griffin was a highly competitive person. If he knew what I was doing, there would be no way he would let me win . . . not emotionally and certainly not financially."

With deliberation, perhaps born from confessional closeness, she placed her hand on mine and squeezed it tightly. "Benjamin, I'm responsible for Griffin's death."

Chapter Twenty-Eight

At thirty thousand feet above the southwestern desert on our return flight to Los Angeles, Samantha Zimmer-Gambil—my boyhood dream girl—had just confessed, for the first time, her involvement with her husband's untimely demise. My expression surely betrayed complete astonishment, unsure if I'd heard her correctly.

"It's my fault Griffin is dead," she quietly repeated, barely audible above the continuous hum of jet engines. "I'm the one who put the idea to kill Griffin into Pete's stupid head. I told Pete about the prenuptial agreement, that if Griffin divorced me I'd get nothing . . . but with Griffin dead . . . ."

Samantha paused, searching my face for some sign of sympathetic understanding. She found none, but continued.

"Pete and I had both been drinking heavily the night I suggested killing Griffin. Of course, I hadn't been serious. It was just inebriated chatter. I'd gone through two bottles of wine myself and Pete had ravenously drunk the entire contents of our liquor cabinet. He was so sloshed I didn't think he'd even remember my suggestion once he sobered up. But the booze bolstered his already overinflated penchant for braggadocio and, to prove that he was fully capable of carrying out my suggestion, Pete bragged to me about killing Jennifer. I was horrified! Until that moment, I truly had no idea that Pete had killed his wife. Even after he told me, I thought maybe it was just something he made up in a drunken stupor as some misguided way of impressing me. But, suddenly I regretted everything I had told Pete about Griffin and the money.

"Pete and I never discussed killing Griffin again. I wasn't even sure if Pete remembered our drunken conversation. That's why, when Griffin was killed and the police ruled it a suicide, I just couldn't let it go at that. I needed to know the truth. Suicide wasn't Griffin's style. Griffin had never seemed particularly distraught over my leaving him, and I couldn't believe he would take his own life over some lowly prostitute. I wanted to blame that whore, but I secretly wondered if Pete had anything to do with it.

"That's why I needed you, Benjamin. I knew you always had a thing for me. How could I *not* know it? So, when I read on the internet that you were single . . . and a lawyer . . . well, I hoped I could use those feelings you once had to my benefit. And when I saw you again after so many years, when you picked me up at the airport that night, I knew I could get you to help me. I used you Benjamin. I'm not proud of myself, but I used you. I knew you would do far more than any probate lawyer would. I knew you would help me find out the truth . . . whether it was a suicide or if someone else killed my husband."

I knew it all along, I suppose. But hearing her actually say the words out loud, that she'd manipulated me into helping her . . . it hurt. It hurt more even than the kick to the ribs I'd taken from Cantu's pock-marked tough guy. Still, I'd do it all over again. Something about Samantha just made me want to be her hero. And knowing that I'd do it all over again—voluntarily—made it somehow more palatable. So, I let it slide, responding without commentary on how it felt to be used by someone you care for.

"Quite frankly," I said to Samantha, "my bollixed investigation was flawed right from the start. I *never* suspected Pete Spivey. Just like you, my money was on Connie Cantu as the culprit. Especially after the police found that holographic will with Griffin leaving her everything. Looked like pretty good motive to me."

"Hindsight is 20/20," Samantha replied. "You were an enormous help in getting all the pieces to fit, Benjamin. Now it's been established that Pete murdered my husband and I no longer need to wonder or worry. You were a greater help than you will ever know."

"Aw shucks, Ma'am," I assured her with lighthearted humility, trying to ease the mood, "that's what I'm here for."

THE AIRPLANE BEGAN GEARING DOWN for its descent into LAX and the clashing of wheels upon tarmac terminated our conversation about this matter. My lawyer's mind knew that Samantha did, indeed, have some limited degree of accomplice liability regarding her husband's death. As far as I was concerned, she certainly had a duty to speak up about her drunken conversation with Pete Spivey. To not do so was withholding crucial evidence. But at the same time, I rationalized, such testimony at trial would not have altered the final verdict as it applied to Spivey. Spivey would still have been convicted. At most, it would have only dragged Samantha down with him. And, as Samantha's attorney, I now had an obligation to remain silent about her mile-high confession to me. It was an obligation that caused me no heartburn—the actual killer had been convicted and justice had been served.

It was only several days later, four miles into my morning beach run, that the thought struck me. Samantha had testified in court that her *assailant* confessed to her about killing his wife, that *this* was how she discovered the man she was sharing a bed with was a murderer—that Pete Spivey had murdered his wife. But Samantha, I now knew, had already learned this during her intoxicated conversation with Pete Spivey the night she suggested killing her husband. The relevance of this was troubling, but I knew there was nothing I could do . . . nothing I should do . . . about it. The attorney/client privilege barred me from divulging to anyone what I had learned.

The California sun shone brightly in the cloudless blue sky; surfers paddled out over waves for the first rides of the day; fishermen cast lines from the concrete Venice Beach Pier—all appeared to be right with the world. But I now suddenly felt heartburn rising up my esophagus.

Part Two
And now, as they say ... The Rest Of The Story

Chapter Twenty-Nine
Samantha Zimmer-Gambil

May 2001

Samantha Gambil sat alone in the kitchen of a house far too large for only one resident. Living here with Griffin, it had not felt so enormous. But now, the wide halls and twenty-foot ceilings seemed overly capacious, cavernous, empty. And cold, she thought, pulling her robe tighter to keep out the chill. Seated at a wrought-iron and glass breakfast table designed to accommodate six, Samantha nursed a cup of steaming tea.

The view through French doors to the outside was gray: a dark May-gray sky had produced a thick, dewy blanket that engulfed the entire backyard. As she stared out at the dampness, dewdrops became raindrops. Samantha watched as droplets began pummeling the surface of the swimming pool. It had a mesmerizing effect. Her mind drifting off to another time; a time when she felt real contentment just being a wife.

Samantha could recall the precise moment her illusion of marital contentment was shattered, changing her life forever. It was December of 1999; the end of the decade; the end of the twentieth century; and six months before the end of her dear, dear Griffin. The memory still as vivid as if it had just occurred yesterday. It began right here, in this very kitchen, with the ringing of the telephone. A call which, in so many ways, she wished she had never answered.

The sound of rain on the roof was like a clock ticking backwards, taking Samantha back in time. Closing her eyes, she began to re-live that December day.

THE KITCHEN COUNTERTOPS WERE CLUTTERED with holiday decorations. Festive Fitz & Floyd holiday plates depicting reindeer pulling a present-laden sleigh were neatly stacked near the sink, a jolly red and white porcelain Santa stood smiling at anyone in the vicinity.

However, Samantha was feeling anything but festive as she slowly hung up the phone, ending the call that had lasted only minutes. Her arm felt numb from squeezing the handset. Although most informative, this had not been a conversation she particularly enjoyed. Her husband, she had just learned, was having an affair. She never suspected such a thing possible. Certainly not from a man like Griffin, a man for whom sex never found its way to the forefront of priorities.

But she had it on good authority: Griffin was seeing another woman. He would meet this woman each time he flew to Honolulu on business, and such business trips had become frequent the last month or two. Griffin was a businessman—a damn good businessman—and Samantha had never before questioned the reasons for his frequent trips.

Griffin had been seen numerous times in the company of a prostitute in Honolulu. *Prostitute*, the term resonated in Samantha's brain until purged and replaced by one more in keeping with her growing anger: a goddamned whore!

How could this be? How could the man she married and trusted do this to her? She had stood by her husband faithfully as his business endured hard times and they pulled in their belts to weather the financial storms together. Only recently was Griffin back on track—the money track—and becoming successful for the second time in his life. Everything was finally returning to normal for them . . . and now this. A goddamned whore!

Was it even considered an *affair* when your husband *pays* to be with another woman? Samantha wasn't completely certain. But she was absolutely certain of one thing . . . her sense of outrage! She had stood by her man in the fine old tradition of Tammy Wynette, only now to find herself more in the role of Hillary Clinton and feeling more the fool for it.

Samantha had always remained faithful to Griffin even though their marriage had never been one of passion. For fifteen years she devoted her best years—her very youth—to a comfortable union, forgoing the pleasures she knew a woman could feel from the *right* man. In her loins she had often longed to be with someone else, someone from her long-ago past who had never been far from her thoughts.

Well, she decided, life was too short to deny herself the passion she had gone so long without. Her husband—it was now obvious—had not been denying *himself* newfound pleasures. Samantha decided she would find her old love, the one who originally led her to womanhood so long ago. She blushed warmly at the recollection of him—losing herself in a swirling amalgam of emotion as she relived the shared singularity of purpose they once enjoyed; so intense was their passion that it eradicated all but the immediate need to satisfy the flesh. Samantha involuntarily trembled at the memory. She had never been able to shake him from her mind or her heart—not even after nearly thirty years.

Painful though it was to learn of her husband's infidelity, Samantha was indebted to the caller. The information he provided allowed Samantha to see her marriage—to see her very life—with new clarity. It was like turning on a light in a darkened room. Samantha now realized what she needed to do. Her entire world was about to change, she knew. She owed the caller for this enlightenment. She wasn't quite sure if the caller's motivation had been as her husband's concerned friend or his formidable foe, but it really didn't matter. She owed Broadus Liberato for calling.

Chapter Thirty
Pete Spivey

June 2001

"As you know, an appeal has been filed," Pete Spivey's attorney began, his client sitting in a chair across from him, staring at the floor. "A criminal defendant has a constitutional right to appeal; not a new trial, mind you, but rather a review by the Court of Appeal to see if the trial court acted in accord with the law." Thirty-five days after the trial convicting Spivey, a Notice of Appeal was filed and a new lawyer, who specializes in appeals, had been handling this next step in Spivey's criminal matter. He and his client were conferring, as they'd done numerous times over the last several months, in a private room at the Inmate Reception Center at Chino State Prison in Chino, California, where Spivey was incarcerated.

"I won't hold my fucking breath . . . I'm never getting outa this joint, am I?" Spivey butted in, suddenly looking up, ending his fascination with the floor. Before his attorney could answer, Pete threw another question his way. "Anything I tell you is still confidential. I mean, even though the trial's over, right?"

"Anything you tell me is protected under the attorney/client privilege, just as it was with your prior lawyer," the appeals attorney assured him for the umpteenth time. "But . . . ."

Pete jumped in again, "You know what the most screwed part about all this is? Fact is, I actually *thought* about killing good old filthy rich Griffin. I really did. In fact, if he hadn't killed himself . . . I might have done it one of these days. But, as it turned out, I am *not* the one who blew the bastard away. I really think he did it himself, you know? Suicide."

The attorney sat passively. He had heard all this before, countless times, from his client.

"Sure, Sammie and me had a very cool connection. That broad is hot! I mean, she carried this thing around for me all those years since high school . . . who knew? She hardly crossed *my* mind since I got outa school. She was just another chick I knew in my younger days, no biggie. But here she was, carrying around this torch for me all those years. I gotta tell ya, by the time she found me and we got . . . *reacquainted*," he emphasized the word, making curly quotes with his fingers, "that torch was so friggin' hot it nearly burned my dick right off! That bitch loved to fuck! She just couldn't get enough of old Pete Spivey.

"But it was her husband what had all the money, ya know what I mean? Sammie was fine livin' on love alone, but I kept thinkin' that with her husband outa the picture, she would inherit all that moolah. And then, when he filed for divorce and Sammie told me about some preternutal . . . ."

"Prenuptial agreement," the attorney corrected. He had heard this story numerous times and each time Spivey fractured the word.

"Yeah, that's it," Spivey concurred. "And because of this friggin' agreement, Sammie would get squat if Griffin divorced her. I knew right then her old man had to get whacked before he could divorce the bitch. I figgered I'd shoot him and make it look like one of them drive by shootings. That way, Sammie would get all the money and I'd be her main squeeze to share the loot with.

"Sounded like a good plan. I was trying to decide just how to do it, when the sonofabitch went and blew his own head off! Waay cool, I got just what I wanted and didn't even have to kill him or nothin'."

The attorney sat staring at his legal pad, working on notes for an entirely different case he had the next day as Pete Spivey droned on.

"Sammie knew it wasn't me what killed her husband. We was both home humping our brains out when he died. Guess that wasn't one of my better performances, because Sammie didn't even remember . . . said I got home late the day Griffin shot himself, but she was wrong . . . that was the night before. I really wish I'd fucked her better, so she would'a remembered."

"Well," the attorney interjected testily without even looking up from the legal pad, "maybe she would've had a more favorable recollection if you hadn't gotten greedy and tried to kill her in her own home."

"I keep tellin' ya, that wasn't me! I was in goddamned Sturgis, South Dakota! It had'ta be someone who sounded like me. Sammie never said she actually *saw* the guy."

"Uh huh," the attorney grunted, still not looking up from the pad. Then, shaking his head in hopeless disbelief added, "And this fellow with a voice *just like yours* confessed to murdering your wife, too. Samantha testified that she heard him. How else would she know about that? Was she lying about you murdering your wife? Looks like she was telling the truth, since you went and admitted the same damn thing to the police. Jesus, Pete!"

"There were thousands upon thousands of other bikers there with me!" Spivey shouted, ignoring everything his lawyer just said about Pete's murdered wife. "The whole damn place looked like a freakin' motorcycle anthill! Thousands of bikes in any direction you looked."

"Yet not a single person who was able to testify as to your whereabouts on the exact day Samantha Gambil was assaulted." The attorney finally looked up at his client.

"Shit! My own fucking lawyer doesn't even believe me! How many times I gotta tell ya. I was up there the whole time, lots of people saw me. I set up shop over at the Buffalo Chip Campground. It's just that I hooked up with some little bimbo with big tits and long brown hair and we made ourselves scarce for two of those days. Unfortunately, those are the same two days the police claim I flew to L.A. and tried to do Sammie in. But it just isn't true, I tell ya. I never left goddamned Sturgis!"

"We've already been through this before, Pete," the attorney said with more than a hint of exasperation. "You can't recall the name of the woman you were with. Your trial lawyer tried to locate this anonymous woman and was totally unsuccessful. Buffalo Chip Campground has absolutely no idea whether you were actually in the campground on the days in question. But, be that as it may, there is also the damning evidence of the plane ticket with your name on it for travel between Rapid City and Los Angeles."

"Nobody ever testified that they saw me on that goddamned plane," Spivey offered in rebuttal.

"True, but the jury convicted you and now I'm working on your appeal." The attorney spoke with finality, gathering up his things in preparation for leaving. "But look, all that's water under the bridge. As I've explained to you before, the Court of Appeal doesn't consider any new evidence, hear witnesses, or retry cases. The Court just looks at things like improper jury instructions, insufficient evidence to support the verdict, things like that. All I can tell you is that I'm working on it and I'll give it my best shot. Keep your fingers crossed."

The attorney left the room as the uniformed officer took Pete Spivey back to his cell.

Chapter Thirty-One
Samantha Zimmer-Gambil

June 2001

It was one of those Southern California early June mornings, so mind-numbingly perfect it almost makes you want to cry: seventy-five degrees without a cloud in the sky, yet almost cool when shaded under a pool-side umbrella. Samantha Zimmer-Gambil reposed atop the Brown Jordan chaise lounge—enjoying the sun as it caressed every inch of her exposed skin. She knew the sun was not really good for her, but was addicted to its warmth. She loved the way it made her skin smell and the healthy glow of tan that made her appear youthful even as it prematurely ravaged her epidermic connecting cells. As a woman well past forty, Samantha rationalized, she was going to end up old and wrinkled whether she spent time in the sun or not—and "tan old" looked better than "pale old" as far as she was concerned.

Squinting into the cloudless sky above, Samantha reveled in the gloriously deep shade of blue. It was a blue unique only to California, the sky never seeming to look quite so rich and flawless anywhere else in the world. She was thankful. Thankful to be alive to enjoy such sensations. Her keen awareness that all this was very nearly snatched away increased her appreciation for all the beauty that life has to offer. Even the sloshing of water recirculating through the swimming pool filter was a comforting sound.

As uplifting as this new appreciation for life was, Samantha was still a troubled soul. Try as she might, she could not purge the events of the last year from her memory; they played over and over in her mind. Her husband was dead, her lover was a murderer . . . and she was accomplice to all of it.

Accomplice? Hell, she was almost certainly the *cause* of it all!

God, how she wished she was Catholic so she could unload all that she knew to some faceless priest under the cloak of the confessional. But she was not Catholic, nor a member of any other congregation for that matter. The only one she could trust was her long time admirer, her attorney.

She trusted Benjamin because she felt certain he would never do anything to harm her . . . and because, as her lawyer, he was prevented from divulging anything she said to him. She tried to tell Benjamin . . . she *wanted* to tell Benjamin . . . *everything*—but stopped just short of doing so. She wasn't certain just how *absolute* the attorney/client privilege was. Also, she was not so sure she could bear Benjamin knowing all the sordid deeds to which she was a party.

But Samantha knew the truth, and it was the truth that plagued her. Pete Spivey had murdered her husband. This was as much a certainty as the clear blue sky under which she now sat. And he very nearly got away with it—a murder for which Samantha herself felt profound responsibility. To murder Griffin had been *her* idea, after all. How could she have been so careless as to actually plant such a notion in Pete's neanderthal mind?

Guilt over her role in causing Griffin's death had enveloped Samantha. As a result, she began to hate herself for setting the wheels of violence in motion. What originally began for Samantha as an exciting rekindling of long dormant passions, reunited with her very first—and, in Samantha's mind, very best—lover from long ago, was instantly extinguished upon learning that this lover was capable of taking human life.

Once she became certain Pete had not only murdered his own wife but Griffin as well, so deep did Samantha's self-loathing become that it overtook all sense of self-worth, allowing her to endure Pete's never-ending sexual overtures, even though—once she knew the ugly truth—his very touch made her skin crawl.

She felt so helpless when the police ruled Griffin's death a suicide. In some sad way she wished they were right—that it *was* a suicide—but she knew Griffin would never take his own life. She knew he had been murdered.

For one brief instant she even dared to consider that perhaps the prostitute had been responsible for Griffin's death. What a relief it would have been to discover Pete was not the killer after all . . . that Samantha was guiltless in the death of her husband. However, that was but a momentary delusional indulgence; Samantha always knew better. She knew it was Pete Spivey who killed Griffin. And, she knew she could not allow him to get away with it.

The police needed to rethink their conclusion. Griffin's death was not suicide! Knowing the truth, Samantha would just have to lead the police to discovering the truth as well. So she had devised a plan to do so. She would fake an attempt on her own life, blame it on Pete and, in the process, frame him for the murder of Griffin . . . a murder she was dead certain he actually did commit.

PETE'S ABSENCE TO SOUTH DAKOTA offered the perfect opportunity. Before he left, Samantha used Pete's credit card to purchase a round trip airline ticket for travel from Rapid City, South Dakota to Los Angeles, California. The ticket was issued to P. Spivey and mailed to Samantha's Woodland Hills home.

Scanning her Arizona driver's license into her home computer, Samantha found it amazingly simple to fabricate a new license identifying her as *Patricia* Spivey—to document her as the P. Spivey on the ticket.

After Pete was gone a few days, Samantha drove to the airport and—using cash—purchased a *second* ticket for travel from Los Angeles to Rapid City . . . one way.

Boarding a plane in L.A., she used the one-way ticket to travel to Rapid City. She then immediately hopped aboard another plane—using the "P. Spivey ticket" purchased with Pete's credit card—and returned right back to where she started, Los Angeles. The male airline personnel who issued her boarding pass in Rapid City paid more attention to her cleavage than to her identification and, once onboard the aircraft, Samantha breathed a sigh of relief that her homemade ID had worked.

Samantha was exhausted from her whirlwind trip to Rapid City and back again as she cruised the parking lot at LAX, searching for a parked car with the window open or the door ajar. Surely some harried traveler might have forgotten to crank up a window as he or she made a mad dash to catch a plane. Only a few minutes of searching, and there it was—a late model American car with the window cracked open just enough so a hand could reach inside.

Stretching the sleeve of her blouse over her hand so as not to leave any fingerprints, Samantha wiggled her arm through the narrow slit created between glass and metal, found the door handle on the inside and opened the car door. She tossed the spent ticket stub from Rapid City to L.A.—with Spivey's name on it—onto the dashboard of the parked car and hurriedly walked away, leaving the car's door wide open.

She hoped, once the news of Spivey's arrest for the murder of Griffin Gambil and assault on Griffin's widow was made public, the owner of the car might come forward with the ticket stub as proof that Spivey was in L.A. to do the deed. That the car with its open door would subsequently invite some joy-riding thief was more than Samantha could have foreseen, and when she later learned of it she could not contain a fit of triumphant laughter; maybe there was justice in the world after all!

Samantha then got into her own car and drove home.

All alone in her big house, Samantha sat at the desk near the old grandfather clock that was Griffin's favorite furnishing and put pen to paper. This was the desk where Griffin so often sat to work during their many years together—a time, she thought, choking back emotion, before her errant words led to his death.

She drafted a brief letter to the only one she could trust, placed it in an envelope and, instead of addressing it, scrawled the words *To be opened in the event of my death by my attorney, Benjamin Harding*. She paper-clipped the envelope to the trust document Benjamin had made for her and placed it in the top desk drawer where it would be easily found by anyone going through her papers.

The letter clearly spelled out Pete Spivey as the man who killed her husband. She added the *lie* that Pete had confessed the murder to her and she now feared for her own life—feared Pete would return from his motorcycle rally and kill her, too. She knew if Benjamin ever read such a letter he would see to it that Spivey would be brought to justice. If anything went wrong with her plan, she imagined this might be the last letter she would ever write . . . to anyone.

Sitting there in the empty house, the dwelling she had shared for many years with the only husband she had ever known, the metronome of ticking from the grandfather clock seemed to mock her; its pendulum swinging back and forth. Tears began burrowing cavernous ravines through her make-up as the image of Griffin's lifeless body with its face blown away haunted her. He did not deserve such a gruesome end. Nobody did.

Samantha had gone about the house closing the windows in each room, turning on the gas jets in the kitchen, and now sat waiting quietly at Griffin's old desk. She knew Gavin came by each day to help out with the probate and anticipated him finding her. More than anticipated—Samantha was *counting* on him to find her. It was her plan that he would arrive in time to save her miserable life.

But if not, if this part of her plan failed, maybe she *deserved* to die. She almost preferred it over living with the guilt. But either way, the important thing was to avenge Griffin's death, to make sure the authorities would now pin the blame where it so clearly belonged, on Pete Spivey.

Samantha felt her body grow weak, the unconscious world overtaking her. The gas was taking effect. But, what if Gavin did not arrive in time to save her?

The irreversible finality of dying struck Samantha like a blow to the head. Suddenly she felt real fear! She tried to rise from the desk, to struggle to her feet, but failing to achieve uprightness, crawled on her hands and knees toward the kitchen—attempting to reach the gas shut-off valve.

The next thing she knew, she was in a hospital bed. Her plan had worked. Gavin had rescued her and she could now point the authorities to Spivey; make him pay—not only for Griffin's death, but for murdering his wife as well. Samantha was making things right!

THOUGH STILL TROUBLED BY THE events of the past year, Samantha saw things so much differently now and felt a growing appreciation—an outright joy— for life and the world in general. Her success at forcing justice upon the man who took Griffin's life added immensely to this joy.

She had come perilously close to succumbing to the noxious gas fumes, but Gavin found her in time and the letter she wrote to be opened upon her death was now moot. Her sworn testimony in court put Griffin's murderer away. For whatever complicity Samantha may have secretly shared in Griffin's death, she was now vindicated. She felt clean and pure as the Valley air she breathed deeply into her lungs.

Samantha turned over on the lounge chair, tanning her backside to match her front. The sun rays feeling warm on her skin, she was glad to be alive.

Chapter Thirty-Two
Ara Ratono

July 2001

Ara Ratono was upset. No, he was *very* upset. Downright hostile! The latest in a string of idiot, incompetent lawyers had lost another of Ratono's legal battles.

Ratono's company was the largest refuse company in three counties. For three decades he'd held what was practically a monopoly. He had built a triple-county empire and was used to getting his way with local government. But recently, trouble arose in the southern-most corner of Ratono's empire. Some Young Turk, newly elected to the Board of Supervisors and looking to make his mark on local government, decided it was his civic duty to break up Ratono's hold on the refuse business in his county. The first step was to arbitrarily lower the rates a refuse company could charge customers, in the hope that a big company like Ratono's would move to a higher-priced county, thereby opening the market for smaller companies that could collect trash more cost-effectively. The measure cut deeply into Ratono's profit margin, and he had no intention of taking it lying down.

Ara Ratono sued the county, alleging the contract his company currently had in place with the county did not allow for interference with the rates he could charge for trash collection, that the measure caused the county to be in breach of contract. The suit was for fifteen million dollars.

And then, after months of legal wrangling, his lawyer had lost the case. California probably had more lawyers than any other state, except maybe New York with its huge population of Jews, Ratono thought to himself contemptuously. Yet, in spite of this plethora of attorneys, he never seemed to be able to find competent legal help no matter how often he changed law firms.

"Blood sucking parasites!" he exploded, fist pounding his desk in rage. "Lawyers take yer money, oh they're always happy to take yer money, then they piss it away on useless legal shit that nobody but a goddamned lawyer ever understands. I've about had it with these asshole lawyers!"

Ara Ratono sat back in his oversized leather swivel-chair, weary with defeat at the hands of the legal system. Who was it that said, *First we kill all the lawyers?* Whoever said that must have felt the same as he was feeling now. "Sometimes a man's got to take things into his own hands, level the playing field a little," he said aloud to himself.

Slowly a smile began to surface across his features, recalling the last time he had leveled the playing field with a lawyer. Back then, Ratono had filed a malpractice lawsuit and a complaint to the State Bar, but it got him nowhere with that arrogant little bastard at the snotty Newport Beach firm, the firm that sucked retainer dollars from him like a suckling pig at a teat then gave his cases to incompetent underlings to manage. This particular underling lawyer proceeded to lose one of Ratono's cases, then flew the coop and quit his job. Chickenshit bastard! Ratono had to actually send someone out and track him down, at a funeral no less. It wasn't that hard. Then the bugger was found hiding out in Venice Beach. Lots of chickenshit weirdos out there in Venice Beach.

Of course, Ara Ratono knew right from the beginning that complaining to the State Bar was pointless. They protect their own, just as he knew they would. Scum-bags always protect fellow scum-bags.

But when the court threw out his malpractice suit and that cocky bastard actually had the balls to give Ratono a snotty smirk right there in the court room—well, that was more than a man should be expected to tolerate. Somebody needed to teach that boy some manners. And there was no shortage of volunteers right here within the ranks of Ratono's loyal employees—trash men, but tough, hard-working trash men—who would be more than happy for a shot at roughing up some sissy lawyer.

The job fell once again to Pat Murphy, one of Ratono's favorite route men, who'd found the dumb-fuck lawyer the first time around. At first Ratono thought Murph might be too soft-hearted for the task; Murph with his friendly Irish face, a large red bulbous nose in the center that gave him an almost clown-like, comical appearance. Everybody loved the affable Murphy, who arrived for work each morning with a friendly greeting toward his fellow trash crew, trading his shiny white four-wheeler Dodge Ram truck for a trash hauler. But Murphy was a large fellow and, when Murph got angry, his normally cartoon-like pock-marked visage became grotesquely distorted, and his eyes could take on a steely look capable of casting fear into the hearts of lesser men.

Ever since Murph's ex-wife took him to the cleaners, her lawyer condemning him to hauling trash for the rest of his life in order to keep the alimony payments coming, Murph had had palatable contempt for lawyers and the, so-called, legal system. Murphy jumped at the opportunity to harass a lawyer.

The smile on Ratono's face broadened as he recalled hearing the details from Pat Murphy, the way he pulled that lawyer punk right out of his fancy sports car and scared him shitless. Reduced that smooth talking, cocky bastard to a sputtering idiot—spewing gibberish about being somebody's sex slave. Hah! That was a good one! Probably thought old Murph was going to have his way with him right there in the garage.

The frosting on the cake was when Murphy trashed the dude's beach pad. That photo taped to the bathroom mirror, what a hoot! Ara Ratono's smile evolved to chuckle causing his shoulders to shake, he found it most amusing. Where Murph got such a photo was anybody's guess, but it was a very *creative* touch. That lawyer punk will probably never be able to enjoy a piece of ass in that pad again . . . too weirded-out and scared to even get it up! Bet that sucker ain't so arrogant anymore. Ratono relished the vision of havoc Pat Murphy had wreaked upon that dip-shit lawyer. A job well done.

Ara Ratono picked up his cell phone, using the walkie-talkie feature, and called Pat Murphy. "Pat," he said jovially, all the hostility he'd been bogged down with earlier now gone, "could ya swing on by the office before heading home tonight? Got another little side job I'd like to discuss with ya. Another lawyer in need of attitude correction."

Chapter Thirty-Three
Gavin Gilchrist Gambil

June 2000
The Day Griffin Gambil Died

Jesus Christ was the undisputed hero of Gavin Gambil's life. Christ had entered Gavin's life when he was in dire need of saving, and Gavin did not turn away from the light. He embraced the Word, was born again and has since lived each day in the Divine radiance of the Lord, encountering each obstacle in life by asking *What would Jesus do?* It was far more than coincidence, Gavin was certain, that his own long-departed mother had bestowed upon him the middle name of Gilchrist—which was *her* maiden name, and means servant of Christ.

Gavin strived to live as Christ-like a life as humanly possible and he was rewarded for his punctiliousness, because now Gavin believed himself to actually be a lot like Jesus.

To Gavin, the similarities were striking. Gavin was both a carpenter and a fisherman, just like his hero. And, just as his hero had converted Mary Magdalene from a life of debauchery, Gavin had saved the soul of Connie Cantu.

Mary Magdalene was a commonly known prostitute in her day. She spent her life in sin, but repented after being shown the light. One day when Simon the Pharisee invited Jesus to dinner, Mary Magdalene came in and threw herself to the floor at Jesus' feet humbling herself. She washed His feet with her tears and dried them with her hair. For such an act of humility and repentance, Jesus forgave her of all her sins. From then on, Mary Magdalene followed Jesus wherever He went and helped Him in any way she could.

Besides Jesus Christ, the person Gavin loved most in all the world was his brother, Griffin. It had pained Gavin deeply that his brother had fallen under the spell of a common whore. So much so that Gavin approached Connie Cantu one evening, a month or so ago, to chastise her for leading his brother astray, and subjecting her to a voracious verbal tirade on the wages of sin. *Charm is deceitful and beauty is vain, but a woman who fears the Lord, she shall be praised! For by grace are ye saved through faith; and that not of yourselves—it is the gift of God!*

Connie Cantu and Gavin had sat that first night for several hours in the darkened living room of her house, Connie listening passively as Gavin continued his didactic diatribe, speaking to her of the Bible and its teachings. *Beloved, I urge you as aliens and strangers to abstain from fleshly lusts which wage war against the soul. And when we find immoral thoughts coming to our minds, purge such thoughts lest ye suffer the consequences of acting thereon. Let us give serious thought to what Proverbs informs us is the inevitable end of immorality—shame, dissipation, and death!*

To Gavin's surprise, his words appeared to have an impact, actually breaking through the evil veil shielding Connie's soul from the light. Displaying a modicum of remorse for her lascivious conduct with Griffin, Gavin was pleased with Connie's receptive reaction to the teachings of the Lord. But what happened next was clearly a sign from God—no less impressive, Gavin thought, than Moses parting the Red Sea.

On this, their very first time together, Connie Cantu sank to her knees and, removing his Sperry Topsiders, began washing Gavin's bare feet with kisses and licks of her tongue. It was an elaborate display and Gavin sat dumbfounded, watching this woman of the streets writhing on the floor in front of him—humbling herself at his feet, caressing each of his toes with her lips. Just like Mary Magdalene.

It was the most *completely religious* experience of his entire life, watching this prostrating sinner at his feet! Just as Mary Magdalene had washed Jesus' feet, this sinner was washing his. And just as Jesus had led Mary Magdalene to salvation, so Gavin was leading Connie.

She remained on her knees a long while, cleansing Gavin's feet over and over with her mouth. Gavin allowed her all the time she needed to free her soul through such humility. Finally, Connie Cantu took her thick, soft hair and dried his feet. Just like Mary Magdalene.

God could not have sent a clearer sign that the conversion of Connie Cantu and the eradication of her sins was Gavin's great calling. Gavin had shown Connie the road to salvation. If pride had not been a sin, Gavin would certainly have felt proud for turning her around. From that moment on, Gavin made it his mission to keep her on the straight and narrow.

SUCCUMBING TO THE LUSTFUL TEMPTATIONS of impure thoughts and immoral pleasures of the flesh, Gavin decided, was neither Connie's nor Griffin's fault entirely. The true culprit was that new, highly technical, instrument of the devil known as the internet. He could not understand people's fascination with this new techno gizmo. And Gavin had played around on the internet himself, so he knew whereof he spoke. He was a Luddite, but justifiably so. He'd used his brother's computer to log on and surf the vast web that lay in cyberspace.

"Web" indeed! The internet—Gavin quickly learned—could suck you in and spin you through deviant worlds best left unexplored, often stranding you in a tangled *web* from which it was difficult to escape. It seemed that no matter where Gavin traveled on the virtual highway, he found himself languishing in pornographic filth!

One time, in an effort to locate the nearest shelter where he might rescue an abandoned cat to keep as company aboard his boat—because cats make excellent sea-going pets—Gavin typed in *kitten* and hit the search button. *Sex Kittens, Teenage Pussy, Pussy Whipped* . . . and a host of similar links appeared on the screen. Gavin was horrified!

But not to be undone, Gavin tried typing *Animals*. His screen instantly became illuminated with *Animal Lust, Sex with Animals, Bestiality, Naked Girls with Animals, Wide Gaping Beavers, Sex Tigresses* . . . Not since the advent of cable TV with its foul language and pornographic late night movies had Gavin found technology so revolting.

The internet was causing a fiendish meltdown of societal values at the hands of Satan. It disgusted Gavin that some people had actually gotten rich from the internet—it wasn't too long ago that stock prices for dot com companies were soaring. But what the Lord giveth, the Lord taketh away.

Could anyone doubt that it was Divine intervention which caused the dot com bust and all the immoral profits derived from internet companies to collapse upon themselves?

The internet was clearly an instrument of evil! One need look no further than the evening news, where on any given night myriad stories concerning the internet could be found. Stories of teenage girls being lured to their doom by middle-aged child molesters; adoption scams offering the false promise of a child to infertile couples in exchange for money; identity thefts ruining the lives and credit of hard-working, upstanding people; internet auctions fraught with fraud ... and wives leaving their husbands for lovers they met on the internet—like Samantha had done to Griffin.

And so it was, Gavin decided, that the internet was ultimately responsible for the immoral coupling of his brother with a woman of the streets cum cyberspace, for it was on the internet that Griffin Gambil and Connie Cantu met.

BUT WHERE GAVIN HAD MANAGED to make strident progress toward the redemption of Connie Cantu, he had met with failure when it came to his only brother. The devil was too firmly entrenched. *Madam Folly frequently passes our way, calling to those who are making their paths straight. She will focus our attention on the passing pleasures of sin, and will minimize the consequences. She will urge us to forget the future and live for the moment. We must not listen to her, for we are but strangers and pilgrims upon the earth!*

Griffin scoffed at Gavin's warnings that hell awaited. "I've come a long way since I've believed in *anything*," he chided. "In fact, I think a person *should* yield to temptation; it may not pass your way again!"

"Please," Gavin implored, "use some common sense, Griffin. Can't you see the internet, this woman, and the devil have all three conspired for you to suffer eternal damnation?"

"Common sense? What's *that* got to do with anything? Common sense is what tells you that the world is flat!" Griffin retorted.

Gavin tried desperately to get the message through to his brother. "Jesus, our Lord and Savior, was the greatest man to ever walk the earth! You can't go wrong if you just follow His example—ask yourself *what would Jesus do?*"

But Griffin would have none of it. "I'd just as soon ask myself 'What would Scooby Doo?'" Griffin laughed vigorously at his own joke about a cartoon dog, openly mocking his younger brother.

Gavin continued his indefatigable attempts to drive a wedge between Griffin and Connie, to put an end to their illicit affair. But each time, the devil prevailed. Eventually, it became clear that Griffin was *never* going to see the light, no matter what Gavin said. Griffin was on the road to eternal damnation and his continuing relationship with Connie would take her with him, thwarting Gavin's greatest accomplishment—saving the soul of Connie Cantu.

Gavin grappled for weeks over what to do, then his epiphany arrived. God sacrificed his only begotten son, Jesus Christ, for the redemption of mankind. Gavin must sacrifice his only beloved brother for the redemption of both Connie's and Griffin's immortal souls. *The righteous hath hope in his death!*

Gavin remembered vividly the day it all came to fruition. "Please Lord! Don't make me do this!" he implored, pounding the steering wheel as he drove his pickup truck toward the Valley. But the Lord had spoken. His will must be done. Cruising slowly along the curbless avenues of Connie Cantu's Encino neighborhood, Gavin spied his brother's car parked on the street, directly in front of her house.

"Dear God, even now he is here embracing evil with her," Gavin thought to himself. Then audibly, but again only to himself, "This must end. I *must* do God's will!"

Gavin stopped his truck several blocks away, stepped out of the cab and opened the toolbox bolted to the truck-bed. Pulling on his work gloves, Gavin rummaged along the bottom of the metal box until he found the gun.

It was a gun Griffin borrowed from Samantha and her home wrecking boyfriend. It was the very same gun Griffin had asked Gavin to wave at Mr. Liberato a few years before to shake him up a little. Gavin wanted no part of that episode with Mr. Liberato, but Griffin convinced him to play along just that one time. Afterwards, Griffin asked Gavin to stash the gun for a while. Gavin did not like guns one bit. So, he hid it in his toolbox until Griffin asked for it back. When Griffin recently wanted to stash the weapon again, Gavin knew just where to hide it. He had Griffin place it at the bottom of the toolbox where it couldn't harm anyone.

Returning to the cab of the truck, Gavin shifted into neutral and silently coasted ahead, stopping less than a car length behind Griffin's parked black Cadillac. He was surprised to see that Griffin was in the car. Gavin sat in his truck, wondering just what to do next.

Apparently, Griffin had not noticed Gavin parked directly behind him. Griffin appeared to be preoccupied, doing something inside his car—writing something it looked like. Gavin got out and approached the Cadillac. He stood outside the car, on the side of the road, watching Griffin . . . but Griffin remained oblivious.

Gavin watched his brother for a long while. He could hear music coming from the car radio. A Phil Collins song. The lyrics seemed aimed right at Gavin, as if Griffin were singing them to Gavin—mocking him yet again: *I don't care what you say, I never did believe you much anyway . . . I don't care no more . . . no more . . . no more . . . no more . . . no more . . .*

Finally, Gavin rapped on the Cadillac's driver side window. Griffin looked up—startled. Then he pushed open the car door with an abruptness that made Gavin jump back, out of the way.

"Look," Griffin spat out the words, "I don't know why the hell your bothering me, but make this quick. I don't have all day."

A voice deep inside Gavin's head repeated rapidly, *Do it! Do it! Do it!* Clearly it was a Devine voice urging him on. In one fluid motion, Gavin raised the gun head high, pulled the trigger and watched in horror as his brother's face flew from his skull onto the dirt and lawn that once belonged to Gavin himself, but now belonged to Connie Cantu. Blood gushing from Griffin's skull sounded like running water, puddling in the lawn.

Righteousness overcame the horrific. As Gavin watched his brother collapse upon the ground in a bloody heap, he calmly whispered, "Proverbs inform us the inevitable end of immorality is shame, dissipation . . . and death! Thy will be done."

But Gavin doubted that his brother heard the words. Griffin had certainly already passed over to the other side.

Chapter Thirty-Four
Connie Cantu

August 2001

Looking out over Ala Wai Yacht Harbor, across the narrow channel where palm trees—caressed by gentle trade winds—were swaying along the red clay shoreline of Ala Moana Park, Connie Cantu smiled to herself. It was good to be home again in Honolulu.

Her time spent on the mainland had not been particularly pleasant. California is highly overrated, she thought. Too hot and dry by day—lack of moisturizing humidity made her skin flake—and too cold at night; as soon as the sun went down, it seemed to take all the heat with it, forcing her to pull on sweaters even in the midst of summer. That's no way to live, she decided. Hawaii was far more to her liking; the moist tropical air felt good against her smooth skin.

But her time in California actually proved quite productive, although she sometimes wondered if it was all worth it. Though the enormous fortune of Griffin Gambil had eluded her, she still came away a far wealthier woman than when she arrived.

The three carat diamond on her left hand also made Connie smile. She was a married woman now. She and Gavin had tied the knot only four months ago. An April wedding for a couple of April fools, Gavin joked lovingly. It was mostly Gavin's idea to get married, but Connie put up no resistance. He wanted to make an honest woman of her, he liked to joke. The very notion caused her smile to widen. They got married right on the beach, like a couple of tourists, and Gavin said it was the happiest day of his life.

Connie, shaded from the afternoon sun by a large umbrella as she reclined in a chair on the aft-deck of the *Waay Mo Bettah*, opened her laptop computer. Checking e-mail was a part of her daily routine, and one she preferred to do in private after Gavin went away fishing each morning. Fifteen messages from potential new slaves; her stable was growing. Tomorrow she would drive down to Kapiolani Boulevard and check her mailbox for monetary offerings. Money, however, was no longer her primary motivator. She was already rather rich, due to an inheritance from her husband's older brother. A windfall she felt more than entitled to, since it was she who had helped him acquire it. Money was nice, but it was the supreme satisfaction derived of watching a grown man writhe and grovel at her feet that set her soul afire. Just as submissives like Griffin Gambil seemed addicted to being on the receiving end of abuse, Connie was equally addicted to being in control and humiliating such submissive males.

She had all but lost interest in her recent subjugation to a male. Playing the subbie was a momentary diversion that was petering out quickly—much like her dabbling with religious conversion. "I didn't claw my way to the top of the food chain to eat vegetables!" she actually muttered aloud, to no one in particular. A smile briefly flirted with the corners of her painted lips as she considered, "Maybe power corrupts, but *absolute* power is very, very cool."

Looking up from the tiny screen she held in her lap, Connie saw *Bite Me*—the fishing skiff her husband used each day, a boat that she had personally christened with such a name—approaching in the distance along the channel. Her husband was returning from his day at sea, hunting fish. She could see him at the helm shaded under the bimini. He waved cheerfully toward Connie. She replied smiling falsely back, with exaggerated effort lifting her arm, moving her hand in a sort of emotionless royal wave. Gavin threw a kiss her way. Slowly shaking her head at this pathetic gesture of affection, her smile stayed glued in place until he looked away, then her waving stopped, her arm flopping down onto the chaise: dead weight.

Gavin had three loves: God, his wife, and fishing. In that order. Yes, Gavin considered himself to be a man of God, alright. What Connie knew that Gavin did not, however, was that she had skillfully choreographed his fall from grace without his even being aware. He had unwittingly sold his soul to the devil; and Connie had brokered the deal.

Watching him approach closer, Connie lazily blew Gavin a return kiss. To her, their four month marriage had already run its course. She was getting bored. Connie was ready to move on and wondered just how long she might be married before some terrible accident would make her a widow. After all, fishing far out on the ocean could be a dangerous pastime; any number of misadventures could claim a man's life. At sea, there would be no witnesses and no one would ever know for certain what happened. She would become the grieving widow, wearing her grief on her sleeve as an item of adornment, but always wondering if there was anyone out there who had seen her husband's end. Such uncertainty might make the loss of a husband almost exciting somehow, Connie speculated. The thrill of the unknown.

But, Connie Cantu-Gambil knew she would make a young and beautiful Asian widow. Young, beautiful and rich, no longer sharing the wealth with a husband. And she certainly had no worries about ever being alone. The world was filled with adoring men more than willing to give up their very *souls* for a woman like her. She knew this to be a fact. She was married to one! Manipulating a man into killing his own brother for her had proven her feminine powers to be boundless. A tittering laugh escaped her lips. It was funny really; men were so very easy to control.

Epilogue
Benjamin Harding

August 2001

Probate officially closed on the Estate of Griffin Gambil nearly one year to the day after his death. The *Order Settling the Final Report of Administrator* and *Petition for Allowance of Statutory Attorney Fees, Allowance of Extraordinary Attorney Fees, Allowance of Administrator's Commission and for Final Distribution and Final Discharge of the Administrator* were signed by the probate judge presiding. Ben Harding collected his fees as probate attorney earned over the course of the year, as did Samantha Zimmer-Gambil for administrative duties. Not the windfall originally anticipated, but he had no complaints. The sum proved adequate compensation for his efforts. *Extraordinary attorney fees* are for those services over and above the scope of what a probate attorney is expected to perform. Ben did not bill the estate anything under that heading. But, just for fun, he'd calculated the amount he *might* have charged for extraordinary attorney fees and the number was so astronomical it made him wince. The court never would have approved, or understood, such fees and expenses, so it was merely a frivolous exercise.

Sitting outside on the deck of his beachfront home, barefoot, shirtless, clad only in ragged shorts as the sun sets beneath the horizon, Benjamin adds a final entry to his journal, diary, memoir, what-have-you:

WE ARE NOW WELL INTO the new millennium and I find myself in a far different world than the one I occupied a brief century ago, before the year 2000. A world no longer containing the two men who triggered profound changes in my life over the course of the last twelve months; my favorite uncle has gone on to his final reward, as has Griffin Gambil. Maybe they will run into each other up there.

Thanks to the generosity of good old Uncle Jack, I remain happily in residence at my inherited little beachfront bungalow. More than twenty pounds lighter than a year ago, this is the best physical condition of my entire life. I'm able to jog pier to pier with little effort and can bike or surf several hours without fatigue. Not bad for a fella who turns fifty next year!

No longer a big-time corporate lawyer with a large firm, I have just single-handedly completed my first probate case; earning only 25% of what I used to make at my old Newport Beach firm, but feeling 125% happier. My life has been irrevocably changed . . . for the better I am convinced.

Waking each morning to the sound of waves crashing, walking out onto the sand and breathing the crisp, cool morning air, looking out at the infinite blue ocean and sky . . . it's a wonderful way to begin each day's journey. It's awesome just knowing that I am living on the very edge of the continent, occupying the last one hundred feet or so of terra firma before the deep blue sea begins its stretch . . . looking out over the horizon and knowing the next major body of land is Hawaii.

There's something very special about residing next to the ocean. Perhaps it's some primeval notion that we all have evolved from the sea that draws me to the water, I don't know. But, whatever it is, I know that I am now in the place where I truly belong. This is the place where I have *always* truly belonged. Cut away all the crap associated with life in the fast lane, of being a high-priced lawyer with a big firm . . . just being near the sea is really all I want out of life! Gad! It only took me forty-nine years to figure that out?

Samantha, the girl of my boyhood dreams, has been thrust back into my life due to my handling the probate of her late husband's estate. Though she may bear little resemblance to the girl I knew thirty years ago, in many ways I find her even more attractive, more alluring. Far too demanding and complicated to be sure, but her presence adds dimension to my life. My heart has hope that one day the friendship she professes for me will become something more. The same hope I have harbored since high school. Some things are timeless.

As her attorney, I suppose, as she has often told me, *I am* the only one she can trust. I carry the limited secrets she has chosen to share with me concerning her husband's death. As her friend, I dare not even ask the myriad questions plaguing my soul concerning her involvement with Pete Spivey and her role in all that has transpired this last year. Perhaps one day I will learn the details to satisfy my inquiring mind. Until such time, I take refuge, smug in the knowledge of the righteous ... that justice was ultimately served—that the man who murdered Griffin Gambil is behind bars. And I feel proud knowing I played an active part in it all.

CHANGE. CHANGE IS UNAVOIDABLE, CONTINUOUS and gradual over time. At least that is how it should be. But, sometimes change is sudden and abrupt. That is how it was for poor Griffin Gambil. None of us are able to predict when our time to occupy these corporeal shells will come to an end. All we can hope, all we can seek, is a life well lived. I plan to spend the rest of mine refining the art of doing *nothing* at Ocean Front Walk.

THE END

About The Author

Michael E. Petrie is a lawyer and a writer whose articles and stories have been featured in numerous local, national and worldwide publications. He was selected most promising new author by South Bay Writers Guild, has won two Erle Stanley Gardner Mystery Writing awards, Texas Bar Journal fiction writing award, and a National Legal Fiction Writing Competition award, drawing many of his story ideas from cases and observations as a lawyer, in often highly complex litigation, in the courts of California, Texas, New York and Washington, D.C.

He lives with his wife, two children, and a golden retriever who is 100+ pounds of pure slobber and love, in a small town at the beach in Southern California where, he says, "Each morning greets us with the sun glistening off the blue Pacific and the laughter of seagulls cheering us on our day." *You're The Only One I Can Trust* is Michael E. Petrie's first novel.

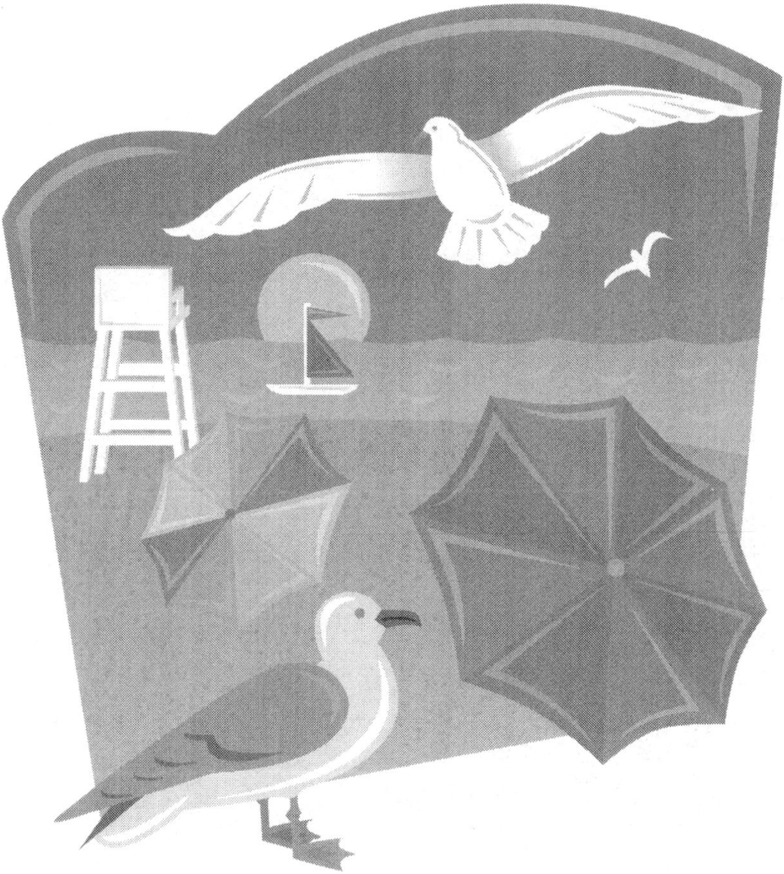

Made in the USA
Lexington, KY
28 January 2016